UNDER THE EARTH, OVER THE SKY

EMILY MCCOSH

OCEANS IN
·THE SKY·

ISBN: 978-1-7354421-2-9 (Hardcover)
ISBN: 978-1-7354421-3-6 (Paperback)
ISBN: 978-1-7354421-4-3 (eBook)

Cover design, illustrations, and formatting by Emily McCosh

Edited by Natalia Leigh (Enchanted Ink Publishing)

Published by Oceans In The Sky Press
OceansInTheSky.com

OCEANS IN
·THE SKY·

Love you Mom & Dad

CHAPTERS

The world is indeed full of peril, and in it there are many dark places; but still there is much that is fair, and though in all the lands love is now mingled with grief, it grows perhaps the greater.

— Tolkien, The Fellowship of the Ring

Rippling Lands

Human Realm

Fair Halls

Heart
of the
Woods

SPRING

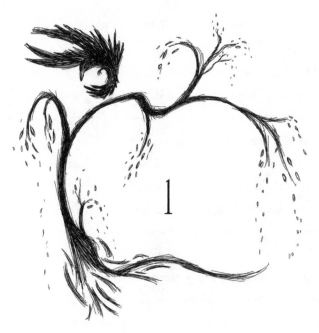

THE KING BENEATH THE EARTH

Seven crows fly to their king beneath the earth. Their wings are heavy with snowmelt, their beaks with gossip. For there are men on the edge of the fair woods, crude weapons in hand, expressions edged with worry, and human feet have not touched the path close to the mountain in a dragon's age.

Eight there are, most closer to forty years than twenty, one man young and nimble with eyes quick as a hawk's. He's heard tales of the fair folk and creatures dwelling within the mountains since childhood. All have. Their thoughts drip in stories told by their grandmothers around fires and whispered in corners, or by the occasional man or woman who pushed the boundaries of the woods and turned up less of themselves than they once were.

These men hunt one of their own. Nothing so dangerous

should be disturbed.

It slides across the footpath, a slice of sunlight in the still-wintering woods. Difficult to discern, none know to call him king, but his fingers are clawed. Slim rough horns slip with grace from a long fall of autumn hair, curling along the sides of his head and down his neck like oak branches huddled with age. Though his skin is translucent, flawless as a fine knife, each time the young man blinks, he glimpses a mess of scars crawling across the perfect limbs. A trick of the light, he's certain.

His clothes are made of strange things, he thinks, scraping at childhood memories for tales his own grandmother told him of how to bargain with a fae. His feet step back before he forces them still lest it be taken as insult.

"What is your name?" the king asks. To his own folk, he is quite ancient. To these men, he was born in a time before their history. He finds humans, with their short lives and short-lived worries, to be amusing. He likes to bother them when they stray near his mountains.

Four men flee, their footsteps no longer silent in haste to be rid of the forest and its wild path. A shout can be heard from one. The young man is left at the lead of those remaining, panic shaking him, considering his options. He glances at the friends who haven't abandoned him. There is a great deal of shuffling steps and tight lips. Wide eyes. Refusing a creature of sunlight and shadow is unwise. So is giving it your name.

"Weapons in my woods, but no name?" the king asks. He is greeted with silence. "Speak."

"There's an . . . um . . ." Blood rumbles in the young man's ears, his pulse in his fingertips. A wood-chopping axe rests in his palm, dulled by age and work, but his grip is gentle. Taking up a weapon against a fae turns his stomach sour. "There's a man farther down the path. He's hiding in an old shack."

"And you seek him out?" The king slips between them, difficult to differentiate where sunlight breaks the trees. They tilt their heads to glimpse his face when they dare. He is curious of their clothes and weapons. Human customs change so in a life as long as his. They carry crude trinkets and toys, not the glistening blades his own kind have crafted, like the one cradled against his spine, but he assumes they do damage.

"He murdered his wife."

The king looks up. His eyes are silver birch bark, made brighter by his autumn hair. He wears no crown, but the horns grace his head as one, and the young man's stomach knots at meeting those eyes. One of his older companions casts him a warning glare, lips pressed, then pales under the king's attention.

"You know this?"

The human's voice grows strong with anger. "He took her into the woods. I mean, she was alive, but he took her. No one's ever had a good thing to say of the man. And he . . . He hits her. Everyone knows. There aren't many other places he could have gone than the shack. It's . . . just forest from here."

The king knows of the little dwelling. His crows—now landing about him, hopping on shadowed feet, doubling in number, tripling, swarming in curiosity—didn't bring him news of those other humans. He listens to the hum of his earth and whispers of his trees and hears a human far off. The shack dwells within the human world, but it's close to the rippling borders of the king's nearest neighbor. He casts a glance into the trees and brushes the chill from his skin.

"You are family to them?"

"N-no. I mean, his family lives far away. She . . . doesn't have anyone else. But we are her *friends*."

"And you seek revenge?"

The human snaps, "We have rules to protect our own. It is not revenge if it is just. Besides, we should've done something for her before . . ."

His companions stiffen at the outburst. One abandons his courage, stumbling down the path. The king regards his retreating form with boredom. "You can follow him back."

"What?"

He slips closer, towering three full heads and more above the tall young human. "These woods are my own. I am their protector. Any justice is mine."

For a moment, there is a swell of pity in the young man's heart for the man in the shack. Only for a moment. He dips his head.

"What is your name?" the king asks, for amusement rather than expectation of an answer.

"What is yours?"

The king flicks his fingers over his shoulder as he turns, dismissing the young man. "Iohmar."

A tongue of sunlight swallows him up, and the men are left blinking like kittens. The young man wonders at the fae name he's heard in ancient war stories and tales told by grandparents many generations removed.

Iohmar finds not a man but a squalling babe.

Hidden in a crate, the infant is butted against the farthest wall from the door, small and plump and strange to the fae king. Few children are born or dwell within his Fair Halls. Several in the last centuries were born before the great war, small and quick and immediate upon their feet, quiet save for the music of their laughter.

Cries from the little human grow loud and harsh as a wounded animal's when Iohmar fits his head through the open window space. Long horns and talons do not make for a comforting sight — he learned long ago.

No grown human appears. Iohmar smells the man, senses him in his woods. Stagnant and foul, the scent of him drifts from the discarded clothes and from a barrel in the corner filled with soiling snow water.

It's troubling he's here, close to Iohmar's borders, reeking of hate and human flesh. He must not believe in the fae to venture so close to the mountains with ill intent in his heart. There was a time Iohmar's kin were a constant presence in the thoughts of humans, but they have long since faded into myth, alive but hardly real, in great part due to Iohmar's own actions. He no longer allows them to steal humans away to the twilight lands, and so they play mischief rather than cause harm. Those men along the path believed, and Iohmar saw their fear bright as sunlight.

Rot hangs in the air, far into the trees, a trail of invisible unkindness. It ruffles him, disturbing in its large presence in a wood so vast.

Maneuvering his head from the window, he drifts into the trees, avoiding mushrooms and squirrels and lizards bothering his bare feet. These woods are not close enough to his own to be filled with his trees' magic, but the branches still shiver as he passes. Here and there, a vine reaches out, and he trails his fingers between leaves and moss and notches of bark. Heavy moisture and the scent of loam fill the air. Still, the smell of rot cuts.

Crows hop about, clicking their displeasure at his lack of attention. They brought him news of the party of men and wish a reward for their concern. He scatters seeds from his palm, and heavy beaks peck between his fingers.

Here the rot is strongest. Iohmar toes at the loose soil, flipping a catch of decaying leaves. The scent is far deeper. Unnatural. Cruel. A body bent. A grave dug in haste. *What creature could commit such an act?* It is unthinkable among Iohmar's folk. His skin crawls with chill for the unknown woman beneath the earth. He brushes his footprints from the soil, smoothing them into the woods. His crows peck the disturbed ground, and he calls them away with a brush of his hand.

Along his return to the shack, he pulls a thistle bud from a near patch of sunlight. Winter is losing her vigor, and the plant doesn't bloom early in spring, but few things will not grow at his bidding.

The babe still cries, more so when Iohmar cracks the window-sill against the tip of his horn. None of his Fair Halls are so small and confining, but he doesn't wish to enter the door. Rolling the leaves between his fingers, he murmurs and presses the pad of his thumb to the child's lips, careful not to touch sharp nails to breakable skin. The little thing blinks but suckles the dripping milk.

Quiet fills the wood, the babe's cries replaced by animal song and the sighs of trees.

The young man from the path mentioned no child. Though rumors of changelings and cursed children still make their way from door to door, Iohmar has not allowed his folk to play such cruel tricks for several centuries, and this one is human as they come, plain and lacking in any magic.

What to do with the child? He cannot leave it.

The babe's mother now lies beneath the earth. Iohmar does not mourn humans, as insignificant as their lives are, but to lose one's kin is a terrible thing. Iohmar knows such pain, and by the hand of another who should be cherished. He has no interest in the child, weak and bland as it is — has never had interest in any child presented to him past fondness for his folk — but pity tightens his chest, a swell of protectiveness. It would be unsafe in his Halls with their wildness and strange magic. Even a king cannot break his own decree.

Heavy footsteps. A human's gruff breath declares its presence before the vile creature appears at the broken-down door.

The babe's father does not see Iohmar at the window, large horns pushed through the small space, a looming monster over a human child. He is nothing but shadow, shade cast from a tree, the slant of sunlight along the wall. Iohmar does not exist in the minds of men he does not wish to. It is only this babe who sees him, suckling milk from his clawed finger.

An unremarkable human, Iohmar thinks, *no uniqueness to his soul to spare him from horrid death. How could a creature kill something he promised to love so dear?* Fae do not marry, do not partake in the strange customs of men, but they know love, perhaps much deeper.

As the spell runs dry, Iohmar drops his fingers, watching the human scrub at his hands in the washing barrel already stinking of filth. There is blood beneath his fingernails.

The child wails, round face pinching, and Iohmar sorts his memories for how a newborn human should appear. They take time not to exist as round grubs struggling to stand. Fae children are not grown for centuries upon centuries, but they are not fat wriggling worms for months and months. *Shouldn't this one be plumper? More colorful in its flesh?* The milk was of assistance, but not much. Unbeknownst to the human muttering along the opposite wall, Iohmar drags the back of his clawed finger down the rags wrapping the little body, searching for signs of discontent. He finds no outward wound, nothing to mend, the faintest strings of magic humans contain weak but existent, so he considers the neglect of the parent across the room that should not be blessed to call itself so.

Round eyes blink up at him, and Iohmar is struck by the color — brown as the rich soils of his mountains stretching to the sky, browner than a fawn's coat and just as warm. He calls to his magic and lets wisps of light dance across the infant's skin, shapeless and warm. A smile crinkles the tiny face, and Iohmar's lips twitch to return the gesture.

Little of his childhood remains in his memories, far past in millennium upon millennium. What he remembers is given to him in dreams and emotions, sensations of warmth in his chest rather than true details. But he remembers the faces of his own father and mother. *How did it appear to them when I gazed into their eyes?*

When his horn cracks the window frame on the way out, the man's gaze finds the space Iohmar occupies. His eyes drift straight past, a hunter trying to catch sight of an animal through a beam of light. His eyebrows pull together, but he returns to his scrubbing without a glance at the babe. There is a curl to his lip. Iohmar touches his magic to the human's heart, hoping for a better explanation, and recoils at what memories he encounters. Swallowing the sour taste rising on his tongue, he is certain of his decision as he gathers twigs and handfuls of fresh sprouted grass from between the trees.

Crows have gathered in greater numbers, hopping about the house and its roots. The man cannot see them. If he could, he would panic. Humans have strange superstitions about birds. *Perhaps for fair reason,* Iohmar considers, tearing a strip from his woven robe to bind the debris. He has not employed such magic in many centuries, this kind taking on a form not its own and consuming the life it is left to take. Iohmar rolls the bundle between his palms and murmurs.

The fair lands are not safe for the boy, but neither is this awful place. Iohmar will find someone suitable to take the infant, but he cannot leave it here in the meantime.

Carefuller and softer than he's accustomed to, he extracts the child from the window. All tears and screams are gone. Those round brown eyes blink at him, a fawn lost in the evening light, a wisp of weight in his palm.

With a rustle and sweep of his robes, he leaves the cursed bundle in the makeshift crib fit for no loved thing and melts into the woods, followed by a shaft of sunlight and a flock of gossiping crows.

THE HALLS BENEATH THE EARTH

Dawn breaks warm with purple twilight as Iohmar passes the human grave.

An overgrown path humans avoid returns him home. Before the crack in the mountains offers him a way to return to Látwill — the lands of Iohmar's people and his Fair Halls — by foot. A mess of gray stones marks the pass, a recent addition in Iohmar's lifetime, less recent in the memories of humans. Vines embrace the crude shrine, mosses of green and orange clinging to the rough surface. Moths living in the thick damp heat of the place where the human and fae world meet bumble about, long tongues finding spring flowers no larger than pebbles.

Iohmar passes the shrine without stopping, running fingers across the nearest stone. He remembers the human in a misty sort of way, gone mad when returning to the human world after dwelling too long in Iohmar's, and remembers acutely the time he discovered the grave, a warning for others to never stray close to the mountains and the twilight lands beyond.

It was soon later Iohmar forbade his kind from bringing the fragile creatures to Látwill. A few days is no worry, but years take too great a toll on the human mind.

Iohmar will return this infant bundle far before then.

Familiar trees extend branches in greeting as he travels the pass, stone cliffs rising on either side, leaving barely enough space for his shoulders. All manner of flowers and creeping vines wrap around his ankles and toes. Their magic, dull and sleepy, is a soothing warmth like weak sunlight. Animals brush their noses against him and scurry away. His crows have dispersed, sated by seeds and breadcrumbs he let fall from his fingers. A deer approaches in a wider section of the path, nose twitching, flowers sprouting along her pale back. Tall as she is, even her head does not reach Iohmar's. She nuzzles his fingers before wandering away into the undergrowth and flowers from which she was born.

Streaks of shadowed trees reach much of Látwill. Iohmar steps through sunlight, avoiding them, but they are not all easy to pass. They tug at his magic. In the distance, the heart of the woods sings to him, awake, trying to draw him into its embrace.

Iohmar . . .

Come sleep, Iohmar...
Årelang wants you...
Croía is here...
You are safe here, sweet lord...

Iohmar shudders at the names of his father and mother and shakes off the trees' heady voices, wondering if the child hears anything at all.

Owls scream overhead. He sees nothing of them but the pale light spilling from their beaks. Obsidian dragonflies drone over the grasses. Wolves circle him. They dwell far into the heart of the trees but emerge at his presence, the pads of their paws whispering along the soil, tails swishing. He glimpses one but senses the presence of the other six as embers are felt near a fire.

The pack's leader flickers among the ferns and mossy branches. Iohmar pauses. So does the creature. Its body is gray, twisted with earth-green vines. A bruise-blue flower falls from its mouth. Its face is flat, built as a diamond in angles and patterns, snout drawn to a point, a mask of flat wood unlike the wolves of any human kingdom. Two sharp eyes with purple irises gaze out at him.

Iohmar knows better than to reach out and keeps his silence. If the creature has something to say, he will speak for himself.

"They rarely come to these trees any longer," says a voice from behind. Iohmar knew of the fae's presence but didn't expect words.

As the wolf trots away, Iohmar turns slightly in the other direction. A face emerges from the dark trunks, body peeking out. It is humanoid in shape, one of Iohmar's few folk who prefer to dwell elsewhere, away from the Fair Halls of his mountain.

Concealing the boy in his robes, Iohmar says, "Hello, Túirt."

Túirt's sharp dark-as-pitch eyes stay fixed on the face of his king, not on what's bundled in his arm. "My sweet lord."

"How are your plums?"

Shuffling from the thicket like a rabbit watching for hawks, Túirt reaches out a long blue-purple limb, shyly presenting Iohmar with a fruit. Unease takes automatic hold, but Iohmar brushes it aside, keeping his expression kind. Túirt is not his friend, but if he were in a foul mood, Iohmar would know by now. Today, he seems to want to please his king.

Taking the plum with the tips of his talons, Iohmar bites into the soft flesh. Sweet and tart flavors flood his tongue, his eyes watering.

"You grow the best fruit, Túirt."

He is a solitary creature and does not hear the magic of his name spoken often. He shudders, and his eyes drift to Iohmar's curled arm.

"What do you have there, my lord?" he asks, starting to side-step closer.

"Nothing for you to worry over," Iohmar says as gently as he can, taking a pointed step away.

Túirt's long face scrunches. The babe shifts, but Iohmar doesn't allow himself to tense. He doesn't know how the fae would react but doesn't want him spreading the information.

"I want to see what you've found," Túirt whines, trying to hop closer, spreading thin lips in a smiling line of needle teeth.

"Enough, Túirt. Go back to your trees."

Command in his voice coupled with the fae's name halts Túirt in his tracks.

"Eeeeehhh." Túirt gives another whine of a noise, scowling at Iohmar and turning for the dark of the trunks, spitting to himself.

Túirt is no true threat, but Iohmar still dislikes angering one of his folk, particularly when they're curious. Sighing, he continues, tossing the pit of the plum aside. He will bring Túirt fresh bread from the Fair Halls to soothe his hurt feelings. He may be a dangerous creature, but he is petty and sated by pretty or sweet things.

Iohmar steps into the nearest sunbeam breaking the fog of trees.

The underside of the highest mountain rises. Rocks mar the lower edge, overgrown with moss, plants, and vines after many millennia. Iohmar remembers the collapse burying him in stone and shadow, a hazy dream from long ago. The storm accompanying the great quake. The sight of it casts spiderwebs of chill across his skin. He lowers his eyes to the infant asleep in the crook of his arm. It is strange to hold something so fragile, so small and helpless. All children in his Halls sit at his feet or hold his fingers, but he's never feared breaking one of them with too careless a touch.

Iohmar's folk dwelling within his mountain will not harm the child. They do not share his small respect for humankind, but he forbade them from bringing humans as pets into the Halls to wither and become discontent, and Iohmar cannot break a law he has so long enforced. But there are those who may steal the babe away to someplace less fair and warm. All fae lands are not so bright and lovely.

For now, the child shall be his little secret.

Lesser folk appear at the base of the mountain. Slow of thought, drunk on the magic hanging heavy within the woods, they sense him as moths discovering a lantern. Some are small and light, floating from the ground. Some waddle along the earth with many limbs and flower-size faces of bark or moss or loam.

"Hello, little things," Iohmar murmurs, reaching to brush his fingers against them. They grab his hands and rub along his legs. None reach his knees in height.

They are not the folk dwelling within the mountain, the ones who would notice the child within his arms. These are not unintelligent, but slow and gentle, dwelling on magic and forest things and often the moon. They are as fae as he, but not the same. He is warmed by their presence, but there is no companionship. He lets them run off once they've made their greetings.

Usually, an outing to the human world would warrant a walk among his people upon returning, a peaceful way to breathe in the warmth and peace of the vast gardens where his folk spend much of their dreaming days.

Today, he carries the child in one of the hidden passages.

The boy has woken, wide-eyed and quiet for a human child, fisting and tugging at his swaddling rags. *Those are the first to go.* Iohmar twines his finger into the filthy garments, dropping the useless things along the forest floor to rot. Insect-tiny fingers pull at his robe when he covers the boy with the excess fabric of his soft sleeves.

Iohmar weaves among the ferns and mushrooms and tree trunks cloaking the mountainside. The fair lands are both above the world and below the mountains, breathtaking in height and deep in seclusion, a concept mortals don't grasp. Should he stand at the highest peak, he would glimpse the tower of the neighboring kingdom and her queen. Iohmar knows by heart the path he found when he was naught a few decades old, still no more than a child himself. By his side walked his friend, the only other of his age running the gardens of the Fair Halls, now long-lost to him. He shakes away the thought of her, the ache of the old wound sewn into his heart.

Here, in a space carpeted by leaves and hidden by ferns, Iohmar can gaze upon the human woods for miles upon miles. Sunlight breaks across the tree-lined horizon — shades of orange and yellow perfect for slipping in and out. Closer to the mountain, they blend into the purple-and-silver twilight of Iohmar's world. Only at high noon do his fair lands bask in sunlight, and only at the peak of midnight do they gaze upon the moon and her stars. Mist hangs where the two realms meet. Darker places mark the densest streaks of trees and the heart of the woods beyond.

Pressing through undergrowth, Iohmar maneuvers roots until the vegetation reveals a tunnel. The scent of cool soil fills his nose, sharp and calming, the distinct cold of rock never seen by the sky. The mountain trembles, as it often does. A shiver. Crystals threaten to cut his bare feet, but he's found his way along the dim of this path enough to know his way. No fae will follow him here.

Time was needed to be comfortable underground once again. Millennia have passed, and he takes strange comfort in the shadows, as he did as a child.

After some wandering, he lifts a pane of glass, swirled as water and milk at the corners and invaded by armies of moss and vines. He drops to the leaf-strewn floor, wriggling his toes in the familiar softness. The dozen clear squares of glass create a section of ceiling, light filtering down. The rest of the ceiling is part of the mountain, woven roots and autumn-hued wood beams nearing the shade of Iohmar's hair. An occasional branch sprouts in, rich with spring buds. Fallen leaves carpet the floor, browning from last autumn, orange and rich with warmth.

The far wall is also paned with glass, revealing another sight of the twilight woods.

My woods. They were his father's and grandfather's and great-grandfather's, many generations before men walked the lands above, rippling a thousand hues of green and auburn and silver. He often watches his people mingle among the trees from his perch far above, never straying too close to the heart of the woods and the slumbering trees and beckoning songs.

Settling the infant in the center of his bed, Iohmar cradles him among the folds of wrinkled covers, and the boy wails.

With a finger to his lips, he leans over and whispers, "Shh . . ."

Quiet. Birdsong filters in. Iohmar opens the nearest pane of glass, letting the birds in to sing. He regards the human creature. He will not tell of its existence until he's decided how to proceed. But for all his years and time spent among the children of his own folk, he's unsure what to do with the babe now it's here, gurgling at the birds along the bedspread.

For a moment, he hesitates. He can tell no one of his bringing the child to Látwill.

Save perhaps one.

This decision may be unwise. He steps from his room, sending Oisín, one of his kingsguard, to fetch Galen. The healer has been a constant part of his existence since childhood. He served Iohmar's own father, and Iohmar struggles to fathom the years the old fae has amassed. Even he cannot imagine existing so long. And the old caretaker is quiet. If Iohmar wishes him to keep this secret, Galen will do so.

Even if he may lecture Iohmar first.

Folding his legs beneath him at the end of the bed, Iohmar rests his chin on the foot of the covers and watches the infant tug at the blankets and crunch leaves between ungraceful fingers. Brown eyes follow the finches and sparrows and chattering songbirds. He seems content, and Iohmar sits so long he's startled when Galen makes a soft noise in the back of his throat.

"I felt when you returned. I wondered why you didn't enter the gardens. What trinket have you found?"

The old creature leans over Iohmar, hands clasped behind his back, silver eyebrows pulled together. Edging around the bed, he plucks the covering from the child and slips a long thin hand beneath, lifting him from the covers. He is less flamboyant than many of their kind. His skin is milk pale, eyes and hair silvery. Black designs streak like ink across his skin, decorating his shoulders and wrists and behind his ears. Iohmar is certain they continue along his body but has never seen the old fae in anything less than his long robes.

He is unassuming and gentle, comforting if not a little severe.

The babe gurgles at him.

"Silly boy," Galen grumbles, and Iohmar bristles at the admonishment. Had anyone else spoken to him so, he'd allow himself to be angry. As it is, he lowers his head without lowering his eyes, expression chill. He is not ashamed. "Why?"

"There was a group of men, off to catch one of their kin. He'd killed his mate and buried her in the woods. The child's mother. I do not understand such human things."

"Hmm . . ." Galen returns the child to the bed. There is a downturn to his lips at Iohmar's story. "It should not be with the man, but it shouldn't be here. You know this."

"Perhaps."

"What will you do with it?"

"Keep it here for now. It has no other kin, and I hope to find some humans appropriate to return it to."

Iohmar has no other idea of what to do with the grub now it's under his protection. It needs to be returned but may have no suitable caretakers. Iohmar was foolish to bring it here. Galen knows as well, a weight to the silence between them, but the old creature has the decency not to say.

Centuries have passed since war shook the foundations of his people, but the babe is a welcome sight to Iohmar, unremarkable as it is, somehow sweeter than the vast beauty of his Halls, simple for him to care for and protect.

Galen makes a soft sound—not displeased nor approving—and brushes his robes as if the child dirtied them. "I can't imagine one of your people would harm it, but news will spread you've broken your own law. I would keep it in your chambers."

"Yes."

Galen opens his mouth, but it takes an extra moment for the words to come out. "And if you need me for anything . . ."

Iohmar draws his eyes from the child to the older face. He didn't have to offer. "I will ask. I thought it appropriate you know it's here. This does not leave these chambers, even to my kingsguard."

Galen bows, the barest tilt of his shoulders, brushing his fingers over Iohmar's arm in respect before he leaves.

Quiet falls, only the shiest whisper of a breeze against the window and flutter of wings. Most of the songbirds have flown back the way they came, those remaining hopping along the bed, interest in the human already lost. He lacks anything shimmering or magic to capture their attention.

Iohmar's own interest intrigues him. His kind are known for stealing humans, selecting someone grown or young with propensity for beauty. An artist, a singer, a chef, beautiful in the face or body, or for any other reason they might find appealing. Humans caught and released without thought were somewhat remarkable for their kind. Even changeling children held some sparkle of beauty to come and therefore drifted into their world without thought or hesitation.

Nothing is remarkable about the tiny thing wiggling on Iohmar's bed.

Even its face, endearing as any newborn's, is rather ugly for a human babe, skin and wisps of hair dull, features set in an unpleasant manner. Iohmar senses no talent beneath the surface ready to break free with age and nurturing.

Still, he is drawn to the creature. Protective. If nothing else, the boy's eyes sparkle when they gaze at him.

Iohmar closes his eyes and turns from the strange thing with a sigh.

His visit to the human world sparked intrigue in Iohmar's heart, a shiver of suspicion.

Perhaps this is fear, he considers as he approaches the borders of his land, the thought sour in the back of his throat.

These are not his borders with the human world, not even with those of the high queen whose kingdom dwells farther from his in a direction often changing, her love letters stashed within his desk. These lands are not far from his own mountains but are far enough Iohmar cannot see them from his window. With a breath and brush of warmth along his skin, he steps through sunbeam after sunbeam until there comes a place where his trees fade and those before him are strange and still and silent. No animals or fae dwell here. This other land is incorrect to even his eyes, sharp as those of any predator bird.

Iohmar breathes. Though he stands too far for his breath to reach the rippling barrier, the shimmer in the atmosphere seems to curve to his presence. His skin has taken a chill he won't be able to shed until his own home surrounds him.

He could draw closer if he wished, twist his fingers into the glistening air, step within the trees of the kingdom beside his.

Murmuring to himself, he draws on the warmth of his own trees, pressing the ever-present sensation of the magic within him, a swirl of warm sunlight threads, outward. No longer does he need to speak when exercising his magic, but it is how he learned as a child, and he takes comfort in the gesture. Reaching the border and beyond, he is met with a void deeper than the tunnels beneath the earth or the space between the burning stars.

A subtle heat smolders behind his breastbone, a familiar rage, an eternal ache, and his fingers twitch to reach for his parents so long-lost to him.

But the creatures dwelling within the stillness are not encroaching. He finds no evidence they are closer to the edges of the trees. And so he lets his magic relax, drain back into his limbs. Stepping into his trees, his feet find the nearest burst of light breaking the canopy.

A beam of warmth returns him home.

3

FEASTS AND LETTERS

Iohmar's new charge requires no special care.

Woven roots coaxed from the wall beside his bed make a simple crib. The boy sleeps most hours, tucked within blankets. It isn't a task to feed him or even to keep him clean. It would be simple, almost, to forget the child exists. Iohmar dines with his folk, wanders his Halls and woods and gardens, and partakes in every aspect expected of and enjoyed by him.

Why did I bring the boy to Látwill?

He visits the human lands once, avoiding those whom he frightened along the path, hiding within sunbeams and shadows, and cannot convince himself any family in the nearest village could care for the boy better than he can. Perhaps he needs to widen his search.

The babe has taken to crying when Iohmar nears him—enough he warded his chambers lest his kingsguard hear—never at any other time. Iohmar knows enough of children, fae or otherwise, to realize such is strange and incorrect behavior.

Shouldn't he scream when he wants food or cleaning or attention? Such is the way of humans, needing and unable to express their wants with words, even the older ones.

The child is frightened of me. The thought comes slow and unwilling. It's happened a handful of times, and Iohmar sighs as he looks down at the boy.

I should not have brought him here, he thinks but does not say the words aloud.

He was remembering his parents. Yes, he must have been. He remembered his parents, and the ache within his chest worsened, and he attempted to soothe it by saving some helpless child. Yes, this must be the reason.

Humans must exist who share the child's bloodline. If not in the nearest village, then elsewhere. There are many ways to reach Látwill from the human lands—Iohmar can find other villages, other cities, other families. It would be correct to deliver the babe to one of them.

His gut churns. Satisfied the child is fed and comfortable, Iohmar leaves him to his crib. The crying fades to a sniffle before ceasing. He suppresses another sigh as he drifts from his chambers.

His kingsguard join him at the end of the corridor. Dressed in soft silver and drapes of comfortable fabric, they do not radiate their usual sharp angles and steel nature. But there is little reason for fine armor and knives in Iohmar's Halls. They are company rather than protection in times of peace. Many have been by Iohmar's side for over a millennium. One was born not so long after Iohmar that they were both considered children within the same few centuries. Each is younger than him by some decades or centuries, but none are close to childhood.

Much like Galen, they do not need permission to join him, but Iohmar invites them with a curl of his fingers. They rise from lounging within the twisted roots and trees lining the walls, drifting behind him with soft steps. Each carries a curved sword full of grace, for the comfort of habit rather than need. Iohmar's own is by his bedside. They are silent save a few words of friendship or the shuffle of one nudging another out of balance. Iohmar smiles. They are the closest to a band of brothers existing among the fae. Five children would never be born to a single family, but they are as close to one another as possible. They have fought by his side. Iohmar remembers the three whose footsteps are here no longer.

"How fair the winds?" he asks.

Only Queen Rúnda of their neighboring lands can call the winds at her bidding. Others can ask and hope their call is answered, but often the wildest gales whip over the mountains of their own accord. Iohmar's folk ride them over the peaks and past the seas and back again, an adventure told of even in human tales, for often the winds carry them past. Iohmar has experienced it many times. His kingsguard never tire of the thrill.

"Bitter cold," says Oisín, walking closest to him, and the others laugh. Iohmar knows each by the sound of their laughter. "Some of the younglings were taking their first trip. Súiler got a girl who latched on to his arm and wouldn't let go. She believed she would fall through the clouds."

Súiler gives a familiar grumble. Iohmar presses his lips together in amusement.

"Glad to know your time was well spent."

Chuckles greet him before being drowned by the merriments of the evening feast. Iohmar lets them disperse to be with whatever friends or lovers they wish.

Iohmar seats himself at the head of the long table occupying half the hall. This is not the throne room, but the chair is carved with vines and streaks of silver and cushioned with fine fabrics and sprouting flowers. It smells of condensed springtime. Not hungry, he picks at the seeds of a pomegranate. The table is spread with food, curved to match the walls at Iohmar's back.

All manner of fae dine here: Creatures with sharp senses and sharper minds, bodies adorned with stones or living things, mosses and growing flowers and fresh shoots of vines. Humanoid faces or those no human would recognize. Lesser creatures, slower in wit and just as precious to him, skitter around the table legs and steal treats for the fun of mischief rather than sitting and dining as they're welcome to. Wine flows. His people feast and drink and break into soft haunting songs, not paying him much mind.

Galen, dressed in blue as deep as the sea, fusses over him and attempts to straighten the edge of his collar until Iohmar shoos him away. He is less formal with his head full of drink, and Iohmar can't have his caretaker smothering him before his subjects.

Picking at one of the smaller creatures tangling its gossamer wings in his hair, he cradles it within his palm while it recovers.

Needle teeth grin up at him. These are the creatures tending to fill the stories of men, with insect wings and flighty minds and small mischievous magic. So quick do the true stories fall to myth. Iohmar considers the men he crossed on the road and the braver of the group to whom he spoke. He held Iohmar's eye and spoke to him when the others fled or cowered.

Perhaps he is worth a visit. After centuries, there is still some curiosity for the human world—it may be an interesting distraction.

He may have knowledge for a suitable human family for the child. The thought sours Iohmar's mood.

There is no reason to be so resistant. He has never wanted a child, never considered himself a caretaker. Protecting his own folk has stretched his magic to the thinnest threads when threatened, and he does not know what he would do with something so small and frail and reliant as a babe.

Does such manner of compassion exist in me? He remembers it once, but it was ages past. He has long since lost any family. His love is for his people. Humans will certainly appreciate the babe far more than Iohmar can.

He sets the creature on the table. It dives between the layers of a cake, and those seated closest giggle and avoid reaching for the food.

The day is damp and drizzling rain when Iohmar takes the boy to the human world. His fair lands are broody with clouds, warm as they always are, but once he takes the mountain pass, droplets catch on his horns, soaking into the shoulders of his robes.

It so rarely rains in Látwill. The sensation sends pleasant shivers across his skin. But the babe, human as he is, won't enjoy the wet. Iohmar folds the blanket around him, covering his squat little face with his long hand.

The boy isn't crying. He did so when Iohmar first lifted him from his crib but soon grew tired of the screaming. Small hiccupping whimpers persist, and Iohmar doesn't know if there is actual fear in the infant's constant gaze or if his mind is playing a cruel trick.

But as he exits the path, passing the grave, the little thing *screams*.

Iohmar winces. They are still close enough to his lands that some passing fae might hear, especially with the echo off the stone cliffsides.

"Shh," he whispers, extending a shred of his magic once more, this time trying to impart a calm sensation over the child.

He doesn't know what's wrong. Even Galen hasn't been able to offer advice, as many children as he's cared for in the past. The babe never cries at Galen's presence.

All the more reason finding some humans is wise, he tells himself. His own determination sounds weak to his ears. He should not be acting in such a way. No one else in his position would. His parents would never have brought the child. Certainly, they would have no qualms about returning it to lands in which it belongs. Queen Rúnda would never act so irresponsibly.

This is the correct course of action, he thinks again, then stops himself from stomping as he walks. He does not throw tantrums, even alone.

No sun shines in the human lands for him to utilize, but Látwill still had its occasional beams breaking the twilight. Iohmar didn't use them and recognizes the wish to walk the entire way as another hesitation, another excuse.

Well, it is too late to correct such behavior. Rain and storm clouds dominate the human lands.

The more Látwill fades to the human woods, the more the babe squirms and cries, even with Iohmar's soothing magic. Stopping under cover of a large pine giving off scent in the damp, somewhere near the path where he found the humans, Iohmar removes his hand from the tiny face, staring down at it.

Flailing two fists, the babe scrunches his face in a scream, feet kicking the swaddle. Iohmar's own face bunches in a frown. His presence may frighten the boy, but he's been quiet for a while.

What has upset him further?

Drawing his fingers down the boy's soft cheek, then his neck and chest, Iohmar searches for the brittle threads of magic even humans maintain. They existed when first he found the child and every time he's checked since, but now he struggles to locate them. The boy, sickly as he is, hasn't been deteriorating in the Fair Halls. Látwill's magic is a warm kind, a healing kind, even if all humans do not take well to it.

The boy's life force is so weak that Iohmar nearly loses it. Panic locks a fist around his chest. He refuses to acknowledge such an unreasonable rush of emotion. He steps from under the branches of the pine, continuing a few yards into the human lands, toward the nearest village, leaving the magic of his woods behind near completely.

More crying. What little magic Iohmar grasps nearly disappears.

Iohmar assumed the boy was thin and small because of the murderer's neglect. Perhaps that was only part of it. Sickness does not exist in the Fair Halls. In the back of his mind, he knows humans are often ill and die even sooner than what short lives they would've lived.

But a child? Do little babes die in the human world?

Iohmar runs in his return to the mountain pass, finding the first beam of sun in his own lands and bringing them both to the base of his mountain. The spark of magic returns, weaker but surviving. The babe does not cease his crying, but it fades to the whimpering level Iohmar is accustomed to at his presence.

"Oh dear," he whispers, and kisses the boy's cheek despite his crying.

When Iohmar returns to his chambers, he sets the babe in his crib. As soon as he backs out of view, the crying ceases.

What should I do with it?

Tossing aside his heavy robe, damp from the rain, he relaxes into the seat of his writing desk, sifting papers rather than dwelling on the new discovery. Letters sit from the neighboring kingdom and his own folk dwelling far from the mountain, but no letter from Queen Rúnda, and his mood darkens further. Soon it will be time to visit, but he feels the distance between her lands and his as a physical weight.

The child wails.

Parchment slips from Iohmar's hold, tearing on his long-clawed finger. He squints at the crib, at the continuing outburst of emotion. Rising, he edges into sight, gazing over the crib's edge. Whimpering turns to a squall.

What does the little grub want? Is the trip to the human lands still present in him? He lifts the boy from the crib by his down blanket. Moss and infant ferns cling to half his desk, eating at the wood, and it's on this soft space Iohmar deposits the bundle.

"What?" he hisses without venom, slipping back to his seat and leaning over the child.

The boy continues to sob, fists flinging about. *Was the babe ever named?* Names hold power in the hearts of the fair folk, so much so many choose never to speak theirs even among their kin, and Iohmar does not sense the presence of a name in the child.

"What to name you?" he muses, regretting the words as they leave his lips. Even suggesting such a thing is unwise. Because it may not be able to live in the human world does not mean he should be considering fae names.

"I do not believe I can return you," he says, to himself rather than the child, resting his chin on the palm of his hand.

Wailing fills the edges of his chambers. Iohmar offers his knuckle, ensuring his talons are not in danger of cutting fragile skin. Suckling his finger, the boy still doesn't cease his crying. Iohmar leans closer, inspecting the color returning to the pale skin with time and care. At least he has done this for the child, even if the boy is frightened by his presence.

All his progress was threatened when Iohmar took him to the realm above.

He runs the backs of his fingers along the babe's soft cheek. The boy blinks wet eyes, the sobs fading. The beginnings of a smile crinkle his plump face.

For the first time, the boy giggles.

Both hands stop flailing, instead reaching for Iohmar's jaw. Iohmar blinks. Lowering his head, he lets the boy's chubby hands pat his cheeks, thump against his horns, and tug the locks of autumn hair spilling over his shoulders. Soft cooing begins. Iohmar blinks again, his eyes hot.

Ridiculous. Fae kings do not cry for a human babe. Delicate as possible, he slips his hands beneath the tiny wriggling body, aware of his claws. He should file them. The thin fabric of his tunic is little barrier. Many scars are hidden within his clothing, ones he is loath to let others touch, but the warm weight of the child is soothing rather than troubling. He checks his magic and finds it clinging to life.

The boy gums Iohmar's shoulder, still making soft nonsensical noises. Drool drips down his collarbone. Iohmar can't bring himself to care.

Leaning back in the large chair, he props his feet against the edge of the desk, hoping Galen won't take this moment to invade his privacy. He could never be caught by his folk acting in such a way. The babe's soft face nuzzles into Iohmar's neck, and he falls into a gurgling sleep.

"Oh dear," he mumbles again. "Galen will be quite unhappy."
He lets the child sleep against his heartbeat.

4

THE HALLS BELOW THE HALLS

Dark things often dwell at the edges of Iohmar's Halls.
Strange creatures reside across his lands, secure under
his protection. Iohmar lets them have their space and their own
magic, and they return their quiet peace. None have ever needed
pushing away as the rippling monsters in their dead lands, though
their magic is often ancient and foreign. Even the most troubled
of fae carry respect for their king beneath the earth. Many live
below the mountain itself.

As days blend into a sweet mess of time, Iohmar wonders about
the knowledge of such creatures.

Neither he nor Galen grasp human time, but Iohmar knows
they age rapidly. So short are their life spans that childhood is but
a blink of an eye even in human standards.

The boy is not growing.

If anything, he is smaller. What color Iohmar nursed to his cheeks has faded, and as he turns the boy's fingers in his, they appear thinner. When he lets him sleep atop his chest—a habit Galen has witnessed and found baffling—the infant is lighter, less of a plump weight and more a wisp to float away. His threads of magic still exist but grow weaker.

Each time Galen visits the king's chambers, Iohmar catches him glancing into the crib.

He has kept his silence about the child, realizing Galen's disapproval and not wishing to engage in the matter, but breaks it now. "He became ill when I attempted to return him to the lands above. His life faded the moment we entered the trees. He seems to be fading here as well, simply slower. Can he be ill? I've never seen a human react in such a way to the Fair Halls."

Galen peers down, fiddling with the blanket, shaking his head in short movements at the new information. "It's difficult to say how humans react to magic. Perhaps it has lasted so long only because of this place."

Iohmar is not easily sickened, not after battles and wounds and death of his own folk, but he forces himself not to shrink. "Would you tell me how to save it, if you knew?"

Offense lights Galen's eyes. "I do not keep truths from you. Just because I disapprove of your decisions does not make me disloyal—"

"I was merely asking."

Silence wraps around them. Iohmar evens his expression, but shame twinges his insides. Galen is dear to him, and Iohmar knows the truth is not being twisted. To imply such was cruel.

Joining his caretaker at the crib, he says, "I apologize. I know you do not approve."

"You are causing trouble for yourself. You haven't named it, have you?"

"No," he says. Like his kin, he cannot lie, and so Galen accepts the word. With greater emotion than he is used to displaying, Iohmar says, "I do not wish the child to die."

The babe grins at them. Under Galen's scrutiny, Iohmar forces his expression not to soften. He lets the tiny fingers wrap around his thumb. Galen's gaze presses against him.

"You are not yet old enough to learn the ways of cheating death, if you ever will. I will never have the gift. Those who may have been able are no longer with us."

Grief weighs in his voice for the wars waged upon their people centuries ago. Everyone lost kin, and the eldest of their kind did not take well to violence and harshness. Some merely faded, returning to the trees and grasses. Though quite ancient, Iohmar was not always the eldest among his folk. Now, finding one older than he is presents a challenge. Within the mountain, it is only his caretaker.

Sometimes, he believes Galen survived for him.

"Do not think on it so much. It is a human thing. There are so many of their kind, and they live such short lives. It may have been suffering there, but it does not appear to be here."

As if to agree, the boy lets out a giggling squeal, tugging at Iohmar's finger and turning his grin to Galen. Iohmar puts his shoulder to the old fae, not wishing his expression to be seen.

Galen sighs. "Do not think on it too much," he offers again, weaker than Iohmar is accustomed to, and brushes his arm as he departs.

Despite its strange effects on humans, Iohmar's magic and that of the heart of the woods, which seeps through his mountains and forests and silver sky, does not harm something small or weak. His magic is a growing kind, a healing, soothing kind balanced in sunlight and shadow.

But it is not enough.

Crouching in the roots circling his forest-facing window, Iohmar casts his magic to the human world above and below, piercing the mist between their worlds, sweeping across each living thing. Night has fallen. Heartbeats reach him. Insects and animals, plants and trees, faint human lives too far to be near the borders of his lands.

Stretching his magic so far drains warmth from his limbs. Returning it to his own body and the surrounding mountain, he dwells in the plants and trees woven within the walls, the birds hopping near his windows, and the human life tucked among blankets. The babe's heartbeat is a bird's wing, soft and quick. Rising, Iohmar slips to the crib and draws his finger down the child's chest. He is rewarded with a soft gurgle. Nothing dark dwells within the little heart, no magic touching him from the lesser creatures of Iohmar's Halls.

Giving in to the grasping hands, he scoops the boy to his chest and stretches along the bed.

"What to do with you?" he whispers. The child drools on his finger. It is a guilty relief to Iohmar that he must keep the boy, not return him to some distant human who may share a scrap of his blood.

The mountains give off a soft rumble, as they often do, but never with such violence as when he was a child, buried in the caverns so far below the earth that nothing living had ever ventured so low. This is a passing tremor. He has encouraged his trees and their roots to reinforce the walls within the mountain, bracing the Halls for any dangerous quakes. The tunnels and their inhabitants are under no threat.

The tunnels.

Slipping into the soft-soled shoes he rarely dons, he folds away the carved door hiding his clothing. A wealth of fine fabric shimmers in the dull light of evening. He runs his fingers along each, testing the weight and texture, the statement made, and selects the darkest of the bunch. It was gifted to him decades ago by the high queen across the realm. Rúnda has a taste for dramatic gifts, but the robe is subtle and powerful. It pools around his shoulders like evening shadow, ink dipped in water. He is well aware of the appearance of his eyes when he wears such dark clothing—bright and piercing and terrible. Fastening the threads down the front, he tucks the child within a fold of fabric near his heart.

Galen would disapprove. He would lose every shred of calm he's maintained since Iohmar was a youngling. But as he was keen to point out, so few remain who know the ways of life and death, so few now the war has come and gone, and Iohmar is powerful but too young by quite some millennia to wield such strength. If he ever will.

There may be some in the shadows of his realm who've been

hidden so long they've learned the art of saving a sick human babe. And those below are secretive. Strange. Unlikely to spread rumor their king brought a human to their lands against his own decree.

"After tonight, I may have to name you," he murmurs against the babe's soft head as he leaves by way of the window cavern, finding his way down instead of up.

It isn't far to the places beneath his Halls. Hours pass, though he soon loses track, and he would be lost if not for his magic.

Tunnels spiderweb beneath his mountains, a labyrinth of lightlessness. Far down, among mushrooms pressing through hard-packed earth, spouting incandescent spores, he feels a creature of pure shadow. In his dark robes and with his quiet footsteps, he would be invisible, bathed in darkness, if not for the subtle glow of his skin. Pale light radiates wherever shadows touch him, as it has since he was a child.

Each time Iohmar glances down, he finds the infant's bright eyes gazing up at him while the boy gums his blanket, never crying.

Iohmar isn't sure for what he's searching. Centuries have fled since he last walked these underground places. Not since he was a boy wandering these tunnels for his lost friend has he found himself so deep within the oppressive earth. Fear no longer settles in his bones, but shadows and mazes of earth hold no comfort.

Small things scurry about his feet, curious and eager to drink from his magic. He lets them crawl across his shoes and cling to the sides of his robes and hems of his pants. They take numerous forms as those above. Some resemble the lizards Iohmar sees roaming human lands, scaled and long with tails and clinging fingers. Others mirror him in miniature, with arms and legs and tiny faces. They are often unclothed and bear strange colors to their skin or scales or feathers. Some, content to exist in the dark, do not see him but smell his magic and hear the brush of his feet. He scoops one from the damp wall, letting the pale creature crawl between his fingers, gaze at him with a tiny noseless face, and flutter off on blue spiderweb wings.

Something much larger pulls itself from the wall. A dozen limbs fumble together, barely a shadow in the lack of light, but the creature casts a strong flame of magic nonetheless. Iohmar edges around it. Even here, in this buried place, nothing is strong enough to cause him true harm, but he doesn't wish to fight with the infant in his hold.

Murmuring, he presses his magic against it, hoping to either warn it back or satisfy it with a burst of power. Tumbling over him, bumping into the opposite wall, it clicks, hissing. It may be large, but it is not as intelligent as even the wolves roaming the heart of the woods.

"Now, now," Iohmar mumbles.

One arm with the tiniest hook of a claw snaps near his face, drawing the slightest sting from his jaw. He dabs at the spot of blood, flicking it away, considering drawing roots to secure the creature.

But it jerks away, hissing louder, frightened by the outpouring of magic at Iohmar's drawn blood. Even this thing, aggressive as it is, will recognize its king.

With a cascade of limbs, it folds itself back into the wall, sending earth and pebbles scattering about Iohmar's feet.

The babe gives a small surprised gurgle. Iohmar doesn't know when the little human decided he was safe in the king's hold. His chest grows tight, and he shoves the sensation away as he returns to his path.

A few resembling his kin living above ground—large and intelligent and drenched in magic—are not difficult to uncover. He doesn't see them within the darkness but feels the watching of their eyes like fingers across his skin. Some appear, attracted by the scuffle, but flee once they've glimpsed him. Drawn to their strong magic, he allows himself to be led by the greatest pull. It is not as intimate a bond as he shares with Galen or his kingsguard— or as he shared with his parents—but he allows his magic to lead him where his eyes would fail.

Hours and hours he wanders, speaking to those who do not shy from his sight, a spare word here and there. None of their names are known to him. Most are hidden within shadow, silent as bones, and he does not draw close enough to see their shapes in the darkness. If they do not acknowledge him, he does not approach.

A room spreads before him, a widening pocket of the tunnel. To his right, Iohmar could continue deeper, far and far down where no one has ventured. He raises his hand as if he can press his palm to the space of darkness his friend was lost to so long ago. He doesn't know if it was even near this place. The air remains chill and light and empty. Iohmar looks at the continuing tunnel until the darkness distorts to his eyes, then turns away.

The little pocket of space he's found has the air of a home. As he navigates tree roots more stone than living thing, touches of life appear along the walls: Braids of roots. A perfect curve to the ceiling.

Cool magic hangs within the small round space. It's not his sun-soaked halls and bright chambers, but it is familiar nonetheless. He cannot determine why it speaks to him so, but it is strong, stronger than any he's come across in a great long time, either above the earth or below.

He sits within the roots and waits.

Eyes closed, he lets his magic seep down, farther and farther than even these dark tunnels. Signs of life fade, left to nothing but rock and precious crystals any human would treasure. Any fae would adore them, for decorating their bodies is a favorite pastime. Iohmar would love to have a mere few between his fingers, to present them to Rúnda, but even his magic could not access them so far in the earth. Instead, he basks in their glow.

Farther down, there is something else, a large presence with some flicker of magic but no life. *A great cavern? Or some underground river destined never to see sunlight?* He allows his thoughts to wander in the cold.

Some hours later, he becomes aware of her magic.

A WOMAN IN THE EARTH

S he is ancient, perhaps older than Iohmar himself.

How is she possible? He blinks, squinting to catch her features. Against the opposite wall, her form is withheld in shadows, part of the darkness itself. With a step, she solidifies, still featureless. Wrapped in shadows, she is no more than ancient magic taking a form matching his. *How would she appear if I were not here?*

Different fae live different life spans. Usually, the larger in form, the less the effects of time. Giant trees of the heart of the woods have lived lives even Iohmar and Galen cannot comprehend. Iohmar may live several more millennia—as his parents would have, as Galen is approaching. Iohmar cannot name this creature's exact years, but as her magic intertwines with his in greeting, he is given an eternity of hazy consciousness.

Silence fills the space. Iohmar is grateful for the babe's calm; it would be wrong of him to first break the quiet of her home.

"My sweet lord," she says, her voice like the long travel of a stream. Such a strange and soft sound for a dark and earthy space.

"My sweet lady," he says with respect.

She steps closer. Magic washes across his senses, prickling his skin. It's very strong to be so tangible. Strange and familiar. For a moment, he is a child exploring his woods and the caverns below, small and unassuming and learning to slip between sunlight and shadow.

"No high lord has ventured so far under the Fair Halls since before my time."

Her words are untrue. Iohmar's own father wandered these dark places searching for his son and the forest friend with whom he played.

"You have the strongest magic I've sensed. How long have you lived beneath the Halls?"

"A long while," she says, stepping once back, then closer. "I've heard you don't allow your people to bring humans to your lands . . ." She pauses. "If I may be so bold."

He doesn't allow himself to tense. "I decided on an exception."

"The king can make any decision he wishes."

Iohmar's kin would not speak to him in such a way. He would not tolerate the disrespect. But he is in her home, her sanctuary, and nearly smiles.

"Indeed I can."

She brushes her hands against her dress. It is a dark thing matching his own, woven in shadow and mist but flecked with earthen green.

Did my childhood friend dress as such? It seems she must have for the way she loved exploring these underground halls.

These tunnels are unearthing painful memories.

Crouching, she leans near, elbows draped over knees. Her body interacts strangely with itself, skin disappearing within itself only to solidify, the dress often becoming indiscernible from her body. She is not within arm's reach but is close enough he smells her skin, matching the stale air and chill earth and stone. The warmth of magic accompanying intelligence is lost to him. Tension knots his shoulders, skin tingling. He sits vulnerable and unarmed, and she is . . . strange.

Forcing his muscles to relax, he stares at her fingers, bare and as dark green and black at the tips as rich paint. Iohmar doesn't know if it's natural or a way she's decorated herself.

She stares at his horns—at least, her featureless face is tilted as such. Of the many odd features of the fae, these are not the strangest, but they are eye-catching, heavy enough he struggled holding his head upright as a child.

A trophy any human would kill to attain.

Her fingers twitch as if she wishes to touch them, but she remains at rest. Iohmar relaxes further. He doesn't wish the hand of any whom he does not know with intimacy to be near his face but does not wish to flinch from her should she reach for them.

"Your name, my sweet lady?" he asks.

"Not important," she says, flicking her fingers. Her face tips as if her gaze travels down his fine robes to the lump along his chest created by the child.

"You know mine," he says.

Doesn't she? Time may pass even stranger here than it does in the above lands. Names may be lost to her in a place such as this.

"I have none."

He smiles. "You mean you won't tell me."

"I mean I have none."

Iohmar blinks. Names are sacred. Some of his kin refuse to acknowledge their own, to keep it for themselves alone, but he can't imagine lacking something so basic to life and magic. Her sightless gaze challenges him to ask, but he does not. He doesn't wish to ignite her anger. He wishes to charm her.

And to plead for her help.

Nodding, he uncurls the babe from his robes. She leans onto the balls of her feet, toes gripping the roots of her floor, and her featureless face ripples.

"Quite unremarkable," she says.

Iohmar bristles but doesn't react.

Didn't I believe the same?

Her face is turned to his. She cocks her head in a sharp, sudden movement, mimicking the songbirds that flutter outside his windows, her ear resting to her shoulder. Long locks of brown hair and smoky shadow spill around her, curled in a messy, unkempt fashion. She is not so vain as Iohmar and the rest of his kind dwelling within the Halls.

Her presence is *so familiar*, a memory he cannot grasp.

"And you wish something of me?"

"The child ails . . ." He pauses at the way her head perks, then continues his tale, explaining the circumstances of his taking the child, the ways he's tended to him, and the worrisome symptoms. She folds her fingers, resting them atop the place her upper lip should be. Iohmar is accustomed to slowness. His people may be quick of emotion and ready for adventure, but long lives make for patient creatures. Often has he waited long stretches for answers.

After a time, she asks, "Why do you seek me out? Surely your magic is millennia stronger than this?"

"It is . . ." Iohmar hesitates. "But this is strange to me. There is nothing to heal, you see. I cannot name what sickens the child, and so I cannot . . . I cannot fix a wound I cannot see."

She nods, face tilted toward the child. "And *why?*"

"Why?"

"You venture to these halls beneath your own, places you never wander, to save a worthless human child you should have left alone by the word of your own decree."

Iohmar glances at the boy, uneasy.

"I wish to save him," he says, hoping the words will suffice.

"I knew as much without requesting. That is not what I asked."

Iohmar bites back an indignant response. He is not an unreasonable king, allowing his people their freedom in all but the most extreme circumstances and encouraging them to speak to him with openness. But he does not appreciate her excavating his emotions. In the silence, her head tilts from him to the child, and the mischief fades from the air.

"You're not as fun as I hoped," she whispers, words so soft he isn't sure they were meant for him.

"Do I know you, sweet lady?" he asks, shaken by the idea his presence was expected.

Her face twitches to his level, the movement angry, but there are no eyes for him to read, no expression among the smoke and shadow.

"Forgive me if I do," he says. "A life so long as mine, not every face can be recalled."

Her fingers return to the space of her upper lip. Tartly, she says, "N-n-n . . . ugh. I knew your son. It is not of importance."

Iohmar recognizes the stuttering. An attempted lie.

But his son?

She believes I am my father, he realizes. *She believes I am my father, and she knew me a long while ago. How strange . . .*

His chest constricts. *She knew my parents.* Acutely aware of his own age and Galen's, her knowledge of his family line takes the breath from his lungs. He opens his lips to pursue the topic, but she gives the same defensive twitch.

"So, you've come to ask me to save this little human?"

Iohmar is king. He could force the subject upon her, and comes close to doing so. Questions catch in the back of his throat. But he is here in her home to beg for assistance. Angering her may cost the child's life. In comparison, the possibility of having met her sometime in the past is small and feeble.

Besides, they must have been near infants for her to mistake him for his father. Though his magic resembles his parents', has the same feel in the air, neither his father nor his mother were adorned with such drastic features as his horns and talons. They were beautiful, both of them, in ways which drew each and every creature, but they were not easy to mistake for their son. If Iohmar has brushed paths with this woman, it mustn't have been of much significance to either of them.

And her question gives him hope. "You know a way? I wasn't certain any would."

"I am unsure. I wonder, what are you willing to sacrifice to make it so?"

It is not a threat. Magic so powerful as theirs does not give life without repercussions. For something so strong even he cannot attempt it . . . the price may be high.

"I wonder what it is I will have to give up."

She makes a noise somewhere between a hum and a chuckle. "Shrewd."

She holds out her hand. Burying his desire to pull the child closer, he removes the remaining fabric hiding him. From the moment he ventured down these tunnels, he knew touch would be necessary. Though this female sets him off-kilter, he senses nothing malicious. Her bond with him is the same as Iohmar maintains with any of his kin. Her magic may not be warm, may remind him of other creatures maleficent and terrifying, but he is aware of the spark of life within her, the strange little beat of her heart, so soft and quick for a creature so large and alive. He knows what it is to meet monsters full of intent to harm, and there is no such thing in this nameless, faceless fae.

And so he maneuvers the child into her hands.

Her skin does not contact his, but he ensures his talons are visible, trimmed smooth but unique, another tell he is not his father. If it registers, she does not show it. She props the child upright, one hand under his bottom, the other cradling his head and shoulders.

Her featureless face, sharp and swirled in darkness, looms close to the boy's. Still, he does not cry.

"Quite small for a human child, isn't he? How old is he?"

"I'm not certain," he admits. "Newborn when I found him. Human children are small."

"Yes." She doesn't sound convinced.

Setting the boy on her knees, she bows her head. Iohmar tastes magic in the air, different from his mountains and sharp as everything about her. It presses around him as a calm bubble of air. Silence falls over the little home, and Iohmar settles in for waiting. He doesn't allow the babe to slip from his sight, but his eyelids droop in the quiet of the room. If he wished, he could press his magic to hers, read her emotions and intent and the details of her talents in the threads of life Látwill has bestowed. But to do so would be invasive and unkind. It isn't a technique he employs unless permission has been given or an advantage needs to be gained to protect.

When she raises her head, Iohmar is comfortable and quiet, tapping his fingers together in his lap. She does not return the child. His hands twitch to retrieve him, but he forces himself still, patient. Waiting. A king controlling his emotions and desires with ease. A king who has seen many millennia and many things worse than someone holding a child he stole from the human lands.

"I find nothing malicious in him, magic or otherwise," she says, inspecting the babe's face as if the soft skin holds answers. "But I suspect you knew such things."

"Yes."

"I cannot tell you for certain what ails him," she says. Iohmar keeps the twist in his heart from showing on his features. "But if I must advise you what instinct tells me, he is too small and frail and young to bear the magic of these lands."

Iohmar blinks.

"He would not have lived in his world, as you discovered — I do not understand human illnesses, so I can't rightfully say why — but he is not faring much better here. I believe your magic may be prolonging his life, but at the same time, he doesn't have the strength to stand up to it."

"My magic does not take strength." Iohmar doesn't enjoy speaking about his life force or the ways in which his magic operates, but this is a known truth.

She shrugs, a roll of each shoulder at separate times. "I cannot tell you why, merely what I believe to be happening. It is as unusual to me as it is to you."

With two fingers, she curls the child's wisps of hair into a pointed twirl. Iohmar waits until he can no longer bear her silence or casual handling of the boy.

"You can think of no way to help?"

"I can think of something. It isn't healing, and you may not appreciate the suggestion. Or the knowledge."

Iohmar knows of darker magics, knows not all power is giving and bright. But it is not something often spoken of — less so since the wars — and none in his Halls bear such gifts. Látwill is a strange land, full of magic straining at its own boundaries, changing as often as it remains rigid, new creatures and magics presenting themselves, even to the king beneath the earth. Iohmar is never surprised to learn of knowledge nonexistent to him. This woman is correct: he may not appreciate the suggestion or the comprehension, but he knows of darkness and death and scars and fear in ways she would be shocked to learn, and it is from these things that such dark magic springs.

No, he may not appreciate it, but it will not shock or disturb him.

He spreads both hands, nodding, encouraging her to speak. Her head cocks, and she leans close to him over the child. Iohmar doesn't allow himself to feel threatened.

"Your father would disapprove," she says, and Iohmar's heart gives so harsh and unexpected a twist that he bares his teeth at her, an unintended snarl of a noise passing his lips before he presses them into a tight line. She should not speak of his parents in ways she does not understand.

But what a strange comment, he thinks a moment later. She still does not recognize him as Iohmar, but as his own father. "Why do you believe I am my father?"

She goes still. Iohmar suspects he has caught her by surprise, or at least caught her speaking words she did not wish to speak. This bout of silence is not comfortable but thick with anger. He leans toward her, ready to demand the return of the child, but she straightens, her shoulders making a show of relaxing.

"I believe you are exactly who you are."

Iohmar is moved once more by a soft wave of recognition, something familiar in the way she speaks or moves, gone before he has time to analyze. She should not be able to unnerve him so.

"I do not know how long you have dwelled here," he says, "but my father and mother have long passed. I am Iohmar —"

"Do you wish for me to explain?"

He pauses, cut short by the sharpness of the words. Usually, he would not allow one of his kind to interrupt, but he suspects she does not understand or does not believe him, so he nods. She rolls one shoulder in a shrug, looking away and losing all interest in gazing at the child.

"You give your magic away and discard the human part of him."

6

STRANGE PROPOSAL

When Iohmar was a boy, his mother changed the shape of her magic. Gifted were her powers, but in strange and subtle ways not easily called to the surface. Iohmar cannot always recall the exact ways in which they worked, but he remembers his father lost, caught once in the strange void of time of the lands beyond their borders. Time passed. She gave him a lifeline back to their mountain and sunlit Halls, distorting the world to aid him, and her magic took a great deal of time to return in strength.

Iohmar clenches his hands. He hasn't cut himself on his talons since he was small, but they dig into his palms now, threatening to break skin.

"Shall I explain it to you, my sweet lord?"

"I would appreciate such," he says, though not kindly. He still doesn't wish to anger her but bristles from her words of his father, the way she digs up his past without thought or effort. She may be powerful, but he does not wish her to forget his strength or his ancient years.

Her attention returns to the boy squirming in her grip. "I do not believe there is anything you can do for him. He is little and human and weak, and should he remain human, I am sure he will not last many days."

"Remain human," Iohmar echoes, testing the words.

"It is possible to shift the magic in creatures, should they be young and weak enough and their own sense of magic undeveloped. He is nothing more than a little ball of moldable life force and human magic. Even then, it's fragile. If he were one of your kin, he could live easily as any fae. They do not weaken and crumble to disease."

"You think to turn him fae," Iohmar says. All anger has left his voice. A far cry this is from his mother warping a foreign forest to release its grip on his father. Skilled as Iohmar is, never has he considered the possibility of *changing* the life force of another creature. Supporting or healing, yes, but never something so drastic. Even the little creatures of sunlight he called often in his childhood—and sometimes still as an adult—didn't have a true life of their own. They existed off his magic, his warmth, and his own heartbeat. Nothing but reflections. His thoughts circle with the new idea presented to him.

She wasn't quite correct. He doesn't appreciate the suggestion, but it intrigues him.

Perhaps his father would not approve, but neither would he

approve of taking a weak and unremarkable human babe.

He notices, also, that she refers to fae as if she is not one, as if she does not dwell below his own Halls and share the connection all his folk share with their king.

"I surprise you," she says.

"Yes."

"You do not appear upset."

"I am . . . considering."

"Mmm . . ."

After a moment, he asks, "Will you explain it to me further?"

"I am not quite sure how to do so," she says, contempt gone, near excitement taking its place at the new idea and an ear to share it with. "If I had to try, I'd say it's a bit like plucking what little magic he was born with and replacing it with a shred of something *other*. Perhaps *changing* him fae is not the correct way to speak it. *Moving* some of the threads of your magic to him . . . Yes, that's better. It should sustain him and grow with time, as that of any child born to these lands. He won't be fae, but neither will he be human."

"My magic," he murmurs.

She hands the child back in a smooth movement, spinning him about and placing him in Iohmar's waiting hands. Relief relaxes his shoulders.

There's no such thing as magic given without worry or consequence. Even Iohmar, with his healing tendencies, cannot give life to one who has lost it. This is not so dire a situation, but neither is it a light matter.

"My magic," he whispers, to be certain.

"It would be a shred, and not taken, just moved. Still a part of you. Your magic is so growing in nature, it shouldn't take too great an effort. Enough to catch on, and the boy should live and sustain his own life, as you or I do. Yours should strengthen as it does at any exertion, but it will not be a pleasant experience."

"You sound quite certain of yourself."

Her shoulders roll again, another shrug.

"How did you learn such things?" he whispers, as if speaking soft enough will prevent her discomfort.

Her voice is not angry but distant, thoughtful. "I'm uncertain. For a long time, I did not know these things. Then I did know them. I don't know when the knowledge came to me."

Iohmar doesn't push the topic, not when long swaths of years are often lost to the whim of time in Látwill. Much of his life is difficult for him to recall, and he can hardly pass judgment upon her for the same, not when she speaks without malice.

He asks, "And the child?"

"It could kill him. There is risk of such, I would think. He will die if you do nothing. With this, he has a chance to live."

"Will it be painful for him?"

Her eyeless gaze is upon him, he is certain, and he forces his skin not to crawl. Raw and vulnerable before someone he doesn't know and who cares not for him, he wishes to curl in upon himself. Even before Galen he is not comfortable expressing such openness. He has lost too much and borne too great of burdens to bear his soul before anyone. But he is king and will act as such even when the title fits as an ill-worn coat.

"I doubt it," she says slowly. "He may be sick for some days, perhaps as ill as you. Human children sicken often as it is. Obviously."

Iohmar knows this is true but is loath to cause the child unnecessary suffering.

"You see no way around such an option?"

"*You* see no way around such an option, else you would not have ventured down to trust a creature you have never known or met."

Iohmar fixes his eyes on the child blinking sweetly up at him, no longer squirming, comforted by his hold. He wishes to think on the decision. He wishes Galen desired to save the child as dearly as he does so he would support his decision and ensure no harm comes to either of them should Iohmar take this strange woman up on her offer and his magic is impacted. But Galen will watch over him regardless of his unwise decisions.

The child will die soon. None in his Halls have the knowledge or ability this woman suggests. If they did, he would have gone to them, even if the secret spread that he brought a forbidden human to his lands.

"Will I immediately be weakened?"

Shadows form her features, but it seems as if she smiles. "I'd suspect minutes or hours. I cannot tell you how long it will last. Based on your strength, I suspect you'll fight it off well."

"You sound uncertain."

"This is strange magic," she says. "And a stranger request."

Iohmar is silenced, irritated by her honesty. If the option had been present, he never would've brought the child here, never would've sought help from anyone besides Galen and his own magic. But he is neither strong nor old nor talented enough for such tasks. Such knowledge has not appeared to him as it has appeared to this woman.

She knows as he does. Iohmar grinds his jaw.

"You have never attempted this before?"

"Never."

"But you know it."

"I do."

A thousand questions spring to mind, none he would dare ask. Her life and challenges are not his concern, as his are none of hers.

"What would I do?"

Another head twitch. "Nothing. Guard your thoughts and allow me access to your magic."

"I wish to think."

"Yes, of course —"

"And I would know your intentions before we continue. I do not know what you wish in return."

Her quiet lasts so long that Iohmar feels a twinge of discomfort. *Will she refuse me now I'm near committed to the act?*

"I don't understand what you mean."

Iohmar blinks. *Has she never come across another fae?* It seems as if she has, for there are many others dwelling beneath the mountain, but to not know thoughts and memories can be shared is a strange thing, especially when she is proposing transferring a shred of Iohmar's magic into the child.

"I wish to know what your thoughts are toward me and the child, just as you need to access my magic to aid him."

"Oh," she says, and something about her tone makes Iohmar believe she's embarrassed.

Then she offers her hand.

Iohmar walls his own thoughts and memories, wrapping them up in tight, safe little bubbles within his mind. He isolates the section of his magic bearing intentions and thought. If he will view hers, she shall have access to his. As it is, she reads him too well. Hiding his intentions would be less humiliating but pointless.

Her fingers brush his palm, maneuvering gracefully around his claws. A heartbeat tiny as a bird's reaches him. Her skin is cool and weightless, and it feels more like running his hand through a cloud when the winds carry him than touching flesh and bone. He suspects she is not entirely a physical being. She twitches at the contact but does not pull away. Touching another creature's magic is a bit like drowning but breathing water at once. If the concept confused her, she's likely unused to it.

Thoughts and emotions pass him as a stream. Distrust. Rawness he did not expect. Anger, hurt, uncertainty, and a strange surprise. Something has shaken her foundations. He pushes past, moving through the stream, not wishing to intrude on anything unessential. Searching for malicious intent, he finds nothing but vague curiosity toward the child, a wondering at how he should be so interesting to a fae high king. Not surprising. Toward him there is a mess of emotion, an irritation at him existing in her home.

But no wish to see him harmed.

She may not nurture the affection toward him the rest of his kin maintain, but there is no cruel intent.

I would welcome her in my Halls, he thinks, forgetting the connection they share. She senses the sentiment, withdrawing her magic and her touch, folding her hands within her lap, posture rigid.

"I meant no offense," he says, softer than before.

She gives a tiny jerk of her chin resembling a nod. "You gave none."

Iohmar bows his head in thought, and she allows him his silence.

Comforted by her lack of malice, Iohmar cradles the child in his palms. This woman, strange as she is, is a beacon of strength even among fae. Had they known each other in childhood, or perhaps under less tense a situation, they may have been friends — rather powerful friends. Iohmar aches to speak to another with understanding of his magic and the power and struggle accompanying it. But he could sense in her emotions and reactions such things are not meant to be, and so he puts the sentiment from his mind.

Instead, he gazes at the child, surrounds himself in the tiny flicker of his life. It is weaker than when Iohmar stole him from his filthy human crib, weaker than even the short time ago when the boy tugged at his hair and patted little hands across his face.

Iohmar's chest squeezes so tight it's difficult to breathe.

He remembers his parents. He does not dwell on what they would think of the child, for they both would be sympathetic but unimpressed with the weakness convincing Iohmar to bring the child against his own laws.

But he remembers their affection toward him, the gentleness of his mother's smile and the warmth of his father's hands. Their companionship was an anchor even when he was past the age to be so demonstrative with his affections. He remembers the cold empty places of those creatures along his farthest borders, remembers his mother and father and kin being stolen from him, remembers the scars from cold magic, decorations along his body he never shows.

His warm Halls will be quite colder should the child leave them, though none but Iohmar and Galen even know of the creature's existence. *You are a fool,* he tells himself, then sighs.

"I wish to save the child," he murmurs.

He does not raise his eyes to her face, for skepticism and judgment would greet him. Instead, he watches the round eyes blinking with trust. If not for the woman across from him, he may have kissed the child's forehead.

"I will need to touch you once more," she says, and he nods, expecting as much.

A rustle of fabric brushes over roots as she slips closer. They are almost knee to knee, not touching.

"You have failed to tell me what you wish of the situation."

"You are high king," she says, and still, though she is close, he cannot determine the shape of her features. "I should not have to ask for anything."

"You cannot wish for nothing."

"The things I wish, you cannot give to me."

"Perhaps, but I wish to give you something."

Her head cocks, considering. For a time, he believes she will not answer, but her tone hardens as she says, "Stay far from these tunnels. They are not your Halls, and we are not part of yours."

He doesn't allow himself to recoil. She has her reasons, and it isn't a surprise those dwelling far in the earth do not welcome a creature who slips through sunbeams as well as shadow, even if he is their lord and king.

"If you wish," he says.

"I wish you to swear it."

Promises are sacred, meaningful things, not words thrown about as humans do. Iohmar has heard of the ways the magic of their lands will overturn should a king break a promise.

"I swear I will bother you no longer."

It is not what she wished, but it appears to be enough. Her chin gives the slightest jerk of a nod.

Leaving nothing but his magic to her touch, Iohmar bows his head, relaxing the tension from his body. She lays one hand across the child's head and places the other to Iohmar's forehead. As before, her skin is cool and ethereal, magic made visible rather than flesh. He breathes around the strange sensation, leaning in to her contact.

And his world changes shape.

AN UNKIND MAGIC

A life as long as Iohmar's does not lend itself to memory.
Iohmar doesn't recall mountains of years unless they're
brought to his attention. Much of his childhood is *known* rather
than *remembered*. Dreamlike to recall. Bright, ethereal, evanescent.
Often, he has difficulty separating dreams from his own history.
Certain folk he cannot recall if they existed before the war.

They visit him now, washing in and out of his thoughts. His
magic is so deep a part of him, his memories and emotions, hates
and loves, a great and colorful tapestry lengthened with years
and wisdom.

This woman plucking at the threads unravels it all.

Emotions he's kept in check have no restraints. He focuses on
not drowning. He will not lash out in return. He requested this.

Agreed to do this. *To protect the child.* And so he will not fight her. *Will not fight. Will not fight. Will not fight.*

As swiftly as it begins, it fades.

Iohmar drifts. Even with the woman's presence on the edge of his mind, he finds himself dwelling on his father. Fae do not often take permanent mates, but he remembers his parents wandering the silvering trees in twilight, calling to him before he could fall from a tree branch too high; his mother's face in a hazy light lost of details, soft and warm, a beam of sunlight rather than true memory; the scent of pomegranate on her skin when she walked beside him.

War flickers along the thoughts, unexpected and unwelcome, and he shoves it aside. No matter what has been done to him, those memories are *not* for the woman to access. His scars ache. *Can she see them?* Not under all his clothes, no.

He thinks of his father and the grandfather he cannot recall in any detail and comes near to weeping. Kings do not weep, so he swallows around a burning throat.

With a snap, he's returned to the small room, vision dipping as waves. Disoriented, he stares at the roots between his hands, at the child cradled in his lap.

How did I come to be in such a place? I walked, didn't I? Traveled the tunnels of my own accord to find someone who terrified me enough she could save the human?

The woman shifts before him, and he notices the lack of her touch. She does not speak. When he raises his head, heavy with the weight of his horns, her face comes close to touching his.

Her eyes are a strange color, he thinks, then remembers before her face held no features.

Her lips peel back. She grasps the largest of his horns. His hand snaps to her wrist, but his blade is hidden along his back, within the folds of his robe —

No, no, I left it in my chambers because I was not leaving my mountain to places enemies roam. His head spins. Even reaching for her leaves him disjointed. Defenseless.

"You," she snarls, "are not little Iohmar."

Her entire body flickers as candlelight against a wall. A roar surrounds his left ear.

She snaps the end of his horn clean off.

Iohmar makes a noise. A scream. His head pounds, flashes of light dancing in his eyes. Before he collapses, he catches sight of the woman gazing at the tip of horn, open shock in her face, before she dissolves into shadow. Iohmar droops forward, desperate not to crush the child as he curls over, waiting for the agony to pass. Breath rasps in his ears. He isn't sure if it's his own or some after-effect of the magicwork. Dizziness seizes him even as he crouches, still as stone.

For a time, he does nothing but fall, no sweet or unbearable memories to soothe or haunt him.

When he surfaces, he is certain the magic has not faded, simply lulled. His insides are raw and hollowed out, magic frayed as it hasn't been since rippling creatures dragged themselves past his borders.

The child is crying, mouth open, eyes scrunched. But there is a magic about him which did not exist before. Iohmar senses its pull, remembering the link between him and his own parents. It's similar but stronger in a way he cannot yet identify.

They are alone in the round room.

Iohmar has not feared the dark since he was a child buried in the mountain's depths. It presses around him, tugs at his hands and horns and clothing. He curls over the babe as if he can shrink from the shadows. Scooping the boy to his chest, he flees the tunnels the way he came.

It seems a lesser time to reach the entrance than it was to venture in. Slowing his steps, Iohmar leans against the cool earth of the wall and calms himself. Familiar crystals glow, casting dim light across the path, and the unease begins to dissipate.

Ridiculous to act in such a way, he thinks, though his limbs are heavier than they've been in centuries, betraying him. *What a foolish thing I've done.*

Before his magic returns him to the sea of memories, he eases down the open window, stumbling on the carpet of leaves. Though he left in the darkness of night, it is once again late and lightless. Strange the way time passes in the tunnels.

Perhaps this is how humans feel. He chuckles. He wouldn't normally find this amusing.

After laying the squalling babe on the bed, he takes a scrap of parchment from his desk, squinting at the trembling in his fingers. The last time his body shook so . . .

He pushes aside war and battles. Galen will appear in the morn, no matter how badly Iohmar wishes him never to see him in such a way, and he isn't sure how long this weakness will last.

Do not be alarmed, and do not call for anyone. All will be explained. The words will not comfort the old fae, but he hasn't time to consider better ones. Folding the paper to stand upright, he sets it on the table beside his bed, words facing the door so Galen is sure to notice. Letting the inky robe fall to a pile at his feet, he kicks off shoes. Still, the boy wails, and Iohmar bends over him with a frown. Lying alongside, he drapes a hand atop the child's chest. There is no pain or true suffering but a sharp discontentment the boy cannot shake.

"Shh," Iohmar whispers to the side of his soft head.

Using the last of his magic available to him, he presses comfort and warmth into the child—the memory of calm water, the weightlessness of wind, the heat of Queen Rúnda's ocean shores—until the boy falls to peaceful sleep. Without bothering to crawl beneath the covers, Iohmar follows.

Once, when he wakes, he is falling to pieces.

Outside, his lands are dark as before, but the stiffness in his muscles and the haze of his thoughts insist it's been days, not mere minutes. He raises his hand. Dust drifts from his fingers. No, not quite dust, but flakes like shredded paper dipped in ink, dissolving to nothing as they leave his skin. Fascinated, he turns both arms over. His claws, once clear and pale, are streaked with darkness like roots reaching into soft soil. He imagines the decorative marks on Galen's body and wants to giggle.

No mirror lies within reach, but placing his fingers on his face, he's certain it must appear the same. His skin is cool and otherworldly under his touch. His horns ache where they meet his skull, the one broken many years ago sending streaks of pain along his scalp. The one broken by the woman throbs in a shallower sensation. They weigh his head as if the entirety of his lands rest upon his hair. He has the presence of mind to recognize he should be frightened, but he is not, and the child is no longer crying, and this is a pleasing thing.

Something brushes his hair, and he's falling back to sleep before his mind can consider it.

Once more does he wake, and he is terrified. Limbs pinned to the bed, tightness in his chest, he is still beneath the tunnels, crushed under the weight of the earth collapsing upon him. He is a child with a mountain atop him and his best friend lost to him, waiting forever and forever and forever for someone to find him.

But he is within his own bed, facing the vast window where silver light is appearing, cool dawn breaking the color of plums. His parents' chambers are alongside his own, closed up as they have been for centuries, overgrown with vines and flowers to fill the void. It's quiet — such are the things he loves greatest in his lands — a silence humans never experience. Even his birds, with heads tucked under wings in sleep, do not sing in the morning stillness.

Peace does not shake the terror in his bones. Not since battles and blood and grief has he felt so weakened and vulnerable. Even with thousands of years in his past, he's never felt so aged and frail. He almost drowned in grief then and will not surrender to it now. Not safe in his chambers.

I am Iohmar. I am alive.

Over and over he thinks the words, small and childlike for a king of the fae, but it calms him better than the quiet. Drawing his eyes from the window, he settles them on the child. Arms spread to either side, resting on his belly with his tiny round face toward Iohmar, the babe is lost to sleep. There is something not quite the same in his appearance, skin no longer frail and devoid of warmth but paler and blue gray as Iohmar's birch-bark eyes. His limbs are slimmer but stronger. Iohmar rests the tips of his fingers against the boy's back.

A thread of magic reaches him, steady and strong.

Noon shimmers bright and warm when Iohmar wakes to strength in his limbs. A chill clings to him, and he basks in the heat. Reaching to his magic, he finds it weak but recovering. There's something new as well, a consistent spark of warmth and life connected to his. He tests it, then brushes his fingers against the child's satin skin. Affection squeezes his heart. Fascinated, he nuzzles his nose into the tiny cheek. Even in sleep, the boy's magic strengthens at the contact, and Iohmar is aware of it without effort. Even with his own parents, there was never this connection of magic.

Inspecting him, he finds the babe resembling one of his own kind: limbs elongated, eyes rounded, elegant, and slim, ears slanted. His skin is papery as bark, expression graceful even in sleep, flowers blossoming in the soft wisps of infant hair. These are his own features, unique to him alone, and Iohmar is pleased at how the boy's magic reflects his own propensities.

The woman succeeded.

But Iohmar's claws, pointed once more, are black as pitch. He runs the pad of his thumb across the sharp tips, testing his ability to change them back and finding them unyielding. An odd change. Iohmar doesn't understand how the two are linked.

It matters not, he reminds himself. There will be time to dwell on his appearance later. For now, he basks in the life of the child he's saved, strong and unique and beating.

My own little boy.

He is aware, then, of another in the room. Before he can tense, Galen's calming presence washes over him, the easy, slow threads of his healing soul. Iohmar rolls onto his back, careful of his traumatized body and unhappy magic.

His old caretaker reclines in the chair woven of soft willow boughs, elbows on the armrests, fingers laced together, expression an absolute storm. Iohmar's seen it before, directed at him as an unruly child, and even once directed at his father, though it never was acknowledged. He awaits the thunder, which never comes.

Testing the waters, he says, " 'Tis a lovely morn."

" 'Tis," Galen agrees.

But Iohmar does not trust such an expression. Gingerly, he sits, testing the ability of his arms to support his weight. They tremble but hold. Galen was watching him sleep, helpless and exposed. Iohmar knows, after all the old fae has seen, it's ridiculous to hate the vulnerability. He tries to put it from his mind. Galen doesn't deserve a cold shoulder.

"Have you seen your appearance?" Galen asks, voice beginning to match his expression.

Iohmar stills, glancing at his talons.

"I don't mean merely those."

Raising his eyebrows, Iohmar slips to his feet, relieved his legs don't shake enough to be visible. He finds his way to the washroom parallel to his desk and the mirror above the water basin.

He looks a terror.

The streaks of shadow invading his talons have seeped into other parts. His horns—two on each side, one larger and one smaller—as well as his hair, are dark as the deepest night. His right eye has turned to pitch, the very center a white dot. The left is as it was. He turns his head side to side, acclimating to the change. His sight is not affected, and neither is the strength of his horns when he touches them. The newly broken edge is rough and incorrect under his fingers. Swallowing, he closes his eyes and accepts the alterations. Strange as it is to have another modify him in a way he cannot correct, he has experimented with his appearance a handful times throughout his long life. No one should think much on it. He will deal with this for the child's health.

He doubts Galen will be so understanding.

As if called by the thought, his caretaker says, "High Queen Rúnda sent you a letter."

"Yes?"

"She wishes you and your court to visit. It wasn't a personal note."

A seed of worry plants itself in the back of his thoughts. He and Rúnda write to each other often, but a formal invitation—the letters Galen reads without permission—could either mean their usual celebrations or something strange and dire. He thinks of the men in his woods and that Rúnda does not need to extend a formal invitation for the usual gatherings between their two courts.

But Galen does not say the letter is urgent. Rúnda would have told him if something were amiss. And so Iohmar puts the thought from his mind. It is nothing he cannot dwell on in a day.

Exhaustion tugs at him. Even the short walk to the washroom put a tremble in his limbs. Strength is returning, but he doesn't wish to push himself. Drifting to his bed, he attempts not to appear weakened. He isn't sure he accomplishes it. The boy doesn't wake when Iohmar reclines along the covers beside him but squirms in his sleep and stuffs his fingers between his lips, drooling. Magic doesn't stop all things, it seems. Iohmar is glad.

"Are you going to tell me what you've done?" Anger is still present in Galen's voice, but Iohmar hears exhaustion as well. *How long has he been watching over his king?* A small, much younger part of him wishes to reach out to his old friend, to hold his hand or ask him to sit close or say something sweet and soothing.

Cursing the dreams and visions he's drowning in, he pushes the desires aside. *I am a king, no longer a child. Not for centuries upon centuries.*

But he owes an explanation. Galen is the only one who knows of the human babe's existence, so he *must* understand what has happened.

With his back to Galen still, he explains in detail, in all aspects he has knowledge of. As he speaks, he runs the pads of his fingers over the child's soft new skin, careful of the sharpness of his talons, which he will need to trim for some time to come, until the child is grown enough to recognize the danger. The boy will never see him as a threat, never the darkness or scars or any such uncomfortable attributes Iohmar harbors. No strangeness or fear shall touch this little life.

And the boy will need a name, for now he is fae, and more importantly, he is Iohmar's.

Galen remains quiet and still throughout the story. When Iohmar finishes his tale, there is nothing but the rustle of trees in the soft breeze and the songs of birds now awake and dancing. Several of his crows hop across the window's edge. A soft sigh whispers behind him, and the downy bed sinks as Galen sits along its side. Iohmar does not turn to him—this is something the old fae hasn't done in many centuries—but neither does he shift or order the caretaker away. His presence is stable, comforting, and Iohmar cannot fault him for his unhappiness.

"So, the boy is yours now," Galen says, no question in his voice.

"Aye, he is my child," Iohmar whispers.

Another sigh, but Galen's long fingers rest on Iohmar's hair, combing softly, tucking the dark strands around his horns— another gesture he has not repeated since Iohmar was shorter than his father's knee. Healing magic slides along his bones, a strange, drowning sense of calm accompanying the easing of pain. Galen's magic is quite effective. Past it, the gentle petting is not how a servant should treat the king beneath the earth, but Iohmar does not shift from the touch.

He closes his eyes and listens to the beat of his son's heart.

SUMMER

8

AN ABUNDANCE OF SHADOWS

Some weeks later, Iohmar finds the paths to Rúnda's court. Galen is near his side, and a selection of his folk travel behind him in song and laughter. His son is tucked within the crook of his arm.

Queen Rúnda sent only one letter, and Iohmar dispatched his crows to her lands before his people departed, thanking her for her invitation and sending news they are on their way. It is not a tradition they take every summer, for years are slippery things not counted well, and even the short time since his experience in the tunnels is not knowable. Iohmar anticipates Rúnda's presence when his skies brighten with summer and her lands turn warm with the changing seasons.

Now, there is the child in his company. Rúnda will have something sharp and grinning to say about the development, and Iohmar finds himself nervous for her judgment, though she has the same fondness for small creatures as all their folk. He glances at the wriggling thing kept in check by his hand.

Lorcan. His little boy.

Iohmar despises nicknames — with greater vigor when sent his direction, though Rúnda has plenty, and he tolerates her eccentric naming rituals — but he's taken to calling the child Lor, a small and gentle word to match the small and gentle creature.

Galen is unimpressed. Often, Iohmar catches him staring at his horns and their changed appearance, or his hair, or into his eyes with direct disapproval. But he isn't scowling to a severe degree. Iohmar has seen worse. The child is growing on Galen, at least to the extent the old fae views him as an individual life rather than something to trouble Iohmar.

Iohmar is not demonstrative. It is a weakness he is aware of and desires not to change. Part is the nature of a king. Part, he suspects, is the war itself and his very own magic. But Lor is in constant need of attention, and Iohmar has no qualms in lavishing it upon him. The boy giggles up at him as he squirms, and Iohmar tickles his belly with trimmed talons. A delighted squeak echoes through the grove of trees. Some of his folk turn to the noise and laugh.

Iohmar rides a great beast the name of which has been long-lost to these lands, a rare thing not seen near his Halls since before even his father was conceived. Iohmar often took to wandering the farthest mountains of Látwill in the times when he was not the fair lord of the land, merely a prince. Once the only other of his age was lost to him, he took refuge in searching the tunnels or straying as far from the mountain as possible.

It was long ago. Details blur, but he remembers the heat of the woods and the shadowy thickness of the air. He was wandering the edge of the heart of the woods, listening to the wolves stalk him, wondering if anyone had passed through the humming giants of trees. Something must be on the other side, though to this day he still knows not what.

The creature was caught among vines. It had been trying to lick the sap of one of the great trunks until it caught itself in climbing thorns. Iohmar had heard descriptions of such beings from his grandfather, of how dangerous were their hooves and teeth, and watched from a distance until the beast's big eyes turned on him. Long and sleek and graceful of limb, it bears diamond-hard scales beneath soft fur the hue of ocean foam. Its body was twice the length of Iohmar's were he to lie alongside it, its legs reaching his head. A long arching neck stretched a dozen hands, a small and soft-featured head resembling a horse's set with large blue eyes.

Its magic made him feel of cool streams and wildflowers, and he remembers quite vividly wondering how it must have been to be in the presence of a dragon if such a ground-dwelling creature could overwhelm him with its sense of life.

Iohmar coaxed the thorns into turning away, though such things are more difficult in the thick, dreary magic of the heart of the woods. The creature touched its soft nose to Iohmar's cheek and visited him often until Iohmar crawled atop its back and was promptly shaken off.

Now, it allows him the honor most any time he requests, though it's a tad temperamental. Iohmar has a kinship with the old beast. A few times, he tried offering it names, but it always turned its head. Some creatures are silent about such matters.

He sets Lor between its shoulder blades. The boy tugs at fistfuls of fur, cooing at each passing tree. Others in Iohmar's court mount wild horses or walk their woods, disappearing into the trees only to return. Iohmar will walk the leaf-carpeted path before the journey comes to a close. His kingsguard bring up the rear of the procession. There is little to threaten them in this time of peace, but such is their usual way, and Iohmar allows them whatever their judgment decides.

There is no set distance between the Fair Halls and Rúnda's court. They will come upon it sometime after they think they might but sometime quite before expected. High noon has appeared and faded several times, and Iohmar is careful not to consider the passage of time too much lest it rearrange itself around his wishes.

At midday, when the sun is hot and the air thick and all manner of twilight creatures have hidden in the shade and tunnels and fallen trees, Iohmar's procession stops. Living diamonds float about them. Names for many of Iohmar's folk were lost to the lands long before he or his lineage was conceived. Most refer to them as gems for their bodies of glass catching and casting off light in a thousand colors. They prefer to wander the trees in soupy twilight rather than brave the treetops in the heat of midday.

It's a sign Rúnda's court is near. Her realm stretches to the vast sands far from here, and the little gems bask in the heat it radiates. Iohmar catches their bodies, light as dandelion tufts, against his fingers and blows them onto Lor's cheeks as he settles them in the tall grass. Galen hovers nearby, hands clasped behind his back. Permission isn't needed to wander where he pleases, but he won't leave his king's side without it. Iohmar shoos him away to do as he wishes. His guard have reclined in a loose circle under the shade of a broad oak. Dáithí, a kingsguard old enough to remember Iohmar's parents, waves and tips into his companion, the little group dissolving into a shoving match. Iohmar finds a comfortable spot in the grass, smiling into his collar. Perhaps he should join them, but he finds himself drawn to solitude as the centuries pass. Even as a child, it was only his one friend he found himself with. His guard do not need their brooding king to dampen their fun.

And he is left alone with Lor, as private a company as he can achieve with his folk wandering, eating and drinking, and edging closer to catch their king's attention. They all wish to be in his favor, to say something which will please or amuse him. Iohmar smiles whenever one of them catches his eye — not in the way he smiles to Rúnda, but gently nonetheless — but is distracted by Lor ripping up fistfuls of grass and watching him with round eyes.

No one is suspicious of the child or even shocked by his unexpected appearance. Well into adulthood, Iohmar hasn't taken a mate or spoken of achieving an heir. But to be gifted a child is no impossible feat, not when deep places in the heart of the woods could provide him a true child of the fae. Children in his realm are created by magic and sacrifice near as often as they are created by lovemaking.

But he didn't wish for a child. No one in his Halls knows this save Galen — for all any of them know he's been planning for a century — but it is odd to him he never desired a child until he was presented with this one. Even now, he does not wish for another or for any babe different from Lor.

Still, it is a story he will allow his people to believe—their woods gifted their king so special and beautiful a child—and it is one Lor will be told until he is old enough to understand the details. He was created by magic for Iohmar and for Iohmar alone. Unique. In a way, it is true, and Iohmar has no qualms about the tale.

Those in the wider lands of Látwill will find no suspicion in the story.

His mind circles about the woman in the tunnels. He extended his magic once it returned to him in fullness and found not even the threads of her dwelling. It should've been easy to sense her once he'd spent time in her presence, but nothing remained. Even if he wished to break his promise, to venture down, she would be long gone. Iohmar hopes his presence did not drive her from a place she cherished, but he cannot help it now. He promised her never to return, after all.

The gems are enamored with Lor, fluttering over his skin as the boy stares in calm interest. Not since the night in the caves has he uttered a cry. Iohmar is near him at all times, and the boy has taken to flapping his tiny fists whenever he is in need of something, even if it is only to be held. Iohmar has not spent any extended time with other fae children and so does not know if this is to be expected. But he sets aside those worries, as the boy is content and the magic tethering them is strong and bright.

"Iohmar . . ." A soft voice draws his attention, and his eyes drift from Lor.

No one approaches his seat near the trees. His folk are gathered in groups, their noise a soft music among the breeze and chiming gems. One fae yelps, his hair turning into a burst of butterflies as he scrambles to his feet, taking off after the culprit. Behind Iohmar lie miles upon miles of forest, nothing but the gentle lumbering creature grazing the long grasses. Extending his magic, he finds nothing unexpected.

Iohmar frowns.

A young fae — young, at least, to him — catches his gazing about and separates from her party, a child of her own tucked within the sleeves of her dress. As she approaches, head lowered in respect, he smiles to welcome her to sit close by. She isn't the one who spoke moments before. Iohmar digs his trimmed talons into the backs of his hands until he catches the gesture and folds his fingers, trying to attain some semblance of elegance.

"Hello, Airgid," he says.

She holds out her child, a hopeful smile on her lips, and the babe wriggles its face out of a cream blanket to gaze at him. He blesses the children who come to his Halls, more a custom than true protection. Blessings are specific, and Iohmar can only give them to those he knows the strengths and weaknesses of, those he knows with intimacy. He gave one to Galen in the past, trying to secure a web of his own magic about the old fae to protect him from dark magics unknown. Galen has no idea the blessing exists and would likely be offended at the idea of needing protection.

But Iohmar takes the girl into his arms and presses a kiss to her forehead. Her features are long and dark and sweet to gaze upon, her eyes like summer lilies. Soft stubs of flesh poke her blanket where wings will one day grow. A loose feather catches in her swaddle. She will fly far and high, and Iohmar's lips tug into the beginnings of a genuine smile when she grins up at him.

"She is quite lovely," he says, passing her back. "Have you chosen her name?"

"Siath."

"A sweet name to match. I am assured your kin are proud."

"We are joyful. It is so rare to have a little babe here with us." She preens her silver hair and casts a cheerful eye at Lor as she speaks—she won't touch Iohmar's child without his permission. Not as flamboyant as some of Iohmar's kin, she stands out nonetheless. "Are you excited for the summer celebration, my lord?"

"It is indeed a time to look forward to."

Iohmar is not so excited as some of the younger fae, who've hardly left the safety of his Halls. They roam the nearby woods and believe themselves adventurous for traveling to the queen's court. But he is eager for Rúnda's company, and traversing her lands puts him no closer to the rippling borders than his own Halls. Sometimes dangerous creatures drag themselves from the darker parts of the woods, but most have learned they've nothing to gain from bothering the king beneath the earth and his folk. It is a pleasant journey.

He listens to the new mother for a time before she returns to her own party. *Did she sense my distraction?* His thoughts dwell still on his parents, those he knew in childhood, and the strange illness, which is taking its time to leave his bones, still there but fading. Iohmar stretches his magic often to chase it away and assure himself of his own strength.

Again, he considers the voice. It was clear as day and just

as strange.

Scooping Lor to his chest, Iohmar searches for Galen and finds him distracted with some of the younger fae. Galen has never taken a mate and does not speak of past lovers to Iohmar. He is the oldest by far in the Halls and takes to being fatherly to anyone he can. Those in the little group he's speaking to grin and tug at his arms to join them.

Smiling, Iohmar takes his chance to slip among the trees. Shade cools the grass beneath his feet. The nameless creature wanders after him before turning aside in favor of a bush plump with bloodred berries. Iohmar left his boots and outermost robe in the clearing, but there is still an overwhelming flow of fabric about him, light as clouds, and a small sword presses against the base of his spine. Blades of grass tickle his feet. Warm patches of earth appear where sunlight reaches the forest floor, the soil cool. Here, it doesn't smell too different from any human forest — warmth on the grass and leaves and flowers, rich earth mixed with damp. The human woods do not smell of magic as these do. Gems wander after him, the soft chime of their bodies adding to the rustle of the forest.

Iohmar closes his eyes. They're heavy, his heartbeat slow. A tendril of discomfort twines up his chest.

When he opens them, there are a great many shadows among the trees. They do not approach, and Iohmar doesn't believe he is being threatened, but they remind him enough of the rippling creatures that he does not sit in the grass as he would with a friend or ally.

"Hello, my shadows," he says.

Many of Látwill's creatures are known to him by name, and many just by their magic, but he is not arrogant enough to believe he knows all. King he may be, but he is a servant and as helpless to these lands as any. He has no name for these creatures, but calling them *something*, even such a little thing as *shadows*, gives him security. He sees them, names them to an extent; therefore, they are his friends. He hopes.

They do not approach but slither between the trees and under the bushes and bunches of grass, where they are too dark for the bright sunlight and the slightest bit too large to fit in their own spaces. Iohmar is fascinated. His heart presses to the inside of his rib cage. No hostility emanates from them. *Will they allow me to touch them?*

He shifts and steps forward. The shadows move, neither retreating nor advancing, taking on a thousand new shapes.

"Hmm," he says aloud, hoping they understand his tongue. "I wonder how I have not seen you before . . . Do you dwell here often?"

Perhaps they have no language he can perceive, which would be a strange thing in and of itself in the twilight lands. Perhaps they have no language at all. Or they refuse to answer. Iohmar stretches his magic. Their presence lingers in the air, a disturbance in the otherwise empty breeze, but they have no discernible intentions.

"We come from my Halls across these woods," he says. "They are far under the mountains and above them. I'm sure you've been there. There is shadow as much as sunlight . . . We are traveling past those mountains there; at least, that is the direction we're headed. At some time, we'll come to sweet Queen Rúnda's court on a visit for the warmest weeks."

He speaks to show his harmless intentions should they understand his language. Slithering and sliding as he speaks, the shadows fall into jittery stillness once he quiets. Lor gives a soft gurgle, and they retreat a small space.

"None in my Halls or the next court over wish you any harm," Iohmar continues, setting a finger on Lor's forehead to calm him. "Is there anything you wish of me?"

These creatures must know him. Born in all who inhabit these lands is innate knowledge, if not love, for their king under the earth. Even those Iohmar does not recognize will understand his heritage. It's strange he was never aware of them in the past.

Taking another step, Iohmar shifts Lor into one arm, reaching out with his free hand, hoping to better understand their form. With the movement, they are gone, leaving nothing but natural shade in their wake. Iohmar wanders another dozen yards into the trees, but neither do they reappear or make noise.

He doesn't believe they could understand his tongue, much less mimic a language. Wondering at the soft voice he heard before, Iohmar turns for his folk resting in the clearing.

"Iohmar . . ."

Iohmar stiffens. There is no sound save for the murmuring of the woods, no one around him for some ways until his magic reaches those in his party eating and drinking. Something—or *someone*—is playing with him. He will not flounder in confusion for their amusement.

Evening his voice, the voice of a king, he says, "If you wish to speak to me, you will step into the light and do so. I will not answer to such slinking about."

He anticipates an answer. A laugh. A taunt. A response of any kind. He receives none.

In a less pleasurable mood, he returns to his folk, refusing to turn, to gaze about in suspicion for watching eyes. He shall not be trifled with, nor shall anyone make him look a fool. Gazing toward the bright canopy, he calms himself, and his expression is perfectly reasonable as he reunites with his folk.

Oisín approaches, hands folded, eyes soft with concern. Like his brethren, he wears no armor, and Iohmar is relieved they are beginning to feel safe once more in their own lands. There is no need to worry them with his grumpiness over strange shadows.

"Are you all right, my lord? You disappeared." Oisín touches the elbow of his sleeve.

"Perfectly. Just wandering." Neither of those things are a lie in their simplest terms, and the words do not struggle to pass his lips.

Oisín's expression evens, and he smiles. Already, the short hours of noon are turning to evening, and Iohmar's party is gathering what they've spread, eager to reach Rúnda's court. Iohmar has not eaten, nor does he wish to, and calls the ancient creature to him with a soft whistle. Galen joins him as Oisín returns to the others, unaware of the remnants of Iohmar's foul mood, combing his fingers into the creature's fur and swaying with wine.

Iohmar seats himself between the creature's downy shoulder blades and feeds Lor from his finger with a whisper and a twist of thistle. He allows his folk to go before him, his kingsguard at the lead as he brings up the end of the procession. Galen watches him but does not question the choice.

The shadows reminded him of those rippling across his borders. Both are some form of strange magic, even if the shadows hold no great power or intent to harm. Their unusual presence is a tug at an uncomfortable old scar. It is unfair for Iohmar to compare them to those other cruel monsters. Resenting his thoughts, he casts his magic far out, passing it over all warm and living and welcoming things. He reaches his mountains and their familiar embrace, past those lands beyond, through the thoughtless winds.

He crashes against the endless void of the rippling lands like a douse of cold water, a bitter sensation bringing a sour taste to his throat even from such a distance.

But nothing moves. Nothing is disturbed. Endlessness greets him on the other side. And he withdraws, with nothing to worry and fret and weep over but his own nightmares.

A GREAT FEASTING

Dusk turns to night several times over before they reach
Rúnda's court.

His people do not shy from darkness, lighting lanterns and singing their way through the hours without light, Iohmar humming
with them. Mist hangs in the deepest forest until it breaks with a
sudden burst of sunlight and salted air, and Iohmar's lands tran-
sition into the queen over the sky's.

Rúnda does not greet them. Her presence is nearby, an explo-
sion of warmth and energy like wind and rivers, a familiar weight
in the back of his mind. Iohmar does not extend his magic enough
to find her—she is likely looking down from some great height—
but relaxes in the joy and affection of her people greeting his.
Later, when the heat of the day has passed and twilight brings

supper and feasting and drinking, she will appear in her dining halls to celebrate with her people and welcome her guests. She will pounce on him with a great many questions appropriate for a lady to ask a lord and sit an acceptable distance so no one watching will become suspicious of the nature of their relationship.

Sometime in the night, one will visit the other's chambers. Nothing prevents them from courting each other, but the privacy makes their meetings all the sweeter.

Rúnda's court is a glorious pillar of ash-gray stone streaked with silver, and it shoots into the sky. Carvings of plants and animals and ancestors long passed wrap its round walls like vines. Iohmar still hasn't seen them all. The tower butts against a cliff-side, a massive knife of rock with no soft mountain slope on either side, a natural wall that's been sung of in the songs of his kin for as long as he can remember, for as long as his grandfather could. Where the wall of rock ends—just past the roundness of the tower growing from it—is the sea, sharp and bitter cold. He cannot glimpse it from this distance, not with the woods between here and there, but its presence and power sit in the magic of the air. Lor will soon see those roaring waves.

Where the forest ends, a step into another realm, is desert. It is vast and empty and devoid of life. Few wander those dunes. Heat is as much a living beast as the wind is about Rúnda's tower.

But it is not the same emptiness as that in the rippling lands.

Those neighboring places could be reached should Iohmar travel far beyond the opposite side of the knife blade of rock, down the shore of the sea until Rúnda's kingdom fades. He hasn't ventured near since leaving his own Halls to drive the creatures from these lands alongside his parents and Rúnda's own mother. A scar still cuts the landscape. Trees have returned to the dead places, he's heard, but the land will never be as it was.

"It was a long time ago now," he murmurs to Lor, gathering the child in the crook of his arm. Lor gurgles.

Rúnda's folk greet him at the woven bridge, welcoming visitors into the palace. Several languages fall on his ears. They are all old dialects, graceful sounds, and there is not a creature in Iohmar's court or Rúnda's who does not understand them upon birth. Iohmar wonders at the shadows and their silence.

None of Rúnda's folk appear particularly like or dislike Iohmar's. They are all shapes and sizes, colors, and features. Some bear animal-like extremities more radical than Iohmar's, some nearing human in their plainness. It is their magic that holds a different tinge, imbued with salt and sea and desert heat, not the damp earth and woods and breath of the trees of Iohmar's. Their talents are spread further and not so concentrated. Where Iohmar's folk excel in singing trees and stones and earth to shape their needs, these people are of the sea and all her terror, the dry forest and the deserts and, with great wildness, the winds.

Iohmar knows there are likely other folk in other lands save for these two and the humans in their own little magic-drained realm, but he has never come across them. His trees extend forever and forever past the heart of the woods. Anyone who ventures in is likely to never find their way out or to come to a place where they lose themselves entirely. No one has crossed Rúnda's deserts or oceans, and far enough in the other direction brings them to the ripplings.

Their world is so vast. So small. When he was a child, Iohmar sometimes imagined the winds could carry him far *up* until they reached the stars.

A woman approaches, half Iohmar's height and with horns of a stag so large and broad they bow her head. Colorful robes brush the mossy ground, and baubles hang from the points of her horns, stones and gems and carved trinkets. Waddling to the side of his mount, she grins at him from a tanned face both smooth and aged. Deer fur creeps along her temples, brown and spotted as a fawn's. Her smile is warm. She never speaks but greets him at every visit. Some memories still catch in his mind of being a child visiting this court and her doing the same to his parents. He smiles in return, touching the tip of her horn with respect when she pats his leg.

Others swarm them, none quite so bold to touch the king beneath the earth, but they smile and welcome their friends. They run their hands along the creature Iohmar rides. The beast shivers and purrs at the attention. Iohmar slips from the creature's back and lets the children—there are many more in Rúnda's court—lead it away with sugars and fruits as they giggle and run rings under its long legs. Dangerous as tales of the creature are, it is never aggressive to any Iohmar holds in regard.

His kingsguard are swallowed up in the welcoming crowd, allowing themselves to be led away; they are safe here and do not need to hover about their king. Iohmar lets his people and their celebration sweep into the tower while he lingers in the shade of the woods.

Galen hovers behind him in the following silence.

"You've been quiet," he says.

"No more so than usual."

"Nothing is troubling you?"

Iohmar squints at him, but Galen's face is concerned, eyes light. "Nothing more than usual."

Galen purses his lips. Lor gives a shriek, reaching for Iohmar's horns. It's become a habit, and Iohmar lowers his face until their noses brush and the boy's arms can reach the curl of his horns. His lips pull into a smile of their own accord. He wanders under the stone gates as Galen drifts after.

"I can hear you thinking," Iohmar murmurs.

"Have you told Rúnda about the babe?"

"No, a letter didn't seem correct. Neither did the crows."

Galen tucks his hands into his long sleeves, stepping beside Iohmar to nod at the child. "Are you going to explain to her the circumstances?"

Chambers are always prepared for Iohmar. He knows by heart the pathway winding up and up and up into the sky. Feasting will begin soon, and he wishes to change from the duller traveling robes draping his shoulders. Instead of continuing into the palace, he turns left and up the nearest stairwell. On his left, thick stone walls rise. On his right, the spiraling hallway is secured with vines and branches so thick that only mere glimpses can be seen down into the palace. Iohmar slips his fingers between the cracks as he ascends.

"I'll decide from moment to moment," he says. Rúnda will think him as foolish as Galen does, and he wishes for her to love Lor.

The staircase leads ever on and on until Iohmar reaches the uppermost levels. One higher would bring him to the quarters of

Rúnda and her queensguard. She's taken him to the roof in the past, and though Iohmar has stood on mountaintops and let the wind fling him over peaks and above the human world, the height of it made his legs weak.

His chambers are as he recalls: small and simple, with shades of dark stone and wood and cloth, rich furs draping the bed. The hearth is already lit and radiating heat. A single window, unobscured by glass, lets in the wild breeze. Scents of salt and sand swirl in, and he breathes like it's his first breath after drowning, tasting them on the back of his tongue. Galen is watching him, but he kicks off his boots and reclines along the bed, sinking deep into the furs, inspecting the ceiling. He coaxes trees to grow within the stone walls whenever he is here. Even so high in the tower, his ceiling is knotted with grizzled branches and smatterings of leaves. Rúnda's ceiling should be sprouting wisteria by now.

"I believe she should know the extent of it," Galen says.

"If you have a point you wish to make, Galen, I humbly request you make it."

His expression remains neat, but Iohmar sees his eye twitch. "It is simply that I believe you may not be telling me the whole story and someone should know . . . in case it becomes greater than you bargained for."

Iohmar stares at a joint of wood in the ceiling. *Have I confessed to Galen the entire story?* The shadows in the woods pick at his thoughts. It is a recent development, unlikely to be related, but with his kingdom and Rúnda's bordering that of the rippling creatures who so upturned their lives, Iohmar is never certain what is relevant. Magic has ways of twisting his mind into knots.

Perhaps he hasn't mentioned all the details, but Lor is healthy, the rippling lands are quiet as they've been since the end of the war, and Iohmar has recovered from his illness. *We are safe.* He shouldn't feel guilty for not dumping his numerous obsessions and worries upon his caretaker, nor upon the woman with whom he has found himself in love.

"Thank you for the input. I will consider it."

When Galen bows his head and turns for the door, Iohmar buries the irritation. The old fae bears many of the same scars, after all.

"Galen, I appreciate the concern."

He doesn't see his expression, but there is a softness to Galen's tone when he says, "I'll join you at the feasting, my sweet lord."

He rolls onto his stomach, one leg draped off the edge of the bed in a much less dignified position. If Rúnda were to walk in, she'd never stop laughing. Lor has no such concepts. The babe disentangles himself from his blanket and, with a joyful squeal, launches onto his belly to wriggle toward Iohmar's face. He may be walking soon. Fae have no set growth for the first years of life. For a time they may grow smaller and larger, older and younger day by day. Already, Lor's limbs are beginning to thin and lengthen, resembling more and more a young fae babe than a human infant. But he may wake smaller tomorrow, or older. His growth will settle into linear progression one day. With the tether of their magic, Iohmar no longer worries when the child wakes smaller.

Lor's skin is pale and a mix of white, blue, and gray, shedding leaves and flowers and papery bark when he's joyful or sad. Iohmar brushes the wisps of greenery from the boy's arms and legs, pleased with how his inherited magic is so similar in affinity to Iohmar's, another thread bonding them. It will be a great pleasure to teach the boy to grasp his magic once he is of age. Iohmar remembers lessons with his mother. His father was as skilled as she was but preferred to teach him swordsmanship and politics. They balanced each other as the mountains and rivers.

Twilight casts purple light across the lands beyond his window. Iohmar slides from the bed before dressing for the feasting. He never carried up the bundle of provisions strapped to the creature's back, but his clothing always manages to find its way to his chambers before he does. It may be Rúnda, or it may be the children who coax the creature away with their treats. It may be the smaller fae who take pleasure in rooting among other folk's items and causing harmless mischief. Iohmar shakes his clothing lest he find his armpits full of mud balls.

The robe that is black as night, Rúnda's gift, was the first he packed, but he selects something lighter for the occasion, a silver thing shimmering like dragonfly wings. He will appear calm and bright as his people, not intense and drawn with shadows. Lor is performing his flailing wriggle toward the edge of the bed. No matter where Iohmar is, the child never wishes to be away from his hold.

Iohmar watches him. The unusual warm sensation in his chest happens regularly these past weeks. Iohmar melts under it.

"Come, little Wisp," he says, scooping the boy from the bed in a flourish. Lor squeals, giggling.

Galen is not hovering outside the door, and his kingsguard are long lost to merriment, so Iohmar walks slowly to the feasting halls with no one watching his every move. Alongside his parents, his old friend lingers in his thoughts, an ever-present weight in the back of his mind since the woman in the caves. Her presence is strange to him, a soft memory nagging under his skin, the sweet girl with whom he used to play, a sister gifted to him by the woods. Never has he forgotten her, but millennia have passed since she existed in his every thought, in every sunbeam he catches upon his skin.

Pausing at one of the many windows overlooking the sea, he murmurs, "Ascia."

Her name is foreign on his tongue, not spoken of since he was a boy, and the wind carries the word away. Lor fusses and looks at him restlessly.

"Hmm," Iohmar hums and continues down the winding stairs. Sounds of celebration reach him.

Eager to see Rúnda, even if they will not touch until the hour is late and quiet, he bounds down the stairs, the wind rushing his friend's name back to him.

Rúnda watches him from across the feasting halls, and Iohmar dips between pretending he doesn't notice and staring back with fervor. Wine makes his head heavy. Fae affect one another easily. On the journey, his people's joyful singing brightened his mood. Here, if the wine weren't enough to make him drunk, the warmth and companionship of the gathering tip him over the edge. He rests the weight of his horns against the chair, bracing his feet along the leg of the table to find a comfortable position. No one seems to notice the undignified posture. *Is Rúnda smiling at me?* It's difficult to tell. His eyes pick up the details of her dark face, the stray hair from her braided curls catching firelight. But so many bodies ripple between them that he can't recognize what she's chosen to wear. The taste of her magic, however, cuts the heavy mess of celebration, hanging over them as the salty air of the ocean shore.

Such is their routine—wait out the celebration and join each other in the evening—but Iohmar finds himself impatient, eager to see her, discontent with the feasting and the cheer. He wishes for her quiet and her company. She'll interrogate him about Lor. Her eyes went to the child the moment she first found him among the crowd, and he saw her eyebrows rise before her people swallowed her up with singing and touch.

Where Iohmar's feasting halls are broad and reach into the mountain's core, Rúnda's are smaller, the ceiling opened into the tower for dozens of stories. Her folk tightrope across walkways spilling up and vines stretching fingers across the space. A chill wild breeze swirls in the upper levels, sometimes dipping and tossing the hair of some unfortunate victim. Colorful paper streams and kites float of their own will in the updrafts. Tables of stone carved with intricate waves and dunes circle the space, a fountain of sweet, clear water bubbling in the center. Children jump in and out while the adults feast, swimming to depths deeper than Iohmar would find appealing. Bodies bustle around the tables, excited feet rarely sitting still. The folk dance and sing and often try to catch the eye of either their queen or the neighboring king come to visit. *Yes, I would much rather be alone with Rúnda.*

Ascia drifts into Iohmar's thoughts. It could be the wine, or perhaps it's the strange haze that's been sitting over him since the illness. Rare is it for fae children to grow with others of their age. She would be Iohmar's age by now, a constant companion and friend. She would've befriended Rúnda and been another for Galen to fuss over. She wouldn't have been his peer, for no one is Iohmar's peer, but a happy shadow balancing him out. Or war could have cut her from him, as it did many others.

Iohmar presses his knuckles to his eyes and tries to think of other things.

What does Rúnda wish to speak to me about? The shadows he met in the woodland meadow were closer to her lands than his, so perhaps she has come across them.

Lor squeaks. Those sitting closest blink and giggle and wave at the child. He's been well-behaved all evening, sitting on Iohmar's knee. Oblivious to Iohmar's dipping mood, he smashes his fingers into the bowl of pudding Iohmar provided. He licks his fingers, dips them back in, and tries to reach for Iohmar's face. The laughter around them grows as he maneuvers Lor's arms out of range. It is all companionable amusement, but Iohmar feels exposed, far too watched for comfort. He slides his boots to the ground, lifts his head from the back of the wooden throne, and scoops Lor into his arms. He needs to leave. Silence will be a welcome companion. Perhaps it's leftover sickness or the child in his arms, but he is uneasy in a way he's never been in the past.

Galen is watching him, and likely Rúnda, but he doesn't search for them. He keeps his head high, his steps slow and carefree, and reaches the cool of the hallway.

There are shadows in the twilight staircase, but they do not move or live.

❧

When the dark hours of night have swept the tower, Rúnda slips into his chambers.

Iohmar is draped along his side, facing the cool of the glass-less window, Lor asleep on the furs before him, shedding happy leaves as he dreams. Fire crackles in the hearth to Iohmar's back. He has no particular fondness for fires, his own Halls warm and balmy, but the warmth is welcome against his back as bitter chills drift past the window. A comforting glow flickers its fingers into the corners of the room.

Rúnda is silent as she sweeps to his bedside. She's clothed in evening dress, a pale gossamer thing shimmering in the firelight and falling about her legs in waves. She bends over him, inspecting Lor, squinting at Iohmar. His eyes are likely difficult to see in the shadows, particularly the one newly dark. She must think him asleep. When her fingers approach his cheek, he snatches her wrists in either hand. His head has cleared, and it doesn't make him dizzy to flip her delicately over Lor and onto his chest. She gasps, and her teeth sparkle in the darkness. Blue blossoms across her dark skin where he touches her, a conscious magic she was born with. She likes to decorate her skin where he touches her, even if it fades soon after his contact is gone.

"Sneak," she hisses, grabbing his wrists in return. Her long fingers are lovely intertwined with his, a contrast against his milky paleness. She braces her thighs around his waist, and now he's the one trapped. She's at least a century younger than him and considerably lighter, though almost as tall, but she holds her own whenever they spar. He could throw her off if he so desired, but he desires nothing less.

She leans her face over his, eyes sweeping across his appearance. She smells sweet, like crushed pine needles and moss.

"What did you do to your horns?" she murmurs. "Your hair as well. Oh, your eye. I don't like your eye such a color at all."

Fae can change great amounts of their appearance, but Iohmar has not since before their first meeting, and neither can he change these strange things back. He holds up their interlocked hands so she can see how his claws — still dulled for Lor — have turned to shadow.

Turned to shadow. Iohmar shakes off the thought. He will not let his worries sour the calm and warmth of the reunion.

Inspecting his fingertips, Rúnda eyes him with an expression somewhere between suspicion and amusement. Her own eyes are black as they have always been, a natural kind, glossy and reflective as gems, never too wide to look innocent or too narrow to appear calculating. They have always seen a great deal of him — more than he's appreciated — since when they first met before the war. He untangles his hands from hers, takes her by the waist, and pulls her down. She lies atop him, chest to chest, her forehead against his, and they soak in each other's warmth.

"You have something you wish to tell me?" His voice is heavy. They haven't seen each other in too long, but he feels himself drawn toward sleep. Rúnda's breath is likewise calm and measured, hardly awake.

"I'll show you in the morning. It is strange, not urgent."

"Hmm," he replies, enjoying the soothing texture of her familiar voice. It must be a strange thing indeed if Rúnda finds it so. He doesn't allow himself to worry. Worry is for the morning.

"You seem to have some things to tell me as well," she says, but he can tell she's asleep once the words leave her lips. He smiles. Lor will be quite the story.

He drapes one arm around her, placing the other hand protectively on Lor's chest, and lets the deep night breeze lull him to sleep.

10

QUEEN OVER THE SKY

Dry heat reaches them before the forest breaks to desert. Iohmar sheds his heavy robe and tugs loose the tight sleeves and neckline of his tunic. Rúnda is dressed wisely in an autumn-orange dress cut up to her hips and wrapping around her shoulders and neck by mere threads. It isn't much thicker than the shimmering thing she wore the night before, but he can't see as much of her skin. It flatters her sweetly.

"You didn't warn me we're going to the sands."

She smiles over her shoulder. The woods don't sparkle as much in comparison. "Poor king. Too hot for your delicate body?"

He scowls while she laughs. Lor appears unaffected by the warmth. He's draped over Iohmar's shoulder, small enough to be held by his feet so he's balanced against Iohmar's neck. As far as he can tell, the boy has fallen asleep, though it's still early, his belly full of milk.

"You could relieve yourself of those clothes," Rúnda suggests deadpan, and Iohmar tosses his robe over her head as the forest breaks for the great sands.

Chuckling, she dumps the fabric at her feet and walks into the blistering heat. She wears no shoes, and Iohmar left his own thin boots in his chambers. Burning heat presses against his soles, the roughness of sand so different from soft mountain peat. He digs his toes in. Lor squeaks, awake and curious, and Iohmar lowers him. The boy does not pull away when he touches the dunes, so Iohmar lets him sit. His skin is near blue against the golden sands. Iohmar's own transparent hands appear a shade cooler. Crouching, he buries his claws in the dune. Lor tries to stuff a fistful of sand into his gums, and Iohmar swats his hand away with a gentle finger.

"Io," Rúnda calls, waving her arms for his attention from the top of the nearest dune, her shape silhouetted against the sandy blue sky. A soft, warm breeze whips her dress around her legs, lifting and depositing her back to the earth as she wanders.

He joins her, Lor returned to his shoulder, robe abandoned. Breezes whip his unadorned hair, tangling it about his horns. Lor tugs on it.

An infinite reach of sand stretches before them. Iohmar has seen Rúnda's desert many times, but it never ceases to strike him as if for the first time. His eyes, so accustomed to greenery and mountains, streams and waterfalls, and caverns of shimmering gems, do not accept a vast eternity of sand. There is no variation in color save for the shade cast by one dune upon another and the moment the land reaches the sky. Even the purplish twilight only tints the desert's hue. Night does not keep the heat from rising in long fingers. Though he has no proof, Iohmar is certain the dunes create their own heat.

And forever on they stretch. No one has reached the other side, or done so and returned, even in the age of dragons far gone. It is of strange amusement to him that a land as confined to boundaries of magic as theirs can stretch so far that their own kind cannot traverse it. Then again, the rules are often broken. To the right of where they stand, the desert breaks against the ocean, and it is so vast in every direction it reaches that all have failed in its crossing as well. Iohmar glimpses its thin haze from the peak of their dune.

The immensity of the place—and Rúnda's presence beside him, Lor fidgeting on his shoulder—expands Iohmar's chest with a warmth other than the desert heat.

He folds his fingers between the queen's. She hums.

As she leads him over the next dune and the next, the forest behind becomes a green sliver. He has no fear of losing his way with her lead. Even without her, it is likely the wind would answer his call. She stops at the bottom of a dune, where the bruised color of the air sends shadows between the waves of sand, and releases his hand. A dozen steps away, she turns to face him, magic building with the feathers of blue traveling up her skin.

She smiles at him, turning her palms to the sky.

Wind rises to her calling—a bitter cold northern gale. It clashes with the heat of the desert as a warm mountain stream meeting the sea. Sand swirls. Rough grains caress his skin. Lor shrieks once, falling quiet when Iohmar shields his face with a hand. She won't let the sand smother them, but the boy may be frightened by the sight. The sound of it is a roar, a thousand insect wings surrounding them. He gazes upward at the pattern the wind creates with sand against the sky, admiring the ease with which Rúnda wields her magic.

The sand separates into Rúnda's fingers, settling in her palms, and the storm quiets. She holds the handful to him, and Iohmar approaches. It's ashy. Small speckles of gray remind him at once of the rotting sickness, though it wasn't the same color. A strange woman dwelling in the caverns far below enters his thoughts. Dreams of his parents and Ascia and battles and scars. Flecks of shadow drifting from his skin. Lor's frail human body asleep on the bed beside him.

He pinches the sand between his fingers, watching it crumble, and kneels to pick at the odd-colored grains he now notices between his feet.

"It seems to gather at the bottoms of the dunes," Rúnda says, her voice carried away by the wind. "I believe it blows off the dunes and collects at the bottom. It has no magic to it, but . . ."

Iohmar knows why she hesitates. Rippling creatures have no magic — it doesn't mean they aren't dangerous.

"When did you notice?" he asks. Lor is reaching for the ground, but Iohmar doesn't want him sitting now.

"Not long ago," she says, contemplation in her voice. "Months. Not many of them."

He understands. Time is tricky. Because Rúnda is younger doesn't mean it doesn't slip through her mind as it does for Iohmar, just as these handfuls of sand slip through his fingers. It isn't worrying on its own — the world changes its color and shape every now and again — but it reminds Iohmar of his sickness. Reminds him of twisting shadows he encountered in the woods. Reminds him of ripplings.

He sits, maneuvering Lor under his chin. Rúnda settles beside him, a great deal of silence between them. He thinks of his parents and Rúnda's mother, of their first evening together, of all the discussions they've sat and considered. He rests his hand on her soft skin, and she covers his fingers with her palm.

"Tell me your thoughts," she whispers.

"Are there new creatures in your lands?"

Rúnda rests her head against his shoulder and considers the sky. "None I am aware of. It must be something strange if you're asking. Has the great king come across a creature he doesn't know?"

"There are just as many I don't know as you."

"Hmm."

"Some ways into your border, my party stopped to rest from the sun. I walked the woods. There were shadows I have never seen before. They were unusual. They moved and lived and gave off a feeling of life all their own. I spoke to them, and I don't know if they didn't understand me or didn't wish to answer."

Rúnda's eyebrows form a furrow along her forehead. "Were they hostile?"

"I sensed nothing. But it is strange to come across creatures in the woods I have never seen or heard or even sensed. I thought they might be yours."

"No, not mine," she whispers. She flicks her fingers, and a handful of sand shifts. "You have no thoughts about what's causing the change?"

Iohmar shakes his head. "It is out of my knowledge. Perhaps it is the shadows, but they caused no change in the forest. Perhaps it is blowing in from beyond the deserts."

Her lips quirk. As long as Iohmar has known her, she's wished to find the other side of both the waves of sand and of water. He believes she will, as many millennia as it might take.

"Then I shall keep observing." She gestures at Lor. "Are you going to tell this story?"

Lor's given up on reaching for the sand and gums at the corner of Iohmar's tunic. Iohmar hands him to Rúnda. Much like him, she's never had much cause to become familiar with children. Her own people bring their little ones to her for blessings, but her hands flutter over the child in uncertainty before taking him. Her eyes alight, and she smiles as she tucks him into the crook of her arm. Her magic intertwines with the child's, becoming familiar with it as she touches each of his toes absently. Petals float from Lor's skin at her petting, blowing out of sight across the sands.

Without looking up, she says, "His magic is . . . different."

Iohmar winces. Rúnda is more observant than most. He doubts others will notice. Protecting his child is now top priority, even from anyone who may simply think less of him. But Rúnda is kind, and she owns a piece of his heart, just as he owns a piece of hers. She deserves truth from him.

"He is . . . from the woods. But it was an unusual circumstance. His magic is strangely bonded to mine."

"Does this, by chance, have something to do with the change in your appearance?"

Iohmar grimaces, fingering the broken tip of his horn. He smoothed the rough edges, as he did the sharp tips of his other horns and talons for Lor's sake, but the bumpy surface remains. Rúnda's eyes follow his hand, but she does not reach out. Despite their toughness, he's always been sensitive to others touching the horns. Ridiculous, but somehow ingrained. Rúnda has permission, of course, but she respects his boundaries.

"Perhaps," he admits, hoping the word doesn't frustrate her. "Walk with me?"

Returning the child, she loops her arm through his, leading him among the dunes. Her skin is petal soft against his. Soon, the salty tang of the sea reaches them alongside the crash of waves over the horizon.

"Iohmar?" she asks.

She will think him foolish if he explains, foolish for bringing the human to Látwill and more so for endangering his own magic to save him. She may still come to love Lor as the boy grows, but how can she view him the same as if he were a true child of the fae, born from love or the heart of the woods? Even Galen does not, and he has known the truth from the first hours the boy was in the twilight lands.

"It was simply strange," Iohmar says. "And no longer dangerous. I promise."

For a moment, her lips quirk down. He knows his chill and secrecy are bothersome. He is awkward with speaking affection, but she is ever patient, never forcing change on his ways. Guilt twines like a vine around his throat.

"I've not quite wrapped my head around it myself," he says. "When I'm sure in full what I've done and the repercussions, I'll explain it to you in full. But I swear to you, there is no more danger. I would tell you without hesitation if there were."

She tilts her head back to gaze at him. He cannot lie, so she knows the uncomfortably heartfelt words are true.

She gives a sharp bark of a laugh, but her eyes are twinkling. "You have too much sugar in your words. But I will be patient with you. You think through things too greatly at times, you realize."

"Yes." Guilt still nags. But he will tell her. When the time is correct. When Lor is as beloved to her as he is to Iohmar. *Truth will not change her feelings toward him then, will it?* He mustn't believe so.

He tugs her closer as they crest a final dune before the sea spreads. Gulls cry and swoop low overhead, feathers shimmering in and out of the wind. Orange-beige dunes dissolve into purple-and-pear sands so bright and ethereal his eyes ache. Ships loom in the distance, beached along the sand. Rúnda releases his arm to dance down to the water, splashing foam. Waves of blue and pearl swirl around her, greeting their queen as Iohmar's trees greet him.

Following, he crouches and dips Lor's feet into the water. The babe gurgles and curls his toes from the cold before dropping them in. Iohmar sets him in the waves. Today, he is large enough to sit on his own, fists gripping Iohmar's fingers. Iohmar's lips curl, and he feels Rúnda's eyes on him. Joining him, she sprinkles clumps of sea foam onto Lor's pale head of hair. He giggles.

"Come," Rúnda says, taking his hand. "I've progress to show you."

She leads him to the ships, great monsters of dark wood and pale sails. Iohmar helped with the trees during their last visit, coaxing ones from the earth that were willing to change their shape for another type of life, drenched in salt and the tug of the gales.

"You've made quite the progress," he says, running his hand along the nearest plank. He also persuaded trees to sprout along the shores, roots clinging to the sand, branches holding the ships in scaffolds. Cherry blossoms sprout from leafless branches, casting soft petals onto the decks and surrounding sands.

"We're close to testing these, I believe." She nods to herself. "Soon."

Past ships haven't withstood the wildness of the waves. And no matter how Rúnda calls her winds to carry her, they won't transport her across the sea for more than a short ways.

So she will make her own way, and Iohmar helps where he can.

He sits in the shadow of the looming craft, setting Lor back into the foam. Rúnda joins him.

"Is there any way I can assist?" he asks.

"Perhaps reinforce the beams where you can, but I believe we have it quite secure." She takes Lor's tiny hands. "By the time this one is older, perhaps we'll have discovered a way across and you both can join in a journey."

The boy will grow with Rúnda's presence. Iohmar's chest tightens until he can't breathe.

"Your face is making quite the funny expression," Rúnda says, maneuvering closer. Fingers of waves tug at her dress. "I believe I should bring you up to the tower top again. Watching you weak at the knees the first time was quite the sight."

"Your queensguard laughed at me."

"Well, I've been spreading rumors. I tell them you're not nearly as frightening as you think you are."

"I don't think I'm frightening," Iohmar says, which is a strange enough mixture of truth and lie that it doesn't struggle to pass his lips.

"Yes, you do. And everyone is always so respectful. The great king beneath the earth . . ."

Iohmar wrinkles his nose.

She grins. "It's fun to see someone snark at you other than Galen. Keeps you on your toes."

"I already have you for that."

"I need reinforcements."

Iohmar bites the inside of his cheek to keep his expression stone and ice. "I have never known you to need reinforcements . . ."

Rúnda leans close enough their noses brush. Her mouth is pulled into a false scowl. He brushes his lips over her eyebrows with the lightest touch, drifting down her temple and ear to a delicate spot along her neck. Blue flickers along her skin, responding to his touch. He rests his mouth and chin there and lets her hair tickle his face.

She sighs.

Her fingers push up his sleeve, trailing the bare skin on his arm. Warmth from her magic settles over him like a blanket. For a moment, he thinks of his refusal to admit Lor's heritage, then stores those thoughts. The danger is over. They need speak of nothing but happy things. The air is somewhere between hot and icy, and Iohmar's eyes are so heavy he could sleep against her shoulder. As he gazes past her wild hair at the miles upon miles of coastline, something shimmers along the sand. It isn't far, but he has to squint to catch a glimpse. Still, the forms don't become clear. He raises his head, leaning around Rúnda.

"What is it?" she asks, turning to follow his gaze. Her eyebrows pucker to match his squint.

Iohmar stretches his magic. There are many creatures in Rúnda's lands who would sense their queen and the king beside her and wish to bask in their magic. Most are familiar to him, both simple and intelligent. Lovely.

No magic meets them. Cold sucks at his skin, and the air is yanked from his lungs so sharply he's certain he won't be able to catch his breath. Even at this distance, he knows them. Empty and thoughtless. Out of their borders. Surrounding him and surrounding him and surrounding him.

Rippling.

11

RIPPLINGS

When first he saw them, Iohmar was a child.

Creatures existed in lands outside Látwill, he knew. His Halls and those of Rúnda and her mother existed in their own haze of mist and woods and desert. But surely there are other lands. Humans dwell not too far from his own mountains, after all. Other things, he would sense far off. As a boy, he imagined he could find dragons, though he outgrew such hopes.

Ripplings were different in their magic in it seemed to not exist at all, but Iohmar could sense their presence even before their borders spread into his.

They were difficult to see, shimmering as mirrors contracting within themselves, giving off a strange cold so different from the chill of the tunnels he and Ascia played in. His skin crawled when he watched them, a natural reaction to something with a void where magic should've existed.

Walking the borders of his land, hiding behind his father's leg, he watched them shift in and out of the strange world bordering theirs, towering over them. The sound of his father's voice has long been lost to him now. He can't recall the tone and pitch of it. Perhaps it was worried. Perhaps curious. Calm, most likely. His father was a tranquil creature in the truest sense of the word, not Galen's type of calm which hides his nerves. His father was not afraid, because he did not understand. He always introduced Iohmar to creatures in their world and in the next. These ripplings were new to them both. Iohmar wasn't sure he liked them, but he was the prince and couldn't make his discomfort known.

Likely, he asked, "What are they?"

Likely, his father gave some answer. Iohmar doesn't remember.

He remembers when they stepped close to the border. When his father spoke to them, received no answer, and so reached out a hand. A stretch of glass and mirror reaching from the border. The rippling way it wrapped about the king's outstretched palm.

His father's littlest finger turned to a wilted, twisted vine. Iohmar remembers the sensation of the injury each time he took his father's hand, a lifeless point against his bright growing magic.

War came much, much later.

A wounded noise rips from Rúnda's throat. She stands out of

Iohmar's grasp, facing the rippling creatures across the sand. He puts his hand on her leg and curls Lor tight to his chest. There are a few of them, and a few can do neither king nor queen harm, not as old and magic filled as they are, but the sight of them raises sickness in Iohmar's throat. He struggles to swallow.

Their rippling borders reach fingers into both kingdoms and perhaps into other lands Iohmar and Rúnda have yet to discover. He's managed to keep them from the human realm. They have no set borders but haven't expanded them since the end of the fighting. Before, it would not have been unusual in and of itself to see them here, rather far from Rúnda's tower, here in a wilderness of sand and sea. But rarely do they venture to the edge now. Iohmar hasn't seen them push their border out—even the little finger of a shimmering wall this is—in centuries, let alone caught them watching.

"What do they want?" Rúnda whispers. Her wounds are not the same as his, but the fear is as potent. He squeezes her leg.

"I don't know."

She huffs a breath, and the silence grows as they watch the creatures. Even from this distance, Iohmar sees them shifting along the sand, never touching the water. Rúnda steps forward. Once, then twice. And still, they do not retreat.

"How dare they come so close?"

Rage laces her soft voice. It echoes in his chest.

"Don't," he says when she steps closer.

"I will not tolerate them here," she says, and she is not his lover, but queen over the sky in the fullest of her power. Iohmar understands and knows he cannot stop her.

"Stay here a moment," she tells him. "These are my lands. And they despise you."

Watching her stray across the sands sours his stomach and brings heat to his eyes. *She does not need my protection.* This he knows. *She does not need my protection.* But neither did his parents need his protection.

Lor has gone quiet and still. When Iohmar glances down, he finds the boy's eyes on the creatures. *Can he see them from such a distance? How can they appear to one so young and uncomprehending?*

To his relief, Rúnda stops when she's still a ways from the creatures. Her dress is a spot of bright sunlight against the purple-orange landscape. He cannot hear her words. His heartbeat throbs behind his ears. A weak chill has settled into his limbs. Such is the way a human would react to fear. Hate for his own ridiculous reaction adds to the burn in his throat.

A minute passes. He counts it out. Then another. Pressing his magic against Rúnda's, he finds no increased distress. The creatures shift before her, and she stands tall and firm. The sea crests around her, roused by her rage. Wind swirls with purple sand.

Then they crawl closer to her, and Iohmar rises. Rúnda does not warn him back. His legs are heavy and aching, and shivers crawl like spiders across his skin. Each step is a strange sensation. Closer and closer, and he's close enough he could defend her. Lor is hidden within his shirt. Up close, the reflective nature of their void bodies is clear and sharp and piercing.

He is close enough to touch Rúnda's back, and the creatures scatter. They have no faces he can discern, no way for him to know if they were looking at him, but his presence sends them back, dragging their gossamer finger of a border along after. It should comfort him they are afraid when he and his queen stand together. Instead, he wishes to curl into a ball and weep.

King beneath the earth, indeed.

Rúnda turns her face to him. Fear must be written into his skin and eyes and magic. She knows he is afraid. So is she. But he hates for her to see it. *She should never see such fear in me.* She doesn't speak.

"What did they want?"

"I don't know. They still don't speak."

Carefully, he steps to the place where the border reached across the sand, then bends and scoops a handful into his palm.

When Rúnda approaches his shoulder, he holds the sand to her, letting the ashy specks drain into her hand.

"Oh," she says, voice shaky.

"They were trying to eat the sand. I suppose some of the grains blew over into the dunes."

"Yes," she says, still staring at the grains.

He wraps his fingers around her arm, warm and solid and safe. He is going to scream.

"Excuse me," he whispers.

He puts his back to her and the retreating border and walks. The wind does not answer him in the same ways it does her. It would toss him about and wish to play, and he cannot bear such. But there is sunlight streaming in little spots where it breaks the twilight and billowing peaks of clouds.

Stepping into a sunbeam, he slips as far from their rippling borders as his magic will take him.

"You weren't easy to find."

Rúnda's voice rouses him. He isn't asleep, but his eyes are closed, thoughts far away. It's dark, and the air is chilled, thousands of stars greeting him.

Rúnda wears the same dress despite the chill. The wind atop the great tower tosses her hair in every direction. Her expression is . . . sad? Calm.

"Forgive me," he says. Acting childish is shameful, but he couldn't be in the presence of anyone, even her.

She shakes her head. "There's nothing to forgive, Io."

He turns his face from her. Understanding is a strange thing, particularly when he doesn't understand it himself. *How can I be so frightened? How can I let creatures with no thoughts or lives or knowledge affect me so? And how is Rúnda so accepting?* He pets Lor's soft hair. The boy is tucked under his shirt and against his skin to keep him warm. It's comforting.

"Do you wish me to leave you to yourself?"

He considers but extends his hand. Slipping to the stone roof, she curls into the crook of his arm, legs folded over his stomach. Her finger slips inside Lor's little palm.

"You must come to me next," he tells her.

"It's been a long time since I've seen your great mountains. Do you still visit the humans?"

Iohmar's heart gives a squeeze.

"Sometimes. I forget how tiny their lives are. I don't go for a time, and suddenly I am a myth their great-great-grandparents tell them about. More and more they do not know what they're looking at. It's easier than ever to make them gaze straight through me as if I am nothing more than a trick of the light."

Her eyes are on him, and his mind remains on the rippling creatures.

"Tell me when you're ready to launch your ships," he whispers.

A smile crinkles her nose. "It will be quite the endeavor. No one's crossed our sea and returned."

"You will. If not, I'll have your winds drag you back to me for a kiss."

She shakes once in a laugh. "They can't reach so far, you know."

"I know. I have my ways. I am more stubborn than your gales."

"Hmm. I'll keep that in mind." She nuzzles his ear with her lips. "You should stay longer this time. I know your people get restless for their own homes, but I believe a longer stay is in order."

His heart aches. "I believe I shall."

She returns his smile. "And then I'll come to you."

Time blends in Rúnda's court as it does in Iohmar's. Most his folk are content with the longer stay—those who aren't wander home through twilight woods. Iohmar is cautious since seeing the ripplings at the sea, but they are safe each time he passes his thoughts over them.

Living shadows don't visit when he wanders the woods with

Lor on his shoulder, Rúnda by his side, and Galen trailing behind with Rúnda's warrior guard and Iohmar's, the little group eager as baby hounds to watch over their king and queen. The rippling creatures don't haunt their steps when they visit the shores again. He and Rúnda are formal with each other in the presence of their people. Fun is to be had with sneaking about, finding places alone, pretending to be nothing but friendly neighboring rulers as they join the feasting only to spend long twilight nights side by side.

Lor is not so sly. Two infant fists reach for the queen each time she appears, a broad grin on his tiny plump cheeks, and he shrieks for her attention. Rúnda holds him whenever Iohmar gives the boy up, and their people watch and smile.

Iohmar sits with Rúnda often in the garden room adjoined to her chambers. It stretches into the knife of cliffside the tower juts from, spilling out the cliff's edge on the other end, where, if Iohmar searches long enough, he can find the streak of ash along the landscape where ripplings invaded long ago. Rúnda's mother, Laoise, is as ancient as Iohmar's parents would be and older than Galen by some time, though none are certain how long. She is a constant occupant of the garden, sitting among the leaves and sweet warmth of the plants. Her magic resembles Rúnda's in its presence, though it's no longer strong and vital as her daughter's, and she knows Iohmar by name even if she does not often speak.

When Iohmar's folk grow too ancient for even the twilight lands, they return to the trees and soils from which they were crafted. Rúnda's folk return to the winds. Strips of colorful cloth decorate the streak of dead land below for each lost. Markings.

Remembrances.

They sit with Laoise often, and Iohmar enjoys her quiet company as he encourages the garden to grow, even as she reminds him of his own mother until his chest aches. Whenever he takes her hand, it is light as nothing, near carried away by the wind. She runs fingers through his hair and over his horns and encourages him to sit close, and though he doesn't tolerate such babying with Galen, he allows her. It pleases Rúnda, and he enjoys her happiness. Besides, no one else haunts these private gardens. His pride can bear it. Laoise smiles at Lor and heaps affection upon her daughter, and Iohmar wonders if she thinks on the ripplings and their war as often as he.

For a time, he is happy to wander Rúnda's lands. But his mountains call to him.

His Halls are home. No matter how Rúnda teases him to stay, she understands his pull to them as he understands her ties to these dunes and seas. It is his soul's anchor, and despite the safety and contentment he finds in his tower chambers, or in sitting in the gardens, or in wandering the forests and deserts, his heart is turning for home. His people know. A large last feast is thrown by unspoken agreement. No matter how little time passes between visits, Rúnda's and Iohmar's folk feast as if they are sending the other to another land for eternity.

That night, Iohmar lies on his stomach under furs, watching Lor sleep in the crib of branches he called forth from the wall. Rúnda lies along his back, skin to skin, her toes wriggling against the soles of his feet. In the dark of the room, he enjoys how she turns her skin an azure blue where she touches him.

She presses her lips between his shoulder blades. "You smell of stone."

"Stone?"

"Mmm. River stones. It's quite lovely."

Iohmar thinks of the sweet, calm cool of water over river rock and smiles into the darkness.

"How do I smell to you?" she asks. Iohmar can't think of a more ridiculous line of conversation.

"Pine. Sand. Warm sand."

"Is that pleasant to you?"

"Yes."

She hums, fingers running along the base of his horns. It's gentle, intimate enough he relaxes into the touch. The small withered horn along the top of his head—he lost it to injury so long ago he can't remember its occurrence—is rather sensitive. Her warm fingers massage with a moth wing's touch. He sighs and reaches back for the slender top of her long ear. She hasn't worn gems in them since he arrived—she grows bored with them every few decades.

"When will you come to my Halls?" he asks.

"Hmm . . . It is warm now. It'll be warm for a time longer. When the chill starts in the air again."

Iohmar knows seasons exist. He has visited Rúnda—and the human world—enough to know most places grow warmer and colder between seasons. His Fair Halls have no such change; they're always balmy and warm, and one is never in need of a hearth or too many blankets. It cools in the darkest hours of the night and is warmest in the brightest hours of the day—never uncomfortable. Seasons are a smell to the air, a sensation along his skin, rather than a change in weather.

"It'll give you time to miss me," she says, her mouth moving above his ear.

He will miss her as soon as he steps foot outside her tower. He is beginning to miss her already, but such words stick in his throat, as they often do, and so he hums as she does when happy and content with him. She presses a kiss to the back of his neck, and he rolls over to catch her in his arms one last time before the seasons change.

12

A BEAM OF SUNLIGHT

Before returning to his mountain, Iohmar visits the human world.

He sees his people to the edge of their trees, taking time to breathe the smell of home and become lost in its magic. When they've wandered through the front gates or into the safety of the trees, he melts into the woods before Galen can figure out his plan and worry. Lor asleep in his arm, he steps into sunlight and skips the thin gradual path between the mountains. Between breaths, he is beside his Halls, then the footpath where he encountered the ragged hunting party. It is overgrown, and spring—or perhaps summer—grasses intrude upon the walking space. Time runs different here, and Iohmar isn't surprised to see undergrowth and be unsure of the seasons.

Lor doesn't so much as stir.

A nearby village draws him. He walks its outer borders in the same way he maneuvered his head into the dilapidated window of the hovel where he first found Lor—a trick of light human eyes peer straight past. It isn't much of a village. A dozen or so cottages are packed close in a clearer section of the woods, the path cutting the center and emerging the opposite end. There is civilization should Iohmar follow it, but this is not a trip for the curiosity of mankind's progression.

Tasting the village on his tongue—a great deal of sweat, salt, mud, animal, water, bread, and other flavors of food—he searches for a familiar thread. It draws him from the cluster of homes and down the human side of the path. Shrines litter the border of the village, knee-high wooden structures stuffed with eggshells, candles, mossy stones, and strips of ink-dipped paper—offerings of friendship to the fae living along the village's borders. Iohmar draws sunlight into his palm until the nearest candles flicker to life. A dog follows him from the marketplace, tail wagging, tongue trying to lick his hand. Lor's large eyes open and follow the creature, and the pup is called away by a woman's voice.

Here in the human bit of the woods, it is peaceful, open between the trees, dull with a lack of wild magic. Pine needles carpet the ground, not so overgrown as the mountains. Another cottage rests a short ways down, others scattered on either side of the path as far as his eyes follow it, and Iohmar drifts to the closest one. A familiar presence gathers here, as familiar as one could be for an insignificant human Iohmar met once for mere minutes.

A child plays with dolls of straw and cloth before the cottage. It is wooden and thatched as the rest of those nearby, unremarkable as the humans dwelling in it, not much to look at after the grandeur of Rúnda's court and the presence of his mountain. Steps away, another shrine, smaller than the rest, is decorated with colorful streams of fabric. A jar of fresh honey nests in the center, and Iohmar dips his finger in to taste and offer Lor.

"Fae," the girl says, and Iohmar's eyes are drawn to her.

She grins at him, dolls forgotten on the pile of straw she's burrowed in. Several teeth are missing, and somewhere in the back of his mind, Iohmar recalls human children lose their teeth before growing new ones. How gruesome. It isn't a phenomenon his kind suffer.

He smiles at her, the disarming gesture meaning a blessing to his own folk. He's noticed the daze it causes humans. Most anything he does is taken as threatening, but he means for the girl to see him, so he tries his best not to appear a terror drawn from her darkest bedtime stories.

Her smile grows larger. Scrambling from the hay, she scuttles up to present him with one of her dolls. Bemused, Iohmar bends to take the ragged thing and watches the girl sprint back to her cottage door. Lor giggles, reaching for the toy, and Iohmar lets him take it.

An old woman shuffles to the porch—her skin crinkled and aged in a way even the oldest of his kin do not experience—and her mouth falls open. It would be comical if the awe were not deserved. Her back is still straight and strong, her hands tanned from sunlight and work, and she does not strike Iohmar as one easily rattled. It is endearing. He nods in respect to the elder, even if he is millennia upon millennia older than she.

Immediately, she stoops in a bow, hands held up as if in offering, mumbling something akin to a prayer.

"Please, calm yourself," Iohmar says before the poor woman can work herself up. She glances up and calls to someone behind her, the name so tense and hissed he doesn't catch it.

A young man appears, confusion in his features. He carries a small hammer in one hand and a wooden box in the other, shirt absent in the heat. He does not, at first, appear to notice Iohmar.

"Grandmother, I—*oh!*"

The box of tools crashes. Iohmar considers the terror at finding a tall horned creature visiting one's child. And doubly so to have his appearance changed from the last time they came into contact. He smiles. It doesn't have the same effect. Silence stretches, and the man who spoke to him on the path does not gather his courage this time.

Remembering the tales humans spread of his folk, he says, "I've not come to rot your eggs or sour your milk, and your children are of no interest to me. You need not worry yourself so."

The grandmother has the bravery to narrow her eyes, and he does not fault her suspicion. Her eyes find the girl, then the babe in Iohmar's arms, then her grandson, and she straightens from her submissive position.

"My own grandmother told me tales of you," she says slowly, choosing her words, and Iohmar has no doubt the stories could've been of him specifically. "But I'm afraid I do not know the proper words for a conversation with a fae."

Humans have many suspicions of his kin, few near truth save

for the warning never to give a fae your name lest they steal you away.

"Don't trouble yourself," he assures her. "I wish to speak to your grandson. I have no interest in stealing him away or tossing about curses. Just a conversation."

Suspicion clouds her expression, but she wipes her hands on the apron atop her skirts and gestures for the girl to go inside. After giving her grandson a meaningful look, she shuffles from view. Iohmar tries not to chuckle. It'll frighten the poor man. The human takes the steps from the porch with great hesitation, pulling a shirt from the back of his belt and over his bare skin. Stopping beside the stack of hay, he stares with wide eyes.

"Is the little girl your daughter?" Iohmar asks. He realizes the hidden threat in his words, unintended but likely terrifying nonetheless.

The human's Adam's apple bobs. "Yes."

"How old is she?"

"Six."

"Is that young for a human child?" Iohmar has never grasped human life spans and isn't sure if they fluctuate as vastly as those of his own kin.

"Um . . . yes?"

"You don't seem certain."

He shrugs, the muscles in his shoulders uncoiling, relaxing. Scratching the back of his neck, he glances at the cottage.

"Um . . . yes, it's young. Very young. She'll, uh . . . be an adult when she's sixteen or seventeen . . . I suppose."

Sixteen or seventeen. How few years. *Do they change so much within the space of a decade?* Iohmar isn't certain of the correlation between seventeen years and the equivalent of a fae child, but it can't be more than an infant. This grandmother—a great-grand-mother to the girl—is naught more than a child in comparison to him.

"And you are how many years?"

"Almost . . . forty . . . I think. I'm not entirely sure the year I was born. It's not important to keep track of."

This makes greater sense. Iohmar does not ask the young man his name. Not yet.

"Have I done something to upset you?" the human asks.

Iohmar remembers this must be rather unnerving. His eyes follow the girl as she peeks out the kitchen window only to be shooed back by the grandmother.

"Not at all. I am simply curious."

"Curious?"

"Yes, curious. Sometimes I wonder why you decided to speak to me along the road that day. Your friends fled."

The man's eyebrows furrow. Much of his face is covered in hair. He has a broad untrimmed beard and thick eyebrows gaining in size when they bunch into a frown. "Someone had to talk to you. You're still interested after all this time?"

This catches Iohmar's attention. "How long is 'all this time'?"

The man blinks. "Five years."

Iohmar considers. It's longer than he would have estimated, but a few years is not much to him, and not to Lor either . . . anymore. He contemplates the man's daughter, who will be an adult in perhaps ten more of these years, and realizes how long a time it must be for the man.

"That is not so very long to me at all," Iohmar says, which doesn't seem to reassure him. The man shuffles his feet and peeks over his shoulder.

"May I . . . May I ask a question?"

"Of course."

"Are you really king of Faeryland? After that day, I described you to my grandmother. She said I'd met the king of Faeryland."

Faeryland. How quaint. "Indeed."

The man's eyes roam Iohmar's appearance as when they first met. *Does the man recognize the change?* It is not unusual for humans to be fascinated by the fae, Iohmar in particular, both by his physical appearance and the clothes he dons. His robes are blue this day, matching the clear of the sky, light and airy, a shock of bright in the dim human woods.

"You must be hundreds of years old then . . ."

"Much more," Iohmar says.

Silence stretches, and Iohmar allows it. He's curious about the man's every reaction. In truth, he's unsure why he decided to come, to seek out the human. Perhaps it's boredom or curiosity or a sense of unease at all the strange little things that have happened since he took Lor from the shack.

Then the man twitches, staring into the woods. "I saw what you did to that man. The one who killed his wife. I've never seen anything like it."

Iohmar waits while the human shudders, a full-body shiver that would reflect in the air if any magic hung so far into the human realm. Iohmar remembers when first he saw such magic employed. Shriveled body pierced and twined with grasses and roots of wildflowers. The beauty of a patch of spring in a winter wood. Overtaking a body.

"We never found her body."

The mother. The poor human creature Iohmar felt deep within the soil. "I did. She was lost long before I arrived, at peace in the earth."

The man's head snaps up. "How do you know?"

Iohmar rolls his shoulder in a shrug. "It's in my nature." At the even stare, he clarifies. "I did her no harm. Truly."

The man twitches again, eyes falling to Lor. Iohmar does not wish to reveal the child's origins to the human. It is likely to upset him.

"So you . . . didn't come here . . . for anything?"

Again, Iohmar sees the girl sneaking peeks out the window. He makes eye contact and smiles. It's returned.

"I mean you no harm." He hopes the sincerity in his voice is not mistaken for a well-tended lie, though humans must know such things are not in fae nature.

"Just curious," the man echoes, beginning to relax in the face. He almost smiles—not comfortable, but reassured.

When Iohmar smiles, the man does not lean away. "I have a fondness for humans that many of my kin do not share. It is an eccentricity of mine, you might say. So, you wish to tell me your name now?"

Hesitating, the man twists the hem of his rough tunic between two fingers. "Would it be horribly offensive if I said no?"

"Not at all. Eventually, I will know."

His mouth bobs open and shut with a click, but he looks confused rather than threatened. Iohmar returns the doll the daughter offered. Hesitating, the human puts his hand near enough to Iohmar's to take the toy.

"Is he your child?" he asks, nodding toward Lor without making eye contact. When Iohmar nods, he blurts, "Is he going to have horns too?"

Iohmar almost laughs. Even if Lor had been born of a physical bond, the boy wouldn't necessarily resemble him. Magic is passed in greater detail and strength than appearance. There is a chance Lor would appear as he does even if he were born of Iohmar's blood, or even if the heart of the woods gave Iohmar the boy.

"No, we don't pass on appearances as your kind does."

"Aaaaaa!" Lor cries, grinning at Iohmar.

The young man starts at the noise. "Oh . . . And you're really not here for anything?"

"You don't believe me?"

"I might if you stopped looking at me like I'm food," he says, then appears startled that the words passed his lips. He takes a step back then forward, staring at the pile of hay as if ignoring Iohmar will make him disappear.

Do I look such a way? Iohmar is taller than the human, a full three heads at least, which can't be comforting. Iohmar considers his expression. He's kept his eyes soft and large and the smile in place much of the time, but his intensity paired with his appearance might be rather worrying for a human, particularly for one who can't understand the motives of the king of Faeryland.

Truly, Iohmar doesn't know what he intended to gain from the interaction. Now he knows how time has passed in the human realm, but such was not necessary information. He finds himself face-to-face with a human as unremarkable as Lor was. The man was brave enough to speak to the fae king along the road, but there's nothing else of note.

"I have no taste for meat," he tells the man, realizing the next moment such words may not be as reassuring as intended. But the human blinks, and Iohmar considers this a worthwhile distraction.

"Ever?"

"Personally, no."

"Oh," he says, watching Lor reach for Iohmar's horns. "This is the first time you've been here?"

An odd question. "I have visited your world countless times. I am usually not so openly seen."

"No, I meant"—he gestures around— "you've never been here before? Right here?"

Iohmar tilts his head, confused. "I have never had cause to."

"But . . ." The human leans forward as if they're conspiring. "The shadows in the woods? The ones climbing around the trees? Those aren't you?"

For a moment, Iohmar loses concentration on his expression. The man backs away, glancing over his shoulder, holding up his hands as if he's frightened.

Shadows? The human is seeing strange shadows on his side of the woods? Iohmar knows humans exaggerate and lie and dream up nonexistent monsters. Iohmar would not be surprised if encountering the man along the path caused him to believe he sees monsters among the trees at all times. But the idea sticks with him, a nagging thought adding to the small things forming a weight in his mind. If it's real, not a figment of the man's imagination, then it's a concern Iohmar may need to address. His lands are the ones bordering the human world. Not often does anything pass from one realm to another, but it is his duty to ensure nothing harmful slips back and forth, even if the living shadows in the meadow were no threat.

"No," Iohmar says gently, aware of how far the man has backed away. "Those weren't me. How often do you see them?"

"Every few months . . . I suppose. Are they dangerous?" He glances at his cottage, at his daughter peeking around the door-frame. Iohmar understands. His first thoughts would go to Lor.

Taking a breath, he thinks of the ripplings sharing his border. His scars rub against the inside of his soft clothes, but he knows the sensation is nothing more than the small and frightened sliver of his mind still caught in an ancient war.

"I do not believe so," he answers. "I am still beginning to know them myself."

Could the shadows have come from the rippling lands?

Frowning, the man looks to his daughter. Iohmar follows his gaze as he melts into the sunbeams between the trees, there one minute and gone the next, and doesn't turn back to see the human's reaction to his sudden disappearance.

13

A SHRED OF SHADOW

Iohmar takes the shadowed way between the human trees.

He doesn't expect to find much. The shadows are unlikely to reveal themselves should he search—secretive beings rarely make themselves known when one is searching—but he patrols the empty woods on his return to his mountains, a sense of duty about the process. He lifts Lor to grip his horns. The weight of the child on his shoulders has become a familiar routine, comforting as nothing else. The boy's bright warmth outshines Iohmar's concerns.

Sunlight sets and rises before Iohmar steps foot on the path between the mountains. Lor is asleep, and Iohmar finds a spot in the greenery to settle, not ready to return to his Halls and their feasts and smiling. He will speak with Galen on the day's events but is unsure of the words. Rúnda will not be there to greet him until the next season, and though he left only days before, it feels a great time. The human grave is close yet unseen. Near as he is to his mountains, he can sit and enjoy their presence.

"Do you know of shadows, little Wisp?" he murmurs, setting the boy in the cross of his legs. Lor wakes with a yawn and grins up at the king. His gums have not yet grown teeth, and Iohmar has no sense of when they will. Milk and soft things will be fed until then. In truth, Iohmar wouldn't mind him staying small and sweet for an eternity.

"Aaaa," Lor coos. Iohmar believes he may be trying to speak these last few days. It wouldn't be too early for a child growing at different stages. Today, he is smaller. He will be bigger and smaller. Iohmar hasn't gone out of his way to teach the boy words, though he might recognize *wisp* before he recognizes his own name.

"Aaaad ddddd aaaa aaaaaaaa." Lor babbles on and on to himself while Iohmar gazes at his woods. It is peaceful here, at the border between his realm and the humans'. Animals prefer one world or the next, but moths flutter among the branches heavy with scent, bodies round with flower nectar, wings often brushing his skin. After landing on Lor's cheeks, they are frightened away by the following joyful scream.

Crows circle overhead, but without their gossip or the promise of a treat, they are uninterested. Heat from Iohmar's twilight lands meets the human sun, mixing into a soupy sky. Sleep pulls his eyelids, and he lets himself curl against the mossy ferns, Lor tucked between his arms and stomach. The boy pulls fistfuls of moss and flings them to either side, rolling with great effort onto his stomach and wiggling his fingers and toes into the soft earth. Pale flowers and tufts of leaves float from his skin happily.

Iohmar dozes, opening his eyes only to assure the boy has not wriggled away. His sleep is dreamless, the heat of the day or his own contentment with the quiet place he has chosen to rest making both his limbs and thoughts heavy.

"Daaaaaaaiiiiaaaaaiiiiiaaaa," Lor gurgles, patting Iohmar's cheek with a tiny fist until he opens his eyes.

"What? Hmm?" he asks, not entirely awake.

"Daaaaaaada . . . Daaaiiidiii . . . Daidí!" the boy coos, and Iohmar's eyes snap open.

He gazes at the boy. *Where did he learn such a word?* Iohmar called his own father as such many times in private but hasn't had a reason to speak it in centuries. Surely he hasn't said or even thought it in the boy's presence. *Could I be sharing my dreams?* He hopes not. They are not often pleasant. Even Iohmar does not comprehend the way their magic is bonded.

"Daidí," Lor says, the noise much more a word this time, and Iohmar's chest gives an odd squeeze. His eyes tingle.

Absolutely unnecessary, he tells himself, then curls over to kiss the child between the eyes. His skin is soft and warm, smelling of plants and the earth he's been digging up.

"My son," he murmurs.

He does not move his face from the child's, and Lor does not squirm, patting Iohmar's cheeks with little fingers as he did when Iohmar first brought him to his Halls beneath the mountain. Their world is calm and quiet, and after a time, Iohmar feels the watchfulness upon them.

When he raises his head, there are shadows about them, fluid and too dark in this bright section between the human world and the Fair Halls.

Lor's birch-silver eyes flicker, taking in the strangeness with a seriousness not fitting an infant. Iohmar does not release him, sitting and scooping him into his lap. His movements are slow, nonthreatening, and he takes in the scene before him as he did the first time he encountered these strange creatures. *What must the human have thought to gaze into the trees and see these same woods gazing at him in return?*

As before, he senses no ill will, but the thought has occurred to him that they may come from the rippling lands. Now that the suspicion has entered his mind, he cannot shed it.

"Hello, my shadows," he says. As before, there's no response.

He carries his weapon against his back within the folds of his robe but does not wish to threaten. Instead, he sets Lor in his lap, holding his empty hands to the woods. The shadows flicker and dip but stay quiet as the night, and Iohmar is grateful at least no strange voice calls to him from deep in the trees. With a great deal of care, he curls his legs under himself and rises, Lor in one arm. His head dips with the weight of his horns and leftover sleep.

"Walk with me," he says with a softness reserved for children and other timid things.

Stepping from the greenery, Iohmar takes the path between the mountains. Past the grave. The shadows slip. Now he notices the places they don't fill. Bits of normal shadows still appear in the far areas of the forest. Surrounding him are these new dark creatures, but they do not fill the trees forever. It is a group of them rather than a strange being overcoming all natural light. Satisfied with this new information, Iohmar does not speak until the path is fully in his lands, sloping up to his mountain.

"There are a few things I'm curious of," he says, hoping words will elicit a reaction. "I do not know what you wish of me or whether you dwell in this land or the next. I wonder if you can understand me. Do you understand and not wish to answer? Or can you not answer? I will speak with you in friendship should you choose to do so."

He pauses, slowing to a standstill while the mountain slopes. He does not wish to lead them to his Halls or the privacy of his chambers. They are closer than before, darkness slipping and slithering mere hands from him. Iohmar crouches, bending his head to the nearest shred of shadow. It is utter darkness, full as night and deep as the fine ink Iohmar uses to write letters.

"But I would request you no longer travel to the human world. They are fragile creatures, often frightened by unusual things. You may upset them."

So close, their presence is more apparent — near a tiny heartbeat, almost imperceptible. He smiles. If these creatures understand expression, Iohmar hopes they see the gentleness and warmth intended.

These could not originate from the rippling lands. Those monsters are all cold and hollow, empty fear. There is nothing similar in the way they are formed.

Wishing to learn but hesitant to approach with Lor in his arms, he holds his hand above the slip of darkness, letting it hover without touching. The shadows bend and dip but do not retreat.

Vaguely, Iohmar is aware of the rest drawing near, blocking the sunlight. He allows his fingers to drift down. The black shards of his talons match the shadows so deeply that they disappear into each other. Even when he presses his hand to the earth below, the shred of night swallowing his pale hand, there is close to no sensation. There is a whisper of a heartbeat as a flutter of hair, a soft sweep of cold reminding him, for a moment, of the ripplings. But this is a different cold, like the cool of the caverns weaving below his Halls.

No way of communication presents itself, no means to form a greater connection. Disappointment tugs at him. He is grateful the contact reveals no harmful intent but wishes further understanding.

He draws back. The shadows cling.

Panic pierces his chest, but he forces himself not to yank away with violence. He thinks of his father's finger swallowed by the rippling monsters, returning shriveled and weak.

These are not the same.

Slowly, he stands, withdrawing his hand. The shadows stick to his skin, stretching as uncooked dough. As they drop, the dark of his talons spreads up his fingers and to his wrist, veins of black as much a part of his skin as his own blood. It bleeds out, dripping into the creatures. His fingertips remain pitch as his talons. Iohmar holds them near his face, touches his lips to them, and frowns at the undesired change to his appearance. He turns his hand in the sunlight and watches his skin shimmer from black to an even deeper blue than Rúnda decorates hers with.

The panic has faded, and the ripplings pick at his thoughts, as does the woman in the caves — helping him save Lor, breaking his horn and sickening his magic until his appearance turned to ink without his knowledge or permission.

She saved Lor, he reminds himself. *And she was much more alive than the shadows. Besides, she is far gone from the tunnels beneath the mountain.*

Perhaps these creatures are not for him to know. There are many things in his lands he has little knowledge and sense of. Perhaps they are not for him to befriend or reject and are simply beyond his knowledge and understanding, magic born in darkness as much the same as Iohmar's was born in both shadow and sunlight, creatures of the deepest parts of his lands even he will never understand.

"I offer my friendship should you desire it," he tells the shadows. He bears strange marks now from saving Lor, his precious boy, and will bear marks from welcoming new creatures to his lands if such is their impact on him.

The shadows snake away as quickly as they appeared, and the tips of Iohmar's fingers remain black as the deepest of night.

AUTUMN

WINDS IN THE MEADOWS

The trees explode with fragrance. Even without changes in weather, Iohmar's woods know the difference between spring and fall, shimmering with darker hues of green and the spare leaf of fire as time changes.

Rúnda declared her tower chill with the beginnings of winter — as she has many times since they spoke of her desert sands — and Iohmar hoards every moment with her now that she's found her way to his Halls. Already, she and her folk have resided here for some time. Iohmar is unsure of the days, the warm weather and feasting blending together in a gentle wave.

He and Rúnda circle each other in the clearing. Fog settles across his mountain nearby, sending the craggy twisted peaks into the purple-silver sky. The trees sway. Their people have gathered in a small round space where the forest breaks, near enough to the heart of the woods that its sleepy magic pulls at them, but not close enough for it to be dangerous. The trees are asleep, not calling to Iohmar, and his folk know never to stray where the mist is permanent.

Galen is playing his lute in the shade, the instrument giving off several tunes mixing into a gentle song. Lor sits between his legs. Blue flowers push up through the grasses. Rúnda twirls a stick in her palm, intensity in her smile. She does not carry a weapon as Iohmar does, though neither would consider drawing on the other. Iohmar finds a matching stick among the grasses and rolls his shoulders.

She strikes first, dancing around him as he deflects and keeps his defenses. Neither is aggressive when their people watch and compare the two leaders good-heartedly. Sometimes, in private, they spar for serious practice, but both their gifts are lent to magic rather than blades. Iohmar can practice with his kingsguard whenever he wishes.

Rúnda tries to dart behind him, to get his back open and vulnerable. Ducking, he swoops up under her arm to catch her off the ground. Her ankle hooks around his, rolling them both to the grass. Laughing, she slithers over him, a beam of light in the honeyed afternoon, hovering in a halo of hair.

"My sweet lord," she says with a grin.

Dáithí laughs from somewhere over the grass, others joining. Iohmar smirks up at her—being bested by her in play is perfectly acceptable with the love between their people.

Rolling from under her, he adjusts his robe and flits out of the way before she can grab at his legs.

"Rú!" Lor takes off from Galen's side for Rúnda at full speed, unstable on the lush woodland floor. He trips over clumps of moss and grass and bounces into her legs, two lithe twig arms wrapping around her left leg.

"Eeee! Hello, little sweet," she says, sweeping him into her hold, nuzzling her nose into the side of his neck. He grabs her ears as he does with Iohmar's horns.

The line of trees opposite the gathering is free of listening ears. Iohmar finds a space under a great oak where they won't be seen by watching eyes. Slipping down shoulder to shoulder, Rúnda intertwines her legs with his. Now they've nothing interesting to offer, their folk return to their laughing and feasting and drinking and finding shady spots to do secret things. Galen watches them over the tops of the grasses for a moment, then focuses on his lute.

Iohmar keeps vigilant for wolves or other creatures lurking to cause mischief, but their little gathering is left alone. Only the creature he sometimes travels with pushes its long limbs from the vegetation, fur drifting in the breeze.

"He is lovely," Rúnda says, releasing Lor to toddle between the trees, never out of Iohmar's sight. "He will stay this age for quite a time, won't he?"

"Most likely. He's been slow to grow."

She smiles against his cheek. "You love him this age."

"Perhaps."

"Hmm," she hums, then laughs. "Does he still crawl into your bed every morning? I used to crawl into my mhamaí's bed when I was small."

Iohmar tries to imagine her as a little thing dancing about the top of her tower, calling to the winds to fly her away.

"Yes, of course," he says, resting the side of his horns against the top of her head. He drank too much wine before they sparred — which didn't help his chances — and sleep is calling.

Since he first learned to toddle, Lor has taken opportunity to follow his father wherever he goes. When Iohmar sits at his desk, Lor crawls under it. When he leaves his chambers, the boy waddles after. When last he received a guest to his Halls — a small group of fae who'd spent their time in the woods and wished to visit their kin in the mountain — their eyes were distracted by the child thinking he could sneak about where Iohmar wouldn't notice.

Most endearingly, he crawls from his bed woven into the wall and hauls himself onto the blankets of Iohmar's. If Iohmar is alone, Lor wriggles under the covers and within the soft shirt Iohmar wears to sleep until he's tucked against his bare chest. In the cool warmth of the morning and solitary space of his chambers, Iohmar doesn't mind the boy touching his scars. Not at this age.

If Rúnda is there, Lor squeezes himself between the two and giggles.

Rúnda pinches Iohmar's darkened fingertips between hers and inspects his talons. He still hasn't told her of how Lor came to be. Or of the woman in the tunnels.

Or of the illness.

He did explain how his fingers came to change color, about how he touched the shadows near his mountain. Like Galen, she did not approve but did not lecture him as Galen had taken it upon himself to do. Still, the desire to protect Lor's existence, and the way he became bonded to Iohmar's magic, has a stranglehold on his words. He trusts Rúnda. He wishes to confide in her. But she hasn't pushed the topic, though she must consider it whenever she looks upon him and sees the difference in his features. What will she think of the king beneath the earth making such a foolish decision for a human child?

Iohmar sighs, and Rúnda drops his hand as if she's caused it. He puts his fingers back over hers.

"What are you thinking on?" she asks.

Iohmar waits until Lor has presented them with a handful of lichens and returns to his scavenging. "I am wondering what you're thinking on."

She flicks him in the ear. "I'm thinking you're worrying yourself into a knot over something and not telling me."

"You've known me for centuries. I worry and complain. Have you only now noticed?"

"Actually, you don't complain," she mumbles. "Perhaps you should."

"Don't I? Perhaps it's my own mind I'm complaining to."

"Io."

"My sweet queen."

"Stubborn."

"Meddling."

"Hah!"

He leans his full weight against her until she collapses. Long grass obscures them from prying eyes.

Guilt nags at him, so he says, "I'm worrying over the shadows.

They're strange. I see them every so often and still cannot tell from where they came."

"Do they approach you?"

"Not since last time." He raises his darkened fingers.

"Hmm," she says, and her tone hardens. "Have you seen them again? The ripples?"

Speaking of them puts a chill along his skin. Rúnda must notice when he shivers. Her hand slides around the back of his neck, but she doesn't mention it.

"No. I check their borders often. I feel them. They're closer to the edges of their land than they once were. But they aren't leaving. And they don't approach the edges while I'm there."

She shifts until his head rests upon her chest, her legs propped over his. He's no longer sleepy, not with the topic of ripplings and shadows, and allows himself to be cradled. Lor's bouncing little flame of magic scurries nearby, in no distress. Iohmar's never experienced such a strong bond between his soul and another— not with so little effort. Even his union with Rúnda was created by time.

"They haven't come to my borders either. I wonder if the two of us together brought them out."

They've been together countless times since, but Iohmar has no better explanation. "Perhaps."

Hopefully it was curiosity. A great number of years have passed since the time on the shores, and the cursed lands have not spread farther.

Placing his hand against her chest, he feels her quick wind-swept heartbeat as the ocean waves. They've fought alongside each other. Confided in each other. He has allowed her near to him as he has allowed no other. She worries as he does about the shadows and ripplings. She should not worry over his little fears and the stories he does not tell her.

Everything about Lor should be told, he thinks, and the words catch in his throat.

"When we are alone, there are things I wish to speak of," he whispers.

Her eyes fall on him. "Oh?"

Wind twines Iohmar's hair, knotting it about his horns, covering his eyes. Laughing, Rúnda presses a kiss to his temple and sits up from under him. "Then I await our being alone. My queensguard is coming."

"Harass them for me."

"Ah, and so are the winds."

"You didn't call them?"

"No, these are wild. Will you join?"

Iohmar sits, watching the frigid gales whip from Rúnda's seas over his mountains, tugging at some of their folk dancing about the clearing. Shouts and whoops ring against the trees. Galen holds tight to his lute and looks quite put upon by the wild chaos.

"No, I believe Lor's still too young, even with me alongside."

Rúnda squints and shakes with a withheld laugh as Lor comes barreling out of the grasses to hide himself against Iohmar's back. "I believe you're correct."

Iohmar smiles.

"I'll be back in a few hours," she says, then darts into the clearing. One of her queensguard, Fainne, meets her with a grin. Though unnecessary and a tad dramatic, Rúnda flings her hands upward. The winds gently lifting those who choose to appear from the trees and step into them suddenly fling their folk upward. Her dress and hair whipping about, Rúnda and several of her guard and Iohmar's follow, shooting straight into the sky until they are no more than dots and swirls of leaves picked up by the gales. Iohmar believes he sees snowflakes brought from elsewhere. They're carried over the mountains and woods opposite the rippling lands.

Sometimes the winds choose to come to Iohmar's folk on their own, carrying them at their whimsy before depositing them back upon his mountain. They've taken them over the human lands enough that the mortal creatures have tales of the fae hunting the skies. With Rúnda alongside, it'll be quite the experience. Though it isn't dangerous, wild and rough magic seems too much to inflict upon Lor when he's only begun to realize he can call butterflies and flowers with his heart. When he's steadier upon his feet and surer of his limbs, Iohmar will enjoy taking him.

As the winds die, Lor peeks around Iohmar's shoulder, staring at the sky, before shrugging and toddling back to his foraging.

Those who did not join the gales return to their eating and drinking, conversations and singing restarting. Someone yips, tussling with another. Galen brushes at his lute as if it gathered dust and shoots Iohmar an offended glance. Iohmar tries not to laugh at the old creature's expression.

Rising, he leaves the celebration and wanders after the rustling shape of Lor exploring the undergrowth. His trees reach their leaves and tender branches to him, caressing his skin and catching his clothes. He brushes at them with his hand, and they drift about in welcome. After the roar of the winds, the quiet is thick and heavy about him.

The thicker trees are still a ways off, but Iohmar is not concerned about the creatures dwelling there. Lor is fae now as any residing in Látwill, and the reactions Iohmar once feared are no longer a danger.

"Daidí, look!" Lor bounces into his leg, presenting him with one of the small blue flowers carpeting the woods.

"Thank you," he says, letting the boy stack a pile into his cupped hands.

They wander the trees. Laughter and music float from the clearing, but the deep quiet of the woods is overtaking. It is not quite near the heart, and the trees' voices are calm with sleep, but Iohmar's head and limbs are still heavy from wine and the heat of the afternoon. It is a welcome silence.

Lor babbles to himself. For a time, he skipped between clumsy noises and speaking a handful of words. His body seems to have settled into knowing how to string together small sentences and comprehend conversations, though he remains shorter or taller depending on the day. It'll be a while yet before he grows in one linear way.

"Daidí," Lor calls, and Iohmar listens without looking up, gazing at the grasses poking between his toes.

"Daidí, look at the creatures!" Lor says, excited now, and Iohmar raises his head.

Shadows surround them. Close. Closer than they've been since the day he touched them. Taking a soft breath, Iohmar unfolds his hands from his robes. Glancing at his stained fingers, he finds them unchanged as ever. Lor is half a dozen paces before him, a bundle of blue flowers in his hands, gazing at the swarming ink about his feet. Iohmar steps closer, meaning to scoop the boy into his arms, and the shadows squeeze, near touching Lor's skin.

"Lor, come here," Iohmar says, throat tight. If they touch Lor, will they cause harm?

Ignoring him, Lor reaches down with a flower, ready to present one to the creatures. He's never known a world where something would mistreat him—even the woods will not touch him with Iohmar present—and all in Iohmar's and Rúnda's courts adore the boy. Lor is too young to have a concept of anything close to horror.

"Lorcan," Iohmar says firmly, with a tone he's never before used on the child.

Startled, Lor turns to him, flower half held out, lips pouting in hurt. His chin trembles.

Iohmar bends and gestures to him, eyes still on the slithering creatures. With the gentlest voice possible, he says, "Come here, Wisp."

Sullen, Lor waddles to him, fistfuls of flowers held out. The shadows slither. Iohmar takes a step toward him, and darkness covers the space between. Sunlight is blocked out. Sound dips. Iohmar stumbles.

Lor steps into the shadows, and every bit of him, magic and all, is swallowed.

CAVERNS BENEATH THE EARTH

Iohmar leaps upon the shadows, and the world is black as pitch. He has fallen before. When he fought back the ripplings. He doesn't remember what led to it but remembers calling to the winds to catch him. Remembers they barely eased his plummet before he met the ground. Remembers pain afterward.

This is not the same type of falling.

Air is stolen from his lungs. For a few long seconds, there is no sight, no touch, and no breath.

He crashes into something damp and unforgiving. Air returns in gasps. His chest aches. For a moment, he lies tense and still, waiting for a threat to make itself known. No magic slithers nearby. One eye cracks open, then the other, and he raises his head, pulling the tip of his horn free of the earth.

Shadows greet him, so full and immense he's certain the dark is its own living thing, not the underground cavern his logical mind knows he's fallen into. Holding his hands before his face, he touches his cheeks without seeing their shape. His skin, which once glowed in the darkness of his tunnels, gives off no light. It hasn't since the illness. He hasn't missed it until this moment. Searching for Lor's magic, he catches hold of it, too far off to determine danger.

"Lor!" he calls, raising his voice above a level which might tremble.

Silence swallows the sound, and not even an echo greets him. Raising his hands and finding nothing impeding, he stands with caution. The largest of his left horns catches on something, and he brushes away what feels to be a branch but has no spark of life. No scent permeates the underground place. Unease rises with his senses denied. Tightness twists the inside of his chest, a sharp string around his heart yearning to find his child. He breathes stale air and does his best to mute the panic.

"Lor?" he tries at less a volume. It seems as if the air itself envelops his words.

His steps are uncertain, the earth damp and hard-packed. Cold seeps into his bare toes. He picks up the faint sense of his son, the soft smell of bark and moss he carries with him, and tries to follow a specific direction. It's too dark to determine if the shadows about him are moving or natural. He will not stop to consider until Lor is safe at his side.

"Da . . ."

It's a whimper so soft Iohmar almost mistakes it for a trick of his mind. But there is light in the darkness, Lor's skin gaining the trait Iohmar lost, and he stumbles into a run.

"Lor," he calls, then hears a sharp cry of surprise. "Lor, listen to my voice. I'm over here, Wisp."

The light grows stronger, bouncing toward him, and Lor's cries become more intense. The boy smacks straight into Iohmar's leg. Iohmar breathes under the crush of relief.

"Daidí," Lor cries. His sobs grow. Iohmar bends and cups the boy's small face within his hands. He still keeps his talons dull, so they cause no harm when he runs his thumbs under Lor's wet eyes. Leaves shed from his skin in upset, disappearing into the dark. Iohmar senses no harm, no more than a bad fright, and moves the hair from his face. His own fingers are visible now, lit against Lor's luminescent skin.

"What's wrong, Wisp?" he asks. Lor covers his face with his hands, mumbling something unintelligible under the sobbing.

Iohmar settles on the cold earth and wraps the boy in his arms. Lor is small enough to fit perfectly against his chest, head tucked under Iohmar's chin. Listening to the sound of his soft cries, the only noise in the immense darkness, he holds him tight enough his tiny body doesn't shake as a leaf in a storm.

"Everything is well," he whispers against the boy's ear. "You're safe. I've found you."

Lor hiccups. Frightened of the dark? Or something else? Iohmar expected tears after being dragged into the earth but didn't expect him to become distressed once he found him. A tug twists his stomach. Turning Lor in his lap until he can tip his face upward, he cradles him in one arm, cupping his chin with

Iohmar strokes his back. "I'm looking for a way out. We're so far down I can't grow our trees."

"Why did those creatures bring us here?"

"I am unsure. There are some things dwelling in these lands even I am not familiar with. Those shadows are strange to me. I don't believe they speak in the ways you and I do."

"Is it like the other fae I can't understand?"

Iohmar frowns. Creatures in the twilight lands understand one another, but this isn't a trait Lor seems to have gained from Iohmar when the woman saved him. Several times in the past, he's noticed Lor's lost expression when creatures speak in other tongues. It isn't unheard of; Iohmar believes he remembers Ascia having difficulties understanding languages not her own, but he isn't sure if such memories are true or dreamt. Hopefully, when the boy is older and his magic is developed, Iohmar will be able to teach him. It hasn't been an issue of concern, but it's something the boy's noticed. Rúnda's noticed the difference as well, though she hasn't spoken of it except to mention it once in passing.

He should have taken today's opportunity to tell her of Lor. He will do so when they leave the cavern.

"I believe not. I don't suspect these creatures can speak at all. If they do, I cannot hear them."

Iohmar listens to the whisper of his feet. He loves the soundless woods, the hissing silence of the desert, and the crash of the ocean, which is an empty and full quiet. This is different, pressing on all sides, and he wishes to be rid of it.

A wall appears. Iohmar bumps into it before recoiling, a start running down his limbs. Lor catches his breath. Iohmar smooths

his other hand. Big eyes blink at him. They're still more human than Iohmar expected, large and round and soft. His son's eyes. He adores them.

"It's quite all right," he tells him. "It's just darkness. We're not frightened of darkness, are we?"

"No." Lor's voice is a hoarse tremble, eyes not reflecting the word. Iohmar wonders if the boy has kept the human ability to twist the truth.

"Are you afraid of the dark, Wisp?"

The boy has never shown aversion to the darkest hours of night. Only when morning twilight has long fallen across the land does he crawl into Iohmar's bed.

Lor murmurs, "I thought you were gone."

Iohmar frowns. He's never left him for more than a few hours, and even then, Galen or Rúnda or one of his kingsguard looked after him. Lor's never been alone or abandoned in his life, not since Iohmar found him.

"Why would you believe such a thing, dearheart?" he asks, nuzzling their noses.

Lor wraps both arms around Iohmar's neck. "I dunno . . ."

"You don't know. Silly boy."

He sits a while longer, soon rising with Lor in his arms. Nothing on the strange unseen floor will harm Lor's bare feet. Darkness swarms them as a living thing, now visible in Lor's light, but doesn't enter the halo he casts. Iohmar wanders, never bumping into any wall or knocking his head on a low ceiling. His toes and fingers are numb with cold. He tucks his hands within the sleeves of his light robes, arms curled under the boy's bottom. He isn't susceptible to cold or heat until it's severe. Even Rúnda's chilly windswept tower does not cause him discomfort. It must be frigid here. Lor does not shiver, tucked against Iohmar's chest and bundled into his long robes. One tiny arm curls between his chest and Iohmar's, his other hand gripping his broken horn. He hasn't lost the habit since he was a little babe. It weighs on Iohmar's head, but he appreciates the burden.

Iohmar's mountains have never been lost to him. Even in the deepest pits of exhaustion and injury, he always connects with the magic in and about him, ever present in his mind whether awake or asleep, drawing from his mountains and trees. Here, it is present, and Lor's as well, a small flame against the cold. But no other life exists. His magic is of use if something exists to cling to. He interacts with his trees. Steps through sunlight. Hides in shadow. Calls to the winds. Calms the mountains when they tremble. Even in the darkest, deepest caves beneath his Halls, even atop Rúnda's tower where nothing exists save the chill and the wind and salt from the sea, he can find life.

Here, nothing exists to reach. This world is cold and dead, so long forgotten and lacking in life it must have been millennia and millennia before Iohmar existed when anyone last stepped foot here.

If anyone ever has.

How can such a place exist? It's so deep even water has not found a path. The air is damp and breathable. If fresh air flows, Iohmar should be able to follow it to the surface, yet he cannot find where it originates. The shadows dragged them down, but nothing exists for Iohmar to see or acknowledge. What do they wish of him? To harm him and his son? What other motives co[uld] they have for bringing them to this buried lifeless place?

Stopping, Iohmar closes his eyes. He acknowledges the feat[her] weight of Lor in his arms, the miles upon miles upon miles deep crushing earth held by nothing but the walls of an inexp[li]cable cavern. He is enveloped, unable to reach past this place. H[e] reaches outward instead of toward the surface and is lost, unrave[l]ing. So vast. So unending. It's as if he's gazing upon Rúnda's ocea[n] in the dark of night without the comfort of warm sand beneath his feet. He draws back. Something brushes his magic. He can't put a name to it. It's nothing alive, but a shape, a disturbance in the earth otherwise even and uninterrupted.

Letting the shape fill his mind, he walks, eyes closed.

"Where are we?" Lor whispers. His tears have ceased, but his voice is shaken, and angry heat fills Iohmar's chest. Whatever the shadows' motivations, they've frightened his child, his sweet little Wisp. He buries the emotion from his voice.

"I'm not sure, Wisp. Somewhere far, far below the mountains."

"Where are we going?"

"I'm not sure of that either."

Lor wriggles against him. Far too young to have a grip on his own magic, he doesn't understand its ways—Iohmar will never understand in full himself—but has been watching his father summon animals and bring forth plants from the earth with a touch of his finger since Iohmar brought him to the Fair Halls. He plays often with the sunlight creatures Iohmar creates and makes small flowers bloom.

His voice grows softer. "Why can't we leave?"

his robes. He shouldn't be so easily startled. Shifting the boy to one arm, he presses a palm to the earth —as damp as the floor — and feels his way until it breaks. He continues toward the massive lifeless presence. Lor's skin grows brighter. He unburies his face from Iohmar's shoulder to gaze at his hand. Iohmar turns Lor's fingers over in his own. Perhaps the deeper the dark, the more he brightens. Iohmar never noticed with his own skin. Strange.

Flecks of leaves swirl to the ground, specks of fading radiance. Lor brightens until Iohmar is holding a beacon of light pale as the farthest stars. It tears at the thick darkness surrounding them. The shadows retreat in swarms.

"What are you trying to show me?" he whispers, more and more believing speech is futile.

A vast cavern stretches before them, long and empty as the one they left, and tall colorless pillars curve toward the ceiling. Iohmar lays his fingers against the nearest one. Each is the width of him plus another and at least a dozen of him in height until their tops disappear in darkness. They are an uncanny pale not matching the gray walls, different than Iohmar's skin or Lor's birch bark complexion. Cold radiates, too rough and lifeless to be ice, too odd in texture and off in color to be stone. When he puts his face near, it is easier to breathe.

Bone. He steps back, gazing up at them, pillar after pillar.

A rib cage.

"Oh," he whispers, chest empty in shock, overwhelmed by the size and knowledge.

Iohmar's grandfather told him stories of his own grandmother, who had been a small thing herself when the last of the dragons were seen. They were not hunted. They did not sicken. They simply ceased to be and fell into human myth so long ago that none now believe they ever existed.

"Oh, great beast," he murmurs, laying his cheek against the cold rib as if some life and magic could be left to pluck out and cherish. Cool air drifts from the surface, but the bones are empty as these cavern walls. He wanders in and around them until he finds the skull, with teeth the size of him and an eye socket double his height.

This, the shape of a head and mouth and eye, Lor recognizes. "What . . . is it?"

"It was a dragon. A great thing that flew. Wiser than any fae."

"What's wrong with it?"

Iohmar realizes. Lor, so small, so young, knowing nothing but life in their bright Halls, has never grasped the concept of something ceasing to be. Death. And Iohmar hates to tell him. Hates it in this dark and empty and old place. But he cannot lie to the boy and does not wish to dismiss his words or dance around an answer.

"It died a very long time ago, before any of us existed," Iohmar says. Lor's eyes stay on the creature, but Iohmar sees confusion. "It's no longer alive. It no longer feels or thinks or breathes or exists in this world. This is a remnant. It is no longer here."

Finally, Lor turns his face up to Iohmar's. Fear is written there, and Iohmar's throat closes.

"Are we . . . ?" Lor trails off.

"No, no. We're not going to cease down here. It is not our time. We're going to find a way out."

Lor blinks, a furrow forming between his eyebrows, and Iohmar says, "I do not lie to you, dearheart."

"I know," Lor whispers, locking his arms around Iohmar's neck, head on his shoulder while his eyes trail the remnants of the great beast. Iohmar gazes upward, finding the place where the skeleton reaches into the roof of the cavern, disappearing into the earth. The other half of the rib cage is buried in the far wall of the cave, and the sight of it tugs at him—a strange dream in his childhood, or a story told to him by his grandparents.

Mumbling an apology to the creature so long buried, he finds one of its great claws and climbs. The bones are rough beneath the soles of his feet. Atop the tallest horn, he reaches upward, stretching onto his toes, and presses his hand to the ceiling of the cave.

There. There, finally, his magic touches something of the world he knows.

Relief wraps around him. Iohmar didn't comprehend the weight of his worry until it eased. Gripping Lor tight with one arm, drawing strength and encouragement from his warmth and familiarity, from the bond created, he stretches his magic taut. Mile upon mile upon mile of cold earth reach him until loam and decaying plants and underground water appears. Past those, so far he brushes it with his magic as a child reaches for a high shelf, he nudges the roots of a tree.

And the earth cracks.

It is as if the whole world shudders. Lor gasps, staring up at the dark ceiling. Though he's witnessed Iohmar practice magic, those were tricks in comparison. So long has it been since Iohmar utilized his magic in such a way. It aches and awakens, and Iohmar isn't sure if it's painful or relieving. He was a king on the battlefield when last he reached so deep within his own life force.

A crack appears, a tiny vine snaking about his wrist so dark and shriveled it's been in the ground for centuries. Iohmar catches the softest hint of fresh air. Satisfied, he shifts Lor higher onto his shoulder.

"Hold to me, both arms and legs. Grasp very tight now," he murmurs. Lor locks his arms around Iohmar's neck, little feet hooking against his sides. Iohmar feels his infant breath against the side of his neck.

He glances at the great skeleton stretching into the dark. There is, once more, a strange tint of magic he almost recognizes. A dream. Shadows. He cannot see them, but his eyes keep believing they catch something out of sight.

Iohmar calls to the roots he's pulled down so far and climbs from the graveyard.

Night has spread across the mountains when a breeze brushes Iohmar's face.

He sucks in the chill as the first breath after sinking to the bottom of the sea, crawling out of the small fissure. Arms aching, legs wobbling, he sits in a meadow and curls Lor against him. The boy relaxes but doesn't relinquish his grip.

Moonlight illuminates the grasses, a brush of lace across the landscape. Not far from the clearing where they feasted, Iohmar finds himself in one of the many grasslands separating his woods. Taking a fistful of fragrant grass, he tucks it into a pocket.

"We're safe, Wisp," he says but doesn't try to peel Lor from his chest.

Rippling lands. Iohmar's skin absorbs the chill of the border, a separate cold from the fresh night air. Straining to see over the trees, the shimmering dead barrier rises into the night. They are close — so very, very close — and Iohmar feels weak.

Standing, he walks not to his mountains but toward the rippling lands, steps and steps closer until he is along the border of the trees where the moonlit meadow ends, and he glimpses the creatures past the trees.

They are there. Inside their border. Not touching his lands, but close. A whisper of breath from entering his world. Faceless and noiseless, mirrors convulsing within themselves. Iohmar does not need eyes and faces to know they are staring into his own.

"What do you want?" he hisses.

Lor starts, turning in Iohmar's arms to gaze at the ripplings.

"Daidí, what are those?" he asks. Never has Iohmar taken him close or even spoken of the existence of these lands and their creatures. Lor knows nothing of the wars. Iohmar doesn't believe it has yet occurred to the child that his father does not have a father and mother of his own.

"They will not hurt you," Iohmar says, because he will not allow it. Monsters shall never touch his child. They shall never again step into his lands and cause his folk harm.

"Da?" Lor asks as the ripples slither close to their border. They do not travel at all like shadows, jerking and uneven in movement. Unnatural.

Iohmar steps against the wall, twining Lor around to his back, the tips of his horns piercing the barrier. It resists him. He could press past if he wished, but he snarls, ready to unleash every scrap of his magic. The sunlight is gone, but his trees are behind him, and he is a creature of shadow as much as of light. They will regret pressing his borders—

A dull twinkle of noise punctures the night as they scatter, disappearing into the corpses of trees on their side of the land. Iohmar feels the lack of their presence, and his legs tremble. He yanks back, staring at shards of moonlight cast off the border. Lor is clinging to his horns, and Iohmar is grateful to absorb confusion rather than fear from the tether of their magic.

He should not have acted in such a way before his son. Not when the threat was not immediate. Tears burn his eyes. He presses his knuckles against them, mortified.

He is stronger than this.

How can he not be stronger than this?

Lor pets his cheek. The boy cannot see his face even if he senses his distress. It's a small comfort.

When he reaches for his magic, it crumbles from his grasp. No sunlight shines in the hours of midnight, but he has stepped into moonlight without difficulty. Even after he climbed from the earth, it should be within his grasp. It flees, and Iohmar notices for the first time his body's frailness. His horns weigh heavy against his head, limbs aching to lie down and sleep.

"Daidí, what's wrong?" Lor whispers.

Holding his hands before him, even in the slight light of the moon, Iohmar sees rot drifting from his skin.

16

ACROSS THE RIPPLING LANDS

Iohmar flees the rippling borders.

He passes the cracked earth without attempting to close it; he will return in time. The ripplings won't break the barrier—not when such a small show of hostility sent them scattering—but Iohmar wishes to be far from them before his body fails.

Was it his use of magic? Stretching his power to its limits never causes weakness. Has the strange rotting sickness been lingering in him all these years? Did saving his little boy do permanent damage? He's felt strong and whole until this moment.

Pulling Lor from his back to his arms, he stretches his magic around him. Testing the bonds between them, he finds bright strings of life and warmth in the back of his thoughts, strong as ever. It grinds at Iohmar to find the bonds. His head spins.

"Daidí?" Lor asks. Iohmar keeps him pressed to his shoulder so he cannot see the sickness drifting from his skin.

"Shh, all is well, dearheart. We'll be home soon." Murmuring and pressing his fingers to Lor's neck, he gathers some semblance of calm, letting it wash the boy into sleep. Lor's limbs relax, a warm, limp weight in his arms. Iohmar grips him closer. If Lor were to wake and see him, he would be terrified. After caverns and dragon bones and ripplings, Iohmar wishes the boy to be comforted. His sleep will be long and deep and comfortable, for Iohmar doesn't believe he will make it to his mountains. Rot and weakness drag him down.

He finds a place in the undergrowth to settle. Warm and soft and cushioned with ferns, the woods here are oppressive, but he is far from the heart of the woods, concealed from prying eyes by trees and flowers and grasses. Creatures of all shapes float about, drawn by his presence, weak as it is, hanging on heavy branches, eager to cling to their king's magic. His folk don't often wander so far. Not even Galen will find him.

Sitting with his back to the tree, he cannot see the rising border. Their presence exists, far off, no longer pushing against or even nearing his lands.

He closes his eyes. Feels strangely hot against the chill air.

Curls in the vegetation.

Maneuvers Lor into the circle of his arms on the mossy ground, held tight to his chest.

Sleeps.

Iohmar is not aware of the hours or days enough to count. Every so often, he awakens and is reassured Lor remains sleeping, expression calm. Flecks of papery rot drift from his skin. An owl with large eyes and a bright mouth watches from the branch of a green-black tree trunk. The rest is unclear, and during one of his lucid moments, he is grateful he's not often awake enough to worry over the severity of the illness.

He dreams of his parents.

Of the warmth and sunlight of his childhood in the Halls beneath the mountain. Ascia laughing and chasing him about. She is nothing but a blur to his dreams. He cannot recall her face or the talents of her magic. Was it similar to his? His mother taking him to the tips of the mountains. His father wandering the orchard. Magic. Swordsmanship. Politics. War. Galen ever present, hovering inside each memory as he does in Iohmar's waking days.

Sometimes he stirs and cannot lift his arms to wrap them around Lor's body. The boy is here, lying alongside him, safe, shedding flowers from his skin, but Iohmar wishes to crush him close, to cuddle him until they are safe and his son forgets all caves and shadows and ripplings. But he cannot reach him. Cannot reach.

Other times, he wishes Rúnda were here, then shudders at the thought of her seeing him in such a way.

Iohmar dreams of his parents.

It was cold the last day.

Rarely are the twilight lands not warm and fair, but a storm turned, as it did every so often. His father and mother were king and queen beneath the earth. Even they did not fully understand the ways of their world. Their mountains are pure magic. Beyond them.

Iohmar is not certain how the war started. It may not have been called *war* if not for the last onslaught. Perhaps they were waiting for no one to expect them. Always, he remembers being a boy, watching the ripplings swallow his father's finger and spit back a lifeless husk. Later, they slithered into Látwill, first dissolving crowds of trees and plots of fertile land. Their shimmering bodies swallowed mountains dead until Daidí and Máthair stood between them.

They withdrew into their lands.

They retreated.

They came back.

Enveloping bodies within their voided forms.

Iohmar remembers one of his father's kingsguard who used to slip him plums and grapes and sugared nuts as he escorted the royal family throughout their mountains. He rarely spoke and could call the littlest creatures in their lands to him with simple thoughts.

Iohmar can no longer recall the fae's face, simply his name — Aoshor — and the twisted vines and shriveled leaves left when the ripplings finished.

They were gentle folk—those dwelling within the mountain. They stitched clothes or fabricated jewelry and pretty knives made for carving. Crafted music and sculpted the Fair Halls. Played tricks on the human lands and one another. Feasted and sang and made love. Iohmar knew the feeling of a sword when sparring with his father. Knew the ways magic drained life or cursed or caused eternal despair. Knew the strength and magnitude of his own given talents. Much as his parents, he used them to aid his folk. Or to play.

His parents stood with Rúnda and her mother, with their small folk barricading themselves within their tower. Iohmar pushed them back. He darkened the sky and pierced them with sunlight and brought trees to drive them back.

He forced them back and forced them back.

From the tip of his mountaintop, when the mist cleared, he watched them break the barriers of Rúnda's land in a shower of mirrors and emptiness.

Rúnda didn't ask how he gained the scars littering his body— not when they first shared a bed or the times afterward. She approached the topic when they were centuries older, swimming in the bruised waves near her tower. It was twilight, and she could see the pale lines crossing his torso better than in the shadowed halls hidden by covers and midnight.

"Mirrors," he told her, and she understood.

She pointed to a single long scar up her spine and across her right shoulder. Iohmar knew it was there, had seen it in the fire-light, felt it under his fingers and considered the few ways a queen over the sky could have gained such an injury.

"When?" he asked.

"When they shattered."

So, it was his fault, if only a little. She'd been there, close enough the aftershocks had reached her body. Shame nagged at him. He drifted up behind her in the waves and kissed the long, thin mark. "Forgive me."

"Forgive you," she mumbled. "You saved us all."

They did not speak of it again for many centuries to come.

When Iohmar called to sunlight and snapped himself away—from his lands to Rúnda's in a step—the remnants of the kingsguard surrounded his father. He knew the shape of him, the dark of his hair, the gentle curve of his shoulder. From a distance, he knew him between the bodies of his protectors.

He called to the magic bonding them and felt none.

Air distorted the borders between the rippling lands and those soon to be Rúnda's. Her mother was nearby, though he couldn't find her shape. The bright sunlit coast opposite the great tower drifted with clinking shards of glass. They'd stung Iohmar's bare skin. His wrist burned from the cut of one of the monsters he'd chased back.

Some of his folk were there. He recognized the remaining husks of their bodies. Others drifted away in the stale winds. Rúnda's folk.

Unburying his father from the exhausted kingsguard, he touched his cheek, laid his face against his as he hadn't done since he was a child. Ropes of vines and tendrils sprouted from his skin, already seeking to tether him to the earth. Each curled away from the foul ground.

"Athair?" he asked and knew there was no one to speak to.

He heard them close by, their rippling bodies clinking and writhing, returning from the border. Iohmar didn't much care.

"Daidí," he said, then kissed him. He tried to remember the last time they'd spoken, days ago before they'd left to assist Rúnda's mother, and exactly what words had been said. It was nothing important. They'd shared a meal and left with a touch of the hands. Nothing important. Nothing at all.

One of the kingsguard gripped his shoulders. He didn't look to see which face was gazing at him, grieved and terrified.

"Iohmar," the voice said. He recognized it vaguely.

"Where is my mother?" he asked, and no words reached his ears. "Where is she? Máthair!"

She should've heard him if she was close. She should've been close.

Casting out his magic, he crashed into the rippling monsters so near it buried him in ice. The air left his lungs. He curled over his father's body until the sensation passed. Living things did not exist there. He felt his own heartbeat, the thrum of his magic, and the lives of his parents' kingsguard—his kingsguard—and a few stragglers. There were others farther off, but he tasted his mother's magic in the air and knew she must've been there.

She must've been there.

"Take him," he said. "Take him."

Arms replaced his own. For a moment, he was held in the circle of kingsguard, unable to bring himself to break free. Shoving from them, he approached the border. Swirls ran up the shimmering gray barrier reaching to the sky—a fingerprint of his mother's magic.

"Máthair!" he called.

The land was dead, a scar plunging into the earth so far that he couldn't reach its end. Uprooted trees and withered flowers littered the ground. He slipped on them. His thoughts were weak, body screaming and strong but exhausted after stealing back his own lands. Rippling shards drew his eyes, and he saw them slinking out of their lands, scavenging for magic leftover in what they'd already consumed.

He slipped from downed tree to downed tree rather than face them.

He found her there, a patch of soft red flowers anchoring themselves to ashy ground. He sobbed. Sobbed. Sobbed and could not remember a time he'd done so since he was a little boy and Ascia had been lost to him.

He pulled roots from the ground—the only things he could call in the dead lands—and eased the flowers from that place. She could not stay there. None of them could.

One was near, near enough Iohmar felt the void of its body

pulling at him, washing him with cold. He stared at it, and though there was no face, he felt it watching, towering three times his height. Sunlight broke the clouds, startling it back. It slithered around the beam of light, almost curious if Iohmar didn't know better.

There were more behind it. Large. Strange. Iohmar wondered if they had parents and children and concepts of what they'd taken.

One of the poppies shriveled under the creature's touch.

Iohmar screamed.

He called the trees. The sunlight and shadows were still there, hidden by all the consuming gray. Trees and roots and soil fused to the remnants of the border his mother had created. He did not have her magic but could reinforce her protection. The creature nearest gave a harsh scream, cut off from its land.

Surrounding himself in shadow, Iohmar pressed out sunlight and heard shattering, a thousand mirrors breaking across his ears. Pain cocooned him, shards of glass coming to pieces, burying themselves in the felled trees, the shimmering border, everything left to contact.

When he raised his head, they'd retreated so deep within their borders that even their soulless forms were no longer within his reach.

He wanted to collapse.

He had to go home. They had to go home.

His kingsguard were bundled where he'd left them, the few remaining who'd come to defend these lands clustered beside them, bodies cut from the shattering. Their eyes were on him.

Iohmar looked at himself, touched a hand to his chest, and found himself more in pieces than together.

The roots of the poppies twined between his fingers.

Calling his sunlight, he drew his folk to him and yanked them home.

Iohmar remembers bringing them home, remembers the trees of the orchard and Galen tending to his ruined body. He thinks Ascia must have been there, but she'd been lost to him so long ago. He hears her voice, his mother's name, his father's, and the names of everyone he has ever known, fae or human or otherwise, all in his thousands of years.

He thinks of the orchard. Dreams of it.

Dreams. Dreams. Dreams.

When he wakes, he feels tears upon his face.

THE ORCHARD

Lor is beside him.

Iohmar wouldn't need more than a breath of magic to wake him, but his limbs quiver when he shifts on the forest floor, and the boy looks so peaceful. Iohmar's certain, though rot no longer drifts, his appearance must be dreadful. His skin is thin to the touch, fragile as if he's thousands of years older. Rolling onto his back with a great deal of care, he tests his muscles. His right shoulder aches. It's the one he slept on. How many days have they been here? Usually his body is not so sensitive.

He spreads his fingers. His talons are sharp and dark as midnight. Pulling his hair over his shoulder, he finds it still washed with ink, his fingers stained from touching the shadows. His skin is translucent as ever, though a little gray with exhaustion. The streaks of rot have faded, leaving no trace on his skin or clothing or even the moss beneath him. He flexes his fingers and watches the tendons move — the piercing scar on his left hand from a shard of rippling glass.

What awful dreams.

He presses his palms to his eyes and finds his cheeks wet. He is a king and far too old to be sobbing like an infant.

Årelang. Croía. He thinks his parents' names and tries to steady his breathing before sitting up. His limbs tremble. He remembers training long and hard as a youngling and how he would wobble when standing for days after. This is not so different a sensation.

Leaves shiver. Iohmar notices the other presence only now, eyes gazing at him from among the trunks.

"Túirt," he says, uneasy but relieved.

The trees here are dense and clustered. He walked farther than he imagined before settling. Were he in his right mind, he would never have settled in these parts of the woods. Túirt must have felt him nearby and come searching.

Was he watching him while he was ill? What does he think of his king lying helplessly on the forest floor?

Túirt slides from the shadows, folding himself on the ground. "I found you sleeping."

A shudder runs across Iohmar's skin, and he struggles to tamp it down. Hesitantly, he says, "Yes?"

Túirt's eyes glance in the direction of the rippling barrier, invisible past the trees. "Thank you for frightening them away. I ensured the wolves didn't bother you while you were asleep."

Iohmar closes his eyes. Wolves were not much a danger, not in the state he was in, but Túirt is not one to give out favors. More so, he doesn't believe the solitary fae will speak of what he witnessed. Not with the look in his eyes. "Thank you, Túirt."

Túirt rocks, arms around his knees, and pets his fingers along Lor's sleeping head. Iohmar allows him the touch. Children are so rare that the creature may never have held one, and it seems no more questions will be asked.

"Do you wish to come to the Halls with me?" he offers, though he wishes to be left in peace.

"No, no, no," Túirt mumbles, rocking quicker. "My trees need singing to. Sweet child."

He strokes Lor's hair, then unfolds from the ground and darts into a gap between the wide trees without a word.

Watching the shadows, Iohmar puts his feet under him, pleased his legs hold his weight. Though his head is heavy, it is no longer on the forefront of his mind. He wriggles his toes in the moss and fallen leaves and brushes at the dirt and tears in his robes from climbing from the earth.

The crack will still be there. He needs to investigate.

But first, he will take Lor home and let his body recover in full. Bending causes his head to throb, but Iohmar pulls Lor against his shoulder and steps into the sunlight.

When he wakes in his own bed, Galen is sitting in the great window feeding his crows. Iohmar's chambers were abandoned when he returned. He sensed Rúnda somewhere in the Halls, and Galen as well, and put Lor to sleep beside him.

He rolls over and stretches, finding his limbs much stronger than before, only the smallest hint of trembling. He needs to change from his soiled clothes, and he flicks dirt from the bed covers.

"You've been gone a great while," Galen says, spreading breadcrumbs along the window.

Iohmar stills. Hours must have passed in the cavern at most. His first sickness was days long, and though this one felt longer, Lor would not have slept past half a dozen days with Iohmar's weak magic influencing him.

"How long?"

"Near two weeks. I made a point to count the days."

Too long. His illness was not so long. Even the blooming grasses had not grown a week's worth, flowers blossoming without withering.

It must have been the tunnels, the shadows dragging him down.

"You are dirty," Galen says when Iohmar doesn't respond.

"Yes."

He doesn't wish to have this conversation.

Touching Lor's cheek and rising from atop the covers, he slips from his filthy robe, tossing it aside. Drifting to the washroom, he fills a basin with warm water and cups it between his hands, staring into the rippling reflection before running it over his arms and across his face and neck and shoulders. Dirt clings in the shallow divots rounding his horns. Galen's eyes are on him from the washroom doorway, and Iohmar shivers, but there's nothing of his bare skin the caretaker hasn't seen.

Iohmar remembers the wounds he returned home with centuries ago. Galen hovering about him all times of day and night, concerned for his healing. Grief weighing the old creature's eyes. Galen tending to Iohmar's injuries when he relented and allowed it. Healing once he permitted himself to be cared for.

He sighs. "The shadows have returned."

Galen cocks his head, taking this as permission to step inside the washroom and inspect him. His fingers flick at smears of soil Iohmar missed. "I thought they return often?"

"They've kept their distance since the time I tried to touch them."

He plucks a leaf from Iohmar's horn. "I am going to comb your hair."

He has that tone that is not to be argued with, and so Iohmar doesn't tell him he's no longer a toddler in need of grooming. Galen works at snags with a bone comb. They can't see each other's expressions.

"They attacked you." It isn't a question.

"I'm not certain." At first, Iohmar believed malicious intent, when they were brought to the cavern and Iohmar hated them for terrifying his son. But once in the dark of their domain, he was at their mercy. They caused neither of them true harm. "I don't believe so."

Iohmar uses a small rough file to shave the sharp tips of his talons. He's never had much use for them and hasn't missed their needle sharpness.

"Some of these scars seem irritated." Galen runs a gentle finger across one of the long pale markings on Iohmar's rib cage. He hisses, brushing Galen away and slipping from the washroom. They no longer pain him except in phantom waves, but the memories are fresh, and he hates the casual touch. Even when Rúnda pays them attention, he struggles not to shy. Only with Lor does he tolerate such behavior, but the boy has so little concept of pain and injury that they are meaningless marks to his eyes. He will find no judgment in his son.

None hurt — though he rubbed against the walls of the tunnels — but he doesn't wish to inspect himself while Galen watches. He tugs a nightshirt over his head, hiding himself within the cloth. The fabric is made from a plant so soft that every moment wearing it is like feeling warm, calm water along his skin. Putting his hand in the pocket of his robe, he finds the fistful of grass he pulled before the illness weakened him.

"I . . . apologize, " Galen says. His voice is so soft and uncertain that Iohmar gives a wave of his hand. No harm was meant. Galen hovers about Iohmar's bedside, inspecting Lor's sleeping face, running fingers over the boy's dirt-streaked forehead and cheeks. The slightest, thinnest wisps of leaves drift.

Wandering to his window, Iohmar gazes at the vast woods bathed in purple twilight. He rubs at the scar Galen fussed over. *Should I tell him of the ripplings watching me from across the border?* He confided in him when they approached along Rúnda's shores. After all this time, he saw the flash of terror in the ancient creature's eyes.

"There is no harm to the shadows when they touch, just strangeness . . . When I am close to them, I can feel their little heartbeats."

Galen joins him, arms tucked within his sleeves. He stares at Iohmar's fingers, expression distant. "They sound like your sunlight creatures, the ones you played with when you were a boy."

Ascia loved when Iohmar created them. Memories of her are returning to him in snippets, never gone, simply difficult to grasp from the past. Her name hangs in the air between them. He still creates those bright creatures, sending them dancing about Lor, slivers of brightness without weight or form or consciousness. *What was her magic?*

"Nearly," he agrees. "But those are extensions of me. No life on their own. These are connected to nothing. They are their own creatures. Do you remember Ascia's magic, Galen?"

At her name, Galen twitches, blinking at the long-forgotten sound. It has been so long. So long since Iohmar spoke her name to anyone. The last time it left his lips, he stood alone with Lor in Rúnda's tower, whispering it for the wild winds to snatch away. His throat burns. Childish.

"No. She played in the tunnels with you. Her magic was quite undeveloped. I'm not sure it had presented itself."

Iohmar nods.

"Might I ask what you're planning to do?"

"I haven't decided . . . They disappeared for quite some time. I'm not sure when I'll encounter them next. And I don't know how to communicate. I need time to think on it. I will not jump to violence."

The rippling creatures slither into his thoughts. Iohmar forces them from his mind. He considers the voice he heard first in the woods on his journey to Rúnda's court, just before discovering the shadows for the first time. Time may blur to him with ease, but the voice remains sharp and clear. He isn't certain the two instances are related.

"Have you . . ." Galen hesitates, and Iohmar turns his eyes back to him. "Have you explained to Rúnda? About . . ." He nods his head toward the sleeping Lor.

Iohmar sighs. "No."

He's accustomed to the frown sent his direction. Rúnda must be sour with him for disappearing as he did, for much longer than the winds would've taken her. He worries she'll think him foolish for his sacrifice. Tampering with one's own magic is a foolish act unbecoming of a leader. Iohmar rubs his eyes. They itch still from the illness, and his skin sits frail and older than his years. His horns are no longer heavy, but his head is filled with mist. He needs to tell Galen of this as well. And he will not test Rúnda's patience and love any longer — not over his petty fears. It is unkind.

"I will talk to her of it before she returns to her tower. I was meaning to before the winds came down from the seas."

Galen nods, the frown smoothing.

A soft whisper reaches Iohmar, Lor stirring on the covers. Glancing over his shoulder, he watches the boy roll until his back is to them. He sighs, a baby bird in the nest of Iohmar's airy blankets.

Lor *screams*.

It's such a foreign noise that Iohmar doesn't recognize what's happening for a horrid moment. Galen starts, tipping into the window as he loses his balance.

"Lor," Iohmar says, leaping to the foot of the bed. "Lor!"

He turns the boy over, taking his wrists. Lor's eyes don't

focus—not until Iohmar gives him a soft shake. Lor blinks, his shrieks cutting off with an echoing abruptness.

"Lor, it's well. All is well." Iohmar drops his wrists in favor of cradling the boy's cheeks, smoothing his hair.

Lor hiccups. Upset, his skin sheds leaves, flower petals drooping and falling. His eyes are glass with tears, lower lip trembling. He stares up at Iohmar as if he doesn't understand him. Iohmar swallows. *What do I do?* The boy has not cried since he was an infant first brought from the human world, and earlier in the dark of the caverns, but such was a simple thing to understand and soothe.

"What's wrong, hmm?" he asks, attempting a calm and unworried voice.

Lor's breath hitches, but he says, "Where . . . where did you go?"

Though he hasn't left the boy's side, Iohmar's stomach twists. "I'm right here."

"I didn't see you," Lor whispers, glancing over his hand at Galen. The old fae is as shaken and confused as Iohmar, frowning at the child. He softens his eyes when Lor looks to him.

Slowly and calmly, Iohmar scoops the boy to his chest. Lor hugs him in return, but Iohmar isn't soothed. Something is wrong. He hates Lor's easy fear. Iohmar isn't certain why the caverns frightened rather than fascinated him. He has always been interested in the tunnels beneath the mountain with their shadows and gems, running ahead of Iohmar into the darkness.

This was different. And the boy knows it.

"Lor . . ." Iohmar starts, unsure. "Did anything happen in the cavern before I found you?"

Mere minutes must've passed before Iohmar found him. It felt an eternity, but Iohmar knows it wasn't.

Lor shakes his head, but Iohmar is not satisfied. "You can tell me if something frightens you, Wisp."

Galen creeps closer, standing in the corner of Iohmar's sight. *What does he think of my softness? Of the way I speak to the boy?* It matters little.

Lor doesn't respond, and Iohmar feels his face twisting into a frown. He shifts the boy until his face is no longer hidden by his shoulder, cradling him as if he were an infant. Lor rubs his eyes and blinks.

Iohmar searches his expression until Lor, unwillingly, says, "I heard a voice."

"A voice?"

Lor hiccups, fiddling with Iohmar's soft tunic. "It was calling for you."

"For me," Iohmar repeats, considering at once the soft voice that spoke his name before he met the shadows. He turns to Galen, but his confusion matches Iohmar's.

"Was the voice familiar?"

Lor shakes his head.

"Is that all it said?"

Lor nods.

"Are you certain?"

Another nod, and Iohmar believes him. It's strange no one addressed him in the oppressive darkness. Perhaps they are linked—the shadows and the voice. He can't imagine why they appear to him but refuse to speak.

"What did the voice want?" Lor asks, putting one of the tie strings from the tunic between his little teeth. Unconsciously, Iohmar rocks him.

"I'm not certain yet," he says. Then, to comfort the boy, adds, "This is a mystery we'll have to figure out, isn't it?"

He searches for a smile, but Lor nuzzles his face into Iohmar's shoulder. Galen's eyes are still confused. Iohmar cannot help him and knows where he wishes to be.

"I am going to take him for a walk," he murmurs, and Galen takes the dismissal, drifting to the door.

As some sort of thank-you, Iohmar says, "You should join us for supper tomorrow—me, Rúnda, and Lor. I need to speak with her tonight."

Galen pauses. It seems to soften him. His eyes gentle, and he bows his head, running his fingers over Lor's temple and Iohmar's shoulder before disappearing.

Iohmar closes his eyes. He needs to visit the quiet of the orchard.

Lor dozes as Iohmar bathes and dresses him. Iohmar daydreams of the crack in the ground. Worry nags. Perhaps he should have told Galen of his encounter with the ripplings. He will tell Rúnda, as always, but the idea doesn't comfort him.

He chooses clothes that are soft against his still-sensitive skin — a weightless pair of trousers, a long loosely spun tunic which catches light in its small filaments, and the heavy black robe Rúnda gifted him. It's stable across his shoulders, and he hopes she will be pleased by the display of her gift. Certainly, she will be cross with him after his disappearance, and he needs to approach the subject gently. One of his lightest crowns of twisted vines he selects to wear when he is out among his folk. Wearing a crown isn't easy around his horns, but this one is open in the back and simpler to slip through his hair. It rests around his temples.

Lor in his arms, he leaves the security of his chambers.

Noon is rising. Sunlight bathes the garden in speckles of light. The grass releases fragrance in the heat, and Iohmar drags his toes through it as he wanders the garden. Rúnda's voice is the first he picks out from among the birdsong. She's sitting with her queensguard, circled under the shade of flowering trees, each of them plucking fruit from the heavy branches. Iohmar idles in the cool of the shadows, not out of sight but unnoticed for the moment. Several of Rúnda's queensguard are older than her, but not Iohmar. They will exist by her side until they are no longer part of these lands. Rúnda feels much the same for them as Iohmar does for his own kingsguard, and so he has affection for them despite having shared few experiences.

They, of so few between the two lands, know the true relationship he and Rúnda share. As far as Iohmar can discern — and he's paid great attention — they appear to approve of their match.

The youngest among them, Fainne, notices him first and smiles with a bow of her head. Her moss-green skin is peppered with light blue freckles, and a dusting of soft feathers fades into her scalp. She joined Rúnda's side within the last few decades. Such practice is not usual. Many of Rúnda's guard have been with her since childhood, but there are exceptions. Fainne can disappear into breezes and pop up miles away, and Rúnda welcomes the opportunity to foster someone young with such a gift. Fainne has never known a time Iohmar did not exist in her queen's life and is always enthusiastic to greet him.

Bowing his head, he steps from the shadows and closer to Rúnda, touching the tip of her ear. Her head lolls back, and she gazes at him with cool eyes. *What does she think of my sudden reappearance?* He smiles and feels it crack his face.

"How are you enjoying the sunlight?" he asks. He dislikes how disingenuous it sounds and assures himself he shall speak with her.

"It's lovely," she says. "It's always quiet here."

There are no wild winds to drag them away. "The gardens are peaceful. I'm visiting the orchard. Shall I join you later?"

She nods, her eyes on Lor asleep on his shoulder. There is curiosity there, and he touches her ear again before he slips from the judgement in her gaze.

The orchards are a swath of rolling trees for miles within Iohmar's Halls. Soaking in limited sunlight and dwelling happily in twilight, the leaves grow in shades of dull color and bear fruit no one in the Fair Halls touches. Iohmar's kind do not decay in the way of the human world, and the winds do not tug their bodies into the skies as with Rúnda's folk. Here, they leave permanent remembrances.

Lor stirs not far into the trees. Iohmar has never brought him here nor explained the significance, though the child has seen the trees from the gardens. Setting him in the grasses, Iohmar watches Lor rub sleep from his eyes and circle the purplish trunks, plucking flowers from their bases, twisting them into little wreaths. Each circlet—sloppy and falling apart in his hands—he hangs on the lowest branch before skipping to the next tree.

"Daidí, I'm sleepy." He waddles through the bluish grasses until he bumps into Iohmar's leg. Iohmar slides his hands under his arms and swoops him up without struggle—the fresh air is sweet and calms the remnants of unsteadiness in his limbs.

"We were asleep a long time, Wisp."

"Why?"

Iohmar's head is weighed by the boy hanging on his horns. Once he grows larger, Iohmar will need to dissuade him from pulling his head down. For now, he cherishes the gesture.

"Well, we had quite the adventure, didn't we?" It isn't a lie, just a dance about the truth. Everyone tires, and Iohmar expended a great deal of magic pulling them from the earth. For all Lor knows, long sleep is needed after such an experience.

He'll realize soon enough. Never did Iohmar plan to explain to the boy he grew sick when he was an infant. But if it happens in the future, an older Lor won't be so easily dissuaded. It overtook Iohmar with such ease, and so close to the rippling lands, in the densest parts of the woods. His mother's magic never failed her once it recovered from saving his father, but it is not so similar a situation as he believed, and he cannot rely on hers to guide his expectations. The corners of his mouth turn down, but he makes his expression neutral before Lor notices.

"Are you still sleepy?" Lor reaches for the leaves of the

nearest tree.

"A little. We will be much better in a while. Do you like the trees here?"

Lor folds a leaf several ways between his fingers. It's spongy and light and bounces back under his touch. "They're strange."

"Yes, they are indeed. Would you like to go for a little walk with me?"

"Yes." Lor drops the leaf at the base of the tree.

Iohmar sets the boy back in the grass, keeping gentle hold of his hand, and wanders toward the center of the orchard. Distance here is as strange a thing as time. Many trees stand between here and the true center, but Iohmar wishes to reach it, and so the lands obey their king. Within a hundred steps, they cross the stream circling the center, reaching two trees twining together toward the twilight sky.

They are large beasts — greener and bluer in hue than the limbs and shaded greens speckling most of the orchard. Intricate designs in no particular pattern sweep their trunks and branches until the thick round leaves flutter in the stillness.

Iohmar lets Lor splash in the creek. Deer blink lazy eyes at the child disturbing their quiet as they graze blue-green grasses. Flowers and branches sprout from their backs, darker foliage to match the shades of the orchard. Large, heavy blooms drift pollen as they walk. Iohmar's crows fly overhead, patterns of noise against the sky. They do not land. Iohmar rests his forehead against the closest trunk and listens to the shiver of life within. The bark is warm against his skin. He does the same with the other. Visits here are rare, and the trees do not notice the difference, but he settles into a nest between the roots, where he feels the dull, slow threads of life—all that remain of his mother and father.

Lor has no concept of this place, and Iohmar does not wish to explain. He would rather the boy see his scars and believe his father born with them. With age, Lor will realize. The memories are here, fresh in his mind, and he believes he cannot form words to explain. Even if he could, they would never pass his lips.

He lays a hand on the nearest root. Poppies spread bright crimson against the trunks and across the grasses and roots. A petal curls around his finger.

Eventually, Lor tires of the stream and shuffles to Iohmar, crawling into his lap with a bundle of grass he's plucked. He does not ask questions, and so Iohmar rests his head against the bark and watches the boy. None of his people wander these trees. It is often silent, left to animals and memory.

Lor pulls the twisted crown from Iohmar's horns, dropping it to the soil before replacing it with the circle of grass and flowers he's created. Iohmar smiles.

"Are you still sleepy?"

"Nope," Lor says in a voice revealing he isn't paying attention.

"Did you hear other voices while you slept? Has anyone else spoken to you?" He doesn't wish to worry the child but needs a better grasp on the strangeness.

"Galen talks to me," he says, and Iohmar smiles again.

"That's good," he says, then allows the topic to drop. If something were frightening him, Lor wouldn't be so disinterested in the conversation.

"I think Rúnda is mad," Lor says, picking a mushroom and

tying bits of grass around its stem. Iohmar presses his lips together. "She seems mad."

Iohmar believed the boy asleep on his shoulder. Perhaps not. "How does she seem mad?"

"She scowls," he says. "But not in the same way you do."

Iohmar thinks of laughing and ruffles the boy's wispy head of hair, sending petals flying. "I'll speak to her."

"What are you going to talk about?"

"Many things. Not entertaining for a little boy."

Lor looks up from his delicate crowns, eyes large, expression serious. "About me?"

The question would be cute if his eyes weren't so worried, a frown forming between his brows, and Iohmar doesn't understand the sudden dip in mood. "Some. You are always on my mind, after all."

Lor continues staring—long enough without blinking that Iohmar's amusement fades to concern—but then returns to his flowers and says, "Galen is grumpy too."

Tension relaxes from Iohmar's shoulders, but he needs to watch him closer. "I'll speak to him as well."

At midnight, before finding Rúnda, Iohmar slips from the glass ceiling above his room. Lor is asleep, and Galen's chambers are close by. The world is quiet. Far in the distance, Iohmar senses the rippling borders.

He finds his way to where he and Lor crawled from the cavern.

He slips among the dark trees until the clearing spreads before him, a swath of gentle shadows in the night. Grass brushes his legs, the soil spongy beneath his feet. He senses the place the earth was torn, a long scar so deep he loses the sense of it eventually. Remembering the press of the earth and the oppressive darkness overwhelming his magic, Iohmar shudders. He looks about, casting out traces of his magic, searching.

The crack is gone.

A THOUSAND EXPLANATIONS

I ohmar stands where the crack formed, digging his toes into the soil. Grass has overgrown it, the earth below scarred but solid beneath a loose layer of peat.

Who in my lands shares my affinity for moving earth and vine and tree and sunlight and shadow? Grass could've sprouted overnight, but healing the earth? Many things about his lands and their magic confound him, but this is a new experience entirely.

Kneeling, he presses his palm to the ground, wriggling his fingers into the soil. He senses it still, the rip in the earth. It is not in his imagination. He sends roots and grasses and flower bulbs down but cannot reach far enough to find the cavern and finds no trace of anything living woven within the crack. No shadows. Healed, but barely. Gaps remain. Whatever magic this is, it is not of the same strength as his.

He stands and turns.

All around are trees and mountains: a ring of soft peaks and his mountain nearest, a sharp towering thing coated with trees and time. Clouds pass between the moon and the land and play with the stars. Iohmar breathes so deep his lungs near burst. Warmth from his people's magic washes over him, a thousand moth wings. Lor's presence is stronger. Lor's and Galen's and Rúnda's, then those in his kingsguard, who have been so near to him since childhood. He can look over them individually, hundreds of lives under his protections. And past them, thousands upon thousands of animals and lone creatures such as Túirt and fae so small they have no thoughts past moonlight and flowers and the embrace of the night air.

Far into the deepest parts of his land, where Iohmar's folk rarely wander, he brushes against the most ancient of trees, woods so grand they reach roots thousands of steps deep. Had Iohmar sought a child of his lands, as his folk believe Lor to be, he would've gone to those trees. Deep in slumber, they stir at his presence, and he withdraws. Some things are not to be disturbed until the need is great.

He stretches far enough to tease the borders of the human world and those of the ripplings. They are restful. He senses none of their cold bodies close enough to be a threat.

The sky he looks toward next, but finds only stray birds streaking the dark air, moths and other nighttime creatures, and the chill magic of the sky. Even the wind does not play tonight, and Iohmar finds nothing of use above.

Satisfied his magic is strong and eager and hiding nothing from his sight, he turns it downward, past fertile earth and into bedrock, past cool underground streams and delicate streaks of crystals. Pressing against the tunnels beneath his mountain, he still finds no trace of the woman who aided him. The grasses and trees about him dance at the overuse of magic, twining around his legs and fingers. Worms and beetles and centipedes and other crawling organisms wriggle from the earth to squirm circles about his feet. Moths are drawn from their forest flowers to land upon his skin.

Iohmar's limbs vibrate with his magic. He is strong. No trace of illness resides in him, not even the sleepy shards that lingered when he walked the orchards with Lor. *Could it have been caused by the expenditure of my magic?* No. This is too natural to him. Too right. Too wonderful.

No, it must have been the shadows or the cavern itself. Or the dragon bones.

Even still, he finds little trace those things ever existed. A scar in the earth carrying on and on and on. The faintest hint of dragon bones and nothing more.

He relaxes, magic fluttering to him with satisfaction. Again, there is a familiar taste of it to the air. He expects to open his eyes and find himself in cold, oppressive earth. But the meadow remains. He recognizes the trace, yet it is lost to him. He must certainly have encountered it before. Years and memories blend, but he has always been sharp at recalling individuals and their talents.

How can I fail to recall something familiar to me?

It must have been long ago if he cannot call to mind the source, long enough he must have been a child. No older than Lor, perhaps. The only clear sources of power he remembers from the time were those of his parents and Galen. The collective warm haze of his guard and all those dwelling within the Halls. His own magic. Ascia's. He remembers her soft and cheerful countenance. A warm, happy little spark of life who couldn't intimidate a soul.

But she is lost to him as his parents.

Perhaps the taste of magic has nothing to do with the shadows and caverns at all. Perhaps it is of no consequence.

"Who are you?" he asks the grasses, feeling foolish for speaking to nothing.

No creature he calls to mind could heal a tear in the earth such as Iohmar created. He wanders toward his mountain, eyes on his feet, paying little attention to the swaying trees and grasses. Insects swarm him, but he brushes them aside, and they drift into the night with fat, lazy bodies.

Even with all its strength, Rúnda's magic does not lend itself to manipulating the earth and living things. A dragon would have no difficulty, if the stories he was told in his youth stand true, but those bones haven't held magic since before he was conceived. If any still exist, they are so far past even Rúnda's kingdom and the rippling lands that he does not recognize them. In his heart, he believes they no longer exist.

And the shadows. Iohmar dipped his fingers into them those years before, as close as one living thing can be to another. There was magic, certainly, and hints of true life, but it was dim and quiet and slow, harmless despite the marks left upon his hand. They may have swallowed him and Lor, but such is a far cry from stitching the earth into place.

If they were trying to communicate, their message was lost to him.

"Strange," he tells himself.

"You are," says a female voice, and Iohmar nearly jumps from his skin. The sharp tip of his horn catches in the trunk of the closest tree. It's been too long since he filed them for Lor's sake.

Now that he's paying attention, he senses her in the air about him.

"What are you doing?" he asks, and Rúnda puts a hand on her hip, raising an eyebrow. Her skin matches the dark of the night, rendering her nigh invisible.

He tries to maneuver his head from the tree, but the bark catches, and a small branch weaves itself around his other horns, welcoming Iohmar's presence. He grabs the horn and pulls his head free, healing over the gash with a splinter of his magic before it bleeds sap. The branches unwind at a lazy pace.

"You startled me," he says, less irritated.

"So I see. Why the magic display?"

If she was following him, she felt it full force. He picks splinters one by one from his horn. Recognizing the nervous gesture, he wipes them all at once, folding his hands before him.

"Don't fold your hands at me, king beneath the earth," she says, locking eyes. "I know you more fully than such."

Iohmar sighs. He holds out his hand. She looks at it, unimpressed, but relents. Her fingers are slim and soft within his, and she steps close to his chest.

"I apologize," he says. "I am trying to work out a few things before I attempt to explain. And I wasn't going to explain while your queensguard was there. I was coming to speak to you."

"Hmm," she hums, eyelids low. She stands under his chin and looks up, close enough to kiss. He does so, a brush of their lips, and when she relaxes, the uncanny strangeness leaves Iohmar's skin. Even in her chill windswept tower she wears slim, delicate clothing. Here, in these warm lands, in the soft dark blues of her evening dress, he feels every bit of her when she leans against him.

Against his skin, she says, "This is not an alternative to explaining."

"I know," he says, drawing her toward the mountain. "Walk with me. I'll explain."

Seated within the glass of Iohmar's wide window, he tells her Lor's story.

She leans against one side of the sill, he the other, their legs intertwined. Lor lies in his bed of roots and down blankets woven within the wall, deep in a sleep and unhearing of their words. Iohmar is calmed by the boy's magic saturating the room, surrounding them.

Each word he drags from his throat.

He begins with the humans tromping the woods. Continues with the murderer in the hut. Rúnda's eyes close when he speaks of the poor woman buried beneath the trees. He tells her of Lor, of the boy's weak little life and soft innocence, and how he couldn't convince himself to leave the helpless thing in the human world, even more so once he realized the boy was too sick to be returned.

He describes the woman in the tunnels. How Lor's magic is bound to his. Life to life.

He explains the caverns and the ripplings watching him through the border. Rúnda shudders. He thinks of scooping her into his arms but can't bring himself to move.

Finally, he explains the illness he thought had long passed, returned for no reason he can determine.

When he finishes, her eyes are no longer on him, so he says, "I'm leaving out details, I'm sure. But that is the greatest amount of it."

"Do you believe the illness will return?"

"I didn't. Now I'm uncertain. If I could pinpoint if it was triggered by something, I would have a stronger theory."

"Will the woman know? The one in the tunnels?"

"She didn't say it would return, and I believe she meant me no harm. She asked I not return. I swore I would not disturb her. Besides, I searched for her magic afterward. It seems she no longer dwells there."

Rúnda nods, but this was another of Iohmar's mistakes, she knows. He should never have made so foolish a commitment.

"Perhaps the second time was because of the shadows."

"Perhaps," he agrees. A linking between the two seems far-fetched, but he has no better idea.

Shame twists his heart. *Was it correct to tell her? To saddle her with the burdens I have placed upon myself?* If he is threatened, it is correct she be aware, not only because he loves her, but also because she is another leader.

But he cannot bring himself to regret these threats to his magic, because Lor is here, sleeping in his bed, healthy and growing and as much a part of Iohmar as his own magic. He can *never* think ill of any decision made to protect the boy.

Even if it labels him a foolish king.

"So, he is human," Rúnda murmurs, gazing at Lor. He cannot read the thoughts in her expression.

Despite it all, his stomach twists. "Yes. I . . . don't wish Lor to know. Not until he's old enough to understand. I don't wish him thinking something terrible will happen to him or to me, particularly not after his fright in the caves. And I don't wish him to worry over all I experienced with the woman to save him."

She gazes at him oddly but shakes her head. "I don't wish him to think it's his fault."

Relief takes hold of him, guilt following for not telling her sooner. He shouldn't be nurturing such weakness in himself.

His parents would not have been so feeble.

"Thank you," he says, desperation in the sound.

Rúnda's eyes render him vulnerable. It is apparent to anyone how dearly he cherishes Lor, but she must notice how deeply the boy impacts each of his thoughts and actions. He shrinks from it. She is another leader, isolated by war, powerful and wise and nearly old as he. Ruling and love for her people are familiar to her. Still, he cannot explain his feelings. As he does not expect to comprehend and understand all which has happened to her, he knows she cannot with him.

"I hope you still love him the same," he whispers and cannot bring himself to be ashamed of the words. He wishes her to love Lor as he does, wishes it with more strength than he can speak.

She smiles a little, worry between her eyebrows. "He is still part of your heart. It is in a different way than I expected, but not important. I am from my mother's heart and magic. She brought me from the woods, and you brought Lor from the human realm. I have no need to see those two things differently."

He reaches for her. Without hesitation, she slips across the window to his side. Sharing closeness and warmth, her fingers tuck between his.

"If any of this becomes dangerous, particularly the . . . ripplings . . . I would wish for you to tell me."

"I have no desire to keep such things from you," he assures her. "Even if I didn't wish to speak of Lor, I was going to explain the ripplings. It is as much for you to know as for me."

He thinks of wrapping his arm about her, of drawing her to his bed. Likely, she would not be averse, but now is not the time. Not after the conversation and all the unsaid fears. Instead, he rests his temple against the top of her head, keeps his horns from cracking her skin, and relaxes into the intimacy. She sighs, a human noise sounding better on her than Iohmar believes it does on him. She presses her face to the thin skin at the base of his neck. Scars are there, not hidden fully by his robes, but he does not push her away.

"I think I should stay longer than planned," she says. "Until you have this figured out. At least until you're certain there is little danger."

Something unwinds in Iohmar's chest, and he closes his eyes, tightening his arm around her. "That may be some time. I am glad."

"Perhaps this was your plan all along. Perhaps you did not fall into a cavern with shadows at all."

If she's teasing, she must not be too cross. He kisses the crown of her head.

"Iohmar," she whispers.

"Hmm?"

"If the illness returns, I hope you will tell me. I will be at your side if you wish it."

He closes his eyes, his throat tight. *What would she think of watching me so vulnerable?* Speaking the words is one thing, but letting her see the reward he has reaped from his actions feels forbidden. He wishes even Galen had not been there the first time. If it should happen again, he would despise Lor seeing him in such a way. He knows his silence and chill are troublesome to Rúnda. Always, he has attempted to speak the words in his heart and fallen short.

He opens his mouth but only says, "I will no longer keep these things from you."

It is not a request for her presence. Certainly, he must be disappointing her, but he cannot bring himself to request his queen tend to him as an infant.

Still, she kisses his neck. "Thank you."

I love you, he thinks, then buries his face in her shoulder.

19

A GHOST IN THE TREES

Rúnda leaves when her oceans and deserts and wild winds call. Uneventful months have passed, as if explaining Lor's history returned their world to its kilter. Both Iohmar and Rúnda tested their magic on the surrounding lands. Trees were blown sideways and flowers uprooted under Rúnda's hand as she tried her own methods of reaching the deepest parts of the earth, but neither found traces of shadows or caverns or odd-yet-familiar magic. The deep scar remains in the earth, lost after Iohmar can trace it no farther. Silent. All is peaceful in his mountains, and Rúnda's worry abates with it.

Even Galen agrees. Iohmar eventually explained the second illness to him and was relieved the old fae was as against the idea of telling Lor as Iohmar. Still, he dealt with a great amount of fuss-ing from the old caretaker.

The rippling borders remain quiet.

Iohmar isn't fool enough to believe all is well, that nothing more shall ever come of such strange events. But he has no leads. No evidence. No trails. No uncanny magic to follow or shadows to attempt conversation. After he expends his magic to near exhaustion and no illness returns, he is at a loss but relieved. Rúnda will not see him ill. Perhaps it is not so broken as he feared.

As he wanders the clearing alone, he wonders if Rúnda's presence frightened the shadows and if they only appear to Iohmar and Lor when the two are alone. But he's wandered the twilight woods with the boy on his shoulder countless times without their appearance.

He stands in the clearing's center, barefoot, and toes at the earth. He casts his magic about with less emphasis than before, but it's still strong. His forests rustle in response, content. Sitting in the tall grass, he enjoys the warm, sweet air of the twilight morning.

"Iohmar?" A whisper lays fingers of chill across his spine.

Standing, he turns and is met with an empty forest. Trees sway. Birds swarm. His crows fly for the far mountains. A badger waddles in a brush of fur, visiting from the human world, casting him an uninterested glance.

Iohmar crosses the open grassland and enters the woods, wandering farther from his mountain. The rippling lands are not far off. Those creatures do not speak —*cannot* speak —and so this must be different.

Lor said the voice in the caverns spoke Iohmar's name.

The trees are cool here, so cocooned within themselves. Butterflies brush his cheeks and land in his hair, their fat bodies full of nectar. When he brushes them away, they explode in a flurry of blue-and-green wings, shimmering as stardust. They are not unusual for these parts of the woods. Glancing out the canopy, he catches the plum hue of the sky.

"Who are you?" he asks and is greeted with silence.

Taking a long, deep breath, he says, "I wish to speak with you, please. You are of my kind, and you dwell in my lands. There is nothing you need fear of me. I would love nothing more than to speak with you. Even if you cannot reveal yourself, we may still speak to each other."

Still, silence.

"My shadows?" he asks in vain. Frustration wells in Iohmar's chest. He wishes to shout and scolds himself for the human desire. None of these little things should overwhelm him, but he finds them unbearable. He is facing a problem he can neither see nor touch nor hear, at least not often enough to put the pieces together. He hates teetering on the edge of politeness and begging.

With purpose, he folds his fingers within his sleeves, appearing the part. "You need not fear me."

Somehow, he doubts this is the issue. But he has no helpful approach other than to be soft and gentle. He is loath to jump to conclusions toward creatures he does not know and has hardly met.

"You frightened me in the caverns. My child was afraid, and I was angry, but I am listening now . . ." he offers, and a shadow flutters between the trees.

This time, there is shape to the twisting, wavering creature, enough so it appears as a child no larger than Lor standing between the trees.

"Where is Iohmar?" it asks in a voice so small and bright and real it knocks him back.

"Me," he whispers, heart leaping, grasping at the thread of communication. "It's I. I'm Iohmar." He steps toward the shadow, offering the hand stained by them long ago.

It flees.

Iohmar runs, chasing it so deep into the woods that he loses sight of his mountains and sky. He's traveled close to the heart before. None of his folk dwell here. It is inhabited by small magic-drunk creatures drifting among the thick trunks and under cool leaves. By wolves. By magic-heavy trees from which all of Látwill draws its power. He knows never to sleep here, for even he, king beneath the earth, would fall for centuries upon centuries under the spell of the deep woods.

He loses the shadow in a mere moment, no sound or sense or trail to follow. He halts in the bruised air, turning a sharp circle but finding no one.

Never has the voice spoken a question. Only his name. *Was it a child's voice Lor heard?* Iohmar isn't certain the boy is old enough to discern the difference.

Thinking of the oppressive, dark cold of the cavern, he shudders.

The shadows have never taken shape.

Rubbing his eyes, he wanders further, listening for noises unusual among the whisper of trees and breath of insects. Hoping something will lead him back to the shadow child.

"I'm following you," he calls, for lack of anything more helpful. "If you tell me what you wish, I'll be able to assist."

Rúnda and Galen do not believe these creatures harmless. Iohmar understands, considering his disappearance into the caverns and the following sickness. But he fell ill for the first time before the shadows ever presented themselves. He has a difficult time believing their nature so malicious, even after they dragged him and Lor into the earth.

How would my parents react? Would they think me too soft? He presses the backs of his talons against his eyelids. Årelang and Crofa were kind creatures but much quicker to their tempers than Iohmar. *Even they would've known there is nothing to be gained by anger and quick judgment.*

"I wish I could speak with you," he whispers to the heavy air so softly no creature is likely to hear, his eyes still closed.

Something brushes his hand.

Iohmar starts, stumbling. Nothing but empty woods. But he *felt* it. Something tangible against the thin skin of his wrist, different from the little heartbeat of the shadows — solid and much more real. His skin remains pale and translucent. Nothing was threatening in the touch, which was soft and light as the butterflies where the woods are still filtered with sunlight. He holds his hands before him — like Lor learning to walk — and drifts them back and forth. Nothing comes into contact with his skin save for the insects fluttering about, pleased by the presence of their king.

Huffing, he wanders deeper. He is nearing the heart of the woods. The air is sweet, fruit and earth and flowers mixing into the softest breeze. There is a hint of rot not belonging. For a moment,

Iohmar believes the fruit is beginning to turn as it drops to the soil. But the scent is incorrect. Iohmar is familiar with the overripe air drifting from the woods to the mountains as the seasons turn. It is not unpleasant. This is different.

He lopes under the low branches, searching for the source. Some of his crows have circled back from the meadow, landing on branches, squawking, crying for his attention. Like many of his folk, they are not at ease in the heart of the woods and would not venture here if not for Iohmar. He strokes the feathers of the nearest ones as he slows to a walk. They hop about his feet. They have no gossip, just desires for treats.

"Do you see shadows?" he asks, and they cock their heads at him, beaks shimmering in the low light. The nearest ones peck his fingers with affection.

Iohmar pulls up the edges of his robe as he hops a creek. The water is slow and sweet and blue as sapphires. It would put him to sleep with a sip. Sand sticks to his toes, rubbing off in the long spongy grasses.

The heart of the woods wraps around him.

Here, the trees are blue with heavy, damp flowers. Trunks press together, so thick he has little room to maneuver.

Iohmar . . . they whisper, some awakening.

Come sleep, sweet lord . . .

Branches tug at him until he breaks free, shaking off the spell. These woods offer many magics and wishes and curses. Should he choose to stay, picking a tree to let wrap around him, he could very well be gifted a child. This is where his folk believe Lor originated. He looks about the sweet, oppressive air and thinks his little wisp of sunlight could never have been born from such a place. But this is where Rúnda was created, her mother making the trip for want of a child of her own. Iohmar was too young to remember the neighboring queen passing the mountains, though his parents told him stories.

She disappeared into the heart of the trees alone, her queensguard left behind, and returned days later with Rúnda in her arms, born of the queen's magic and force of will and the strength of the trees. He wonders what of her magic she gave up to attain the piece of her heart that is her daughter.

Iohmar lays his hand on the closest trunk, damp with nectar overflowing the flowers.

This is where Ascia came from. Deep in the heart of the woods. Alone. Perhaps someone entered to gain a child but was too weak for the trees. Fae have been consumed in such places. Iohmar was too young then to understand; he merely loved Ascia for being the sibling he'd longed for. A little sister to protect.

Tried to protect.

Iohmar circles a tree and is met with the eyes of a wolf.

Its face hovers inches from his, unrelenting in its presence, and Iohmar locks his body into stillness, pinpricks of unease along his skin. Heavy paws stand on the low twisting branch of the tree, elevating its face to his level. Others circle nearby. This one's hot breath curdles in the air. Two eyes, plum purple and blue as the trees, latch on to his, a low growl in its throat.

"Shh . . ." he whispers, gathering enough magic to set his entire mountain to sleep, washing it over the creature.

It gives a shudder, relaxing its body enough that Iohmar is safe to step around.

The footfalls of the pack follow.

The rotting scent grows, thick and cloying and swirling about him as a living thing. He remembers the woman buried in the place where his woods met the human world. Remembers Lor's human mother. Melancholy envelopes him, and he cups the nearest flower in the palm of his hand. Nectar drips between his fingers. The insects have thinned to almost nothing. Strange they do not land to drink from the flower.

Iohmar lets it drop to the forest floor, and particles come free in his hand. He opens his palm, staring at the bits drifting away. For a moment, he is certain they are the shadowy, papery particles that drift from his skin when he falls ill.

But no, these are not light and airy, disappearing into nothing. They crumble in his fingers with ashy weight. He shakes the branches of another tree, and more swirl to the grasses. Wolves circle, eyes on the ash, growls low in their throats. The small blue-green leaves are in the same condition. One dissolves in his gentle fist. Several branches are withered and lifeless. Carefully, Iohmar brings the handful to his face and breathes in its smell.

Rot. A familiar magic.

Or a familiar *lack* of magic.

Iohmar stares long and hard before he remembers the appearance of the rot, the withering of the trees.

The sight of the world when the rippling creatures slipped from their borders.

HEART OF THE WOODS

In the deepest forest, where the heart of the woods is thickest, the trees ancient and sleeping and powerful, Iohmar finds ripplings.

It is so small a thing, small enough he did not sense it and the trees did not wake and cry out to him: a finger of their border, crawling among the trees, eating at the mosses and grasses and lichens, not disturbing the great trunks but withering the smallest leaves and causing the fruit to rot in upset.

Putting his hand to the nearest tree, he leans his forehead against the damp bark, much as he did with his parents' trees in the great orchard. It sleeps, even under a gentle wash of his magic, slow and sad and always thinking. A nearby branch twines around him but does not drag him close, instead pushing him toward the border, the abomination cutting the air. No sickness has reached the trees' hearts, and Iohmar almost weeps with relief he found the ripplings before greater damage could be done.

Did the shadows find the rot? Was the shadow child leading me to warn me? It still has not reappeared.

Creeping closer, Iohmar raises his hand to the barrier, unable to bring himself to touch it. There is scant light here, not enough to catch along the mirrors and voids of their bodies. He senses them now, little creatures too small to be of terrible harm to him should he come into contact with their draining bodies. They're not much like the great rippling beasts he faced protecting his mountains and nothing resembling the ones that stole away his father and mother.

But they are many. And they will grow. If he does not push them back, they will feed on the heart of the woods until the trees and flowers and grasses and all manner of creatures are consumed. And Iohmar's lands will die and become theirs.

They will swallow him up. Him and Galen and Rúnda. Lor. Iohmar shudders.

Memories from his sickness are upon him still, ever present. He did not tell Rúnda of them, or Galen. But he thinks of his mother's voice often, the way his father held himself when he walked, the sensation of their magic in the mountains and trees.

His scars weigh upon his skin. Now, they press against the insides of his robes, aching at the closeness of the monsters. He doesn't know if it's a real sensation or imagined. But he *hurts*. One of those creatures could slip from their border as they did by Rúnda's sea. They could approach Lor.

He imagines his son seeing them. One swallowing up his little fingers, the soft skin and the smile he turns upon Iohmar each day. Iohmar digs his talons into the border and rips.

He has not trimmed them these last few weeks, distracted by Rúnda and Lor and magic and feasting, and they always grow quickly when his magic is in sharp display.

A hollow shattering pierces the bruised air, so high-pitched and deep it doesn't reach him until his ears ache in protest. Not a physical, living thing in and of itself, the border does not break. It is an extension of the ripplings' inverse magic, fortified by Iohmar's to keep them out if possible and dissuade them if not.

His claws leave streaks convulsing and shimmering, casting off light from somewhere Iohmar cannot see. The barrier withdraws a few paces within itself, away from the heart of the woods. A scar is left upon the forest floor from where they consumed the growth. The soles of his feet tingle and ache when he steps onto the rotted ground.

"How you dare come here," he whispers, though neither he nor his parents discovered if they can speak or understand. He steps forward, palms raised, prepared to pull roots from the earth and trees from far away to drag the border back. Magic tingles along his skin, begging to be released.

One rises before him, face-to-face. Iohmar is so close the creature must feel his breath. It's a shapeless, lifeless form, rippling in and in and in on itself, the sound of its body as breaking glass. All air leaves Iohmar's lungs. He has not been this close to one. Never this close. Not since . . .

Not since he gathered his mother's flowers from the rotted fields of Rúnda's kingdom.

"Why will you not *leave me alone?*" he whispers. Silly, childish, and worthless, speaking such things to a mindless monster.

It twitches. Had it a form or recognizable body, Iohmar would've sworn it cocked its head at him. He tilts his own in return. Small as they are since last he forced them back —matching his height instead of towering as trees— Iohmar is less panicked by its size and power than by the terror accompanying it. He lowers his hand.

The creature watches him, but Iohmar knows better than to reach out. Long ago, he watched his father do as such, watched his finger shrivel to a lifeless husk. Iohmar remembers what was done to his folk centuries later.

"Why?" he whispers and again is met with a strange twitch.

Others swarm, rippling across their lifeless ground, nonthreatening as they can be but causing his skin to crawl. This one is still —as near to still as ever he's seen. Never has he known one to be so quiet and unmoving.

Softly, he lets his magic wash over the borders. He does not press past, does not wish to threaten and provoke an attack, but touches gently at the place his land meets theirs.

The creature slams into the border.

Knocked to the rotting ground, Iohmar calls for his trees, waking the slumbering giants about him. The nearest is pulled awake, perhaps for the first time in centuries, and crashes its giant trunk against the border, uninterested in capturing their king, only in coming to his aid. Branches are swallowed within the shimmering air, but trees wake under his call, beating themselves against the shattering border until it slithers back.

Rising, Iohmar rouses all manner of trees and vines and roots, past the heart of the woods and from his twilight forests, wrapping around and dragging back the convulsing border until it is far from his lands, back in their own, and the long streak of rot they left is a lifeless, wicked scar cutting the forest.

My forest.

The creatures are still watching, hovering within their border as it's pushed back and pushed back.

"Leave me alone," he tells them, not caring how they do not comprehend. He is too angry. *How am I so angry?* When they fail to back away, he screams, *"Leave me alone!"*

Trees toss themselves against the border, ground trembling, and the ripplings flee so deep within their own lands that he no longer senses their magic or even a shred of their existence.

Iohmar curls against the mossy trunk of a fallen tree and weeps.

Returning to his mountain, Iohmar slips into his chambers by the glass roof and finds the edge of Lor's crib. It is midnight now, the entire day and evening lost to the heart of the woods.

Galen is asleep in the willow chair, chin on his chest. All the lands must have felt the impact of Iohmar's magic, the way in which he dragged the rippling barrier away from their trees. His caretaker will have waited up for him.

Iohmar is grateful he fell into slumber. He cannot face him.

Drawing a hand across Lor's soft hair, he presses his nose to the boy's cheek, satisfied he is peaceful and sleeping and not a shred of rippling has or will ever touch him.

Under his touch, Lor rolls under his blankets and puts his tiny hands to Iohmar's cheeks.

"Daidí?" he mumbles, voice full of sleep.

"I'm here, Wisp. All is well. Go back to sleep."

"Mmm." After nuzzling their noses, Lor rolls back onto his stomach and burrows into the covers. Iohmar smooths his hair until his breaths are even with slumber. Strings of magic bonding them warm and soothe his frayed nerves.

Iohmar slips back out the glass ceiling, finding his way to the top of his mountain.

There is a great outcropping of stone stretching into the sky. Often, when he was a child, he sat with Ascia in the heat of noon, creating little sunlight creatures to chase them about.

He perches on the edge. The moon and her stars gaze down upon him. Perhaps the shadows do not follow him everywhere, do not hear each word he speaks, but they have been following him this day.

"Thank you," he whispers, and the wind breathes the words back as it carries them all down across his mountains.

WINTER

21

A HUMAN VISITOR

Twelve of Iohmar's crows fly to him one early winter.

A nip to the warm air signals the difference in seasons. Rúnda will arrive soon. There is no change to his woods, no encroaching border.

But a storm is gathering, one of the rare monster downpours Látwill experiences every few centuries. Iohmar accepts some of the shyer fae into the mountain. Woods and underground places ill protect his folk in such tempests—they are always welcome in the Halls, but most only come when they'll be otherwise soaked.

Iohmar makes a point to wander and greet remaining stragglers. His throne room is utilized little, a smaller room within the mountain adjacent to the feasting halls. A chair of pale woven roots and emerald moss awaits him, but Iohmar remembers sitting against his father's leg when Årelang was king beneath the earth. It lies incorrect in his chest to take the seat as his own.

Three creatures barely reaching his knee scurry in the opening to the wide doors at the base of the mountain. Putting on his best smile for small, timid fae, Iohmar bends and gives each a touch on their bark-encrusted heads.

"Welcome back," he says and accepts the handful of acorns each presents. "I will plant them in the gardens."

Their shimmery round eyes flicker around his shoulders, and a giggle begins behind the throne. A smile and pair of eyes emerge.

Iohmar restrains a laugh. "Lor, stop your sneaking and come down here."

The boy bounds down the moss-carpeted roots and hides against the back of Iohmar's shoulder. The goblins blink and shuffle at the child they've never seen but have likely heard of.

Grinning, Lor hugs each one of them, sending them scattering happily off to find some damp, root-bound place in the mountains to wait out the storm. Iohmar lets the laugh bubble up from his chest.

"The crows are in your room," Lor says, tiny hands clasped behind his back, mimicking Galen's posture. "They're making a mess, and they don't listen to me."

"Let's see what gossip they have, shall we? Ah, look who made it . . ."

Túirt appears around the edge of the great door. The hallway and throne room are mostly empty; everyone is hiding away or organizing their distractions for the storm. Food and various supplies have already been amassed, but final stock is being taken. Twitchy and uncomfortable in the open underground space among other fae, Túirt folds himself through the door, hurrying to Iohmar. A basket of woven grasses is clasped to his chest, brimming with plums, though he has already left hundreds at the base of the mountain over the past weeks.

"Thank you for arriving, Túirt. I was beginning to worry," Iohmar says, letting the basket of fruit be thrust upon him.

"Hello, Túirt!" Lor grins up at him.

Túirt blushes at all the attention, mumbling hello and ducking away into the nearest hallway to find some place he wishes to hide. Lor waves at his retreating form.

Tucking the acorns into his pocket and grasping the basket under an arm, Iohmar follows Lor from the throne room and up the solitary walkways to his chambers. Crows are indeed making a mess of his room, scattering leaves from his ceiling and papers from his writing desk. They cackle their laughing caws when he shoos them, taking a seat at his desk.

Lor is now tall enough to stand beside Iohmar and peek over the edge at his correspondence. He learned to write in a matter of hours once Iohmar sat him down to learn and likes to copy Iohmar's letters to better practice "sounding wise." Iohmar smiles.

The boy boosts himself onto the moss-covered edge of the desk, biting the end of one of Iohmar's quills between his front teeth. There are many strange human quirks he's maintained, but all in the mountain adore him, and no one is suspicious their king brought a human boy into the lands beneath the earth.

Soon, Iohmar will need to tell the boy his origins. But not yet.

The birds hop across his bed and along the floor, cawing and pecking his fingers. One lands atop Lor's pale head of hair, and he giggles.

"Daidí, when are you going to teach me to understand them?" In the private of Iohmar's chambers, Lor still calls his father by the affectionate title, not the formal, respectful one Iohmar was calling his own father at his age. His heart grows warm each time the word touches his ears.

Lor's little eyebrows are pulled into a furrow. No matter how often he is reassured, Lor is troubled by the differences in his magic. Iohmar has told him countless times that not all born to Látwill know its languages.

"It'll come in time. I was older than you when first I learned. One day you'll be able to understand their intentions. I'll give you a little guidance, but most of it will come naturally."

Not all his folk understand Iohmar's crows. It is possible Lor will never understand, or it will take a great deal of teaching. But he was created of Iohmar's own magic — he may not have the same specific talents, but the roots are the same. Even if he struggles in small things, Iohmar is not concerned for the boy's ability to protect and rule when Iohmar grows too frail in the coming millennia.

Lor wrinkles his nose and plucks the crow from his head, cradling the large bird in his lap. He may be growing taller, but he hardly reaches the king's knee.

Iohmar no longer picks him up in public, though he does often in private, and the boy still takes his hand when they walk the gardens. Iohmar will never tell him it is inappropriate of a growing prince. Formalities are for others. His father would disapprove. His mother would as well, but she would have tolerated it better.

Lor knows his grandparents' names now and the significance of the orchard, but little do they speak of it since Iohmar explained.

"When is Rúnda arriving?" he asks as Iohmar listens to the whisper of his crows.

"Soon," he says, distracted by their gossip. "In the next few days, I assume, if they can hurry past the rain."

"I want to go visit her next. You still wouldn't let me climb the tower last time."

"And I shan't this time either."

"*Daidí,*" Lor whines under his breath, but Iohmar isn't paying attention.

He listens until his crows have finished their gossip, then drops breadcrumbs and seeds across his desk as they bounce and peck greedily. Lor's expression is still drooping.

"Lor, do you wish to write to Laoise this time?"

In the seasons when Rúnda visits him, Iohmar has taken up the habit of writing short letters to her mother. Though Laoise rarely speaks to him in person and never sends a response, Rúnda assures him she reads all his letters to her mother, and they make her smile.

The last time they visited the windy tower, Iohmar introduced her to Lor. She stopped admiring her daughter's garden long enough to pick the boy up and claim him for much of the visit. Iohmar remembers the smile upon Rúnda's lips and the way it lit her eyes.

Lor grins, troubles forgotten. "Really?"

"Yes. Draft the letter, and we'll go over it later."

Lor presses his lips together, a withheld smile. "I know you're off to do some sneaky kingly thing, but I don't care. I'll write the letter."

Iohmar performs his best insulted expression. "I'm not sneaking."

"I'm not *that* young, you know."

He is, but Iohmar doesn't say so. He remembers Lor's age in a vague, dreamy sort of way, when the world was sunlight and playful winds and Ascia pretending adventurer by his side. He doesn't wish to injure the boy's infant pride. Standing, he hands him a sheet of parchment and a pen and kisses the crown of his head.

"Sneaking," Lor whisper-sings as Iohmar slides on a soft blue robe and slips from his chambers. He restrains himself from rolling his eyes, a quirk Lor picked up from somewhere and that has been rubbing off on his father. Galen finds the action utterly baffling and bordering on the edge of enraging. Iohmar finds it worth his time to watch the old fae flustered by such a harmless and human action.

Iohmar leaves his Halls not by the wide front gate surrounded by trees and scooping vines but by the tunnels he often takes to the human world. He would have crawled out the bright opening into the mountain, but Lor may have followed, and Iohmar wishes to keep the path to the human lands a secret until he is older and has gained enough discretion.

He takes the same path where he found the men upon the borders of his woods, winding and ancient and overgrown. Spare raindrops pelt him, and wind twines his hair, but the storm has not yet arrived. He need not travel far. The human awaiting him is not upon the path nor in the human village but sheltered in a cluster of old pines and twisted oaks, needles carpeting the ground, dry moss stretching upon lower branches of trees.

Iohmar watches for a time, hidden in the shadows he calls about himself. She is unremarkable, a bland human with a matching expression and features. Her dress is simple peasant's clothing, a coat and pants and a worn skirt over the top. Her feet are propped near a lazy fire, and she gazes about with unease.

She reminds Iohmar of someone, though he can't put his finger on who. He has not visited the human world in a great time.

When he slips from the shadows, the woman starts. Her eyes roll across him, settling upon his horns and face and eyes. Were he to step closer, he's certain his size and appearance would startle her back.

Still, as politely as he can, he asks, "Why are you in my woods, little human?"

She is not young by means of her own species, though to Iohmar she is an infant. Fine wrinkles around her eyes are not a great indication of age.

For a long while, she stares, and he allows her to consider her words. She carries no belongings save for a sack with the smell of food. She must have come with purpose, knowing her footsteps traveled along the borders between her world and the fae's. She is brave, so Iohmar allows her time to gather her thoughts.

"You are the great king beneath the earth," she says, voice uncertain but not afraid. She folds her hands in her lap, making an effort to meet his eyes without fear.

Iohmar smiles, the faintest curl of his lips. Copying her posture, he folds his hands before him. "Yes."

"My father told me of you," she says, eyes intense.

Was it the man upon the path those decades ago? He was brave enough to speak to him, with a grandmother who was suspicious and a daughter who gave him a toy. Iohmar cocks his head at her.

"And who was your father?"

"He never gave you his name," she says. "But you visited his home once, decades ago. And before, when a group of men in our village went to find a man who murdered his wife. My father said you stopped him along the way."

Iohmar stares. Though she is quite young to him, she must be a good halfway into her life. He believes he knows the answer but asks, "And how fares your father?"

The furrow of her eyebrows is sympathetic. "My father passed away over a year ago now."

She does not lower her eyes, but there is sadness in them, less strength. Melancholy lodges in Iohmar's chest. The human was a mild curiosity, someone he visited once. Never did he learn the man's name. He was a wise man for such a discretion, but Iohmar doesn't allow himself to smile at the memory. The woman would misread.

But Iohmar remembers his father and mother, their lives no more than the souls of soft trees. This is as much understanding as he can share with a human: The sympathy he grew for them after war came to his own lands. Grief and strength and loss.

So he bows his head and shoulders to her. "I am sorry for not realizing. Time passes quite differently in my world than it does in yours."

The woman nods. Iohmar suspects she expected nothing different. Softly, she says, "I remember you."

"You gave me a doll."

She smiles. Iohmar steps farther from the shadows, crouching and plucking a pine needle from the forest floor. Fiddling puts humans at ease, and he is smaller now, nearer to her level. He can stand still for so long, and it unnerves them. Her posture relaxes.

"I am grateful you have told me," Iohmar says. "I suspect there is more reason you've come to the edge of the woods."

She shifts. "When my father was old, he wished I would tell you something once he was gone. You had a conversation the last time he saw you. He said there was something that seemed to frighten you, and he wanted me to tell you that after time passed . . . the thing he was telling you about never returned. He never saw it again after last he spoke to you."

A short quiet follows, and she continues, "I don't know what he was speaking of, but it was important to him, and he believed you would not cause me harm."

"I will not cause you harm," Iohmar whispers. He looks at the pine needles crumbling between his fingers. Shadows. The human man saw shadows among his trees. After his visit, they were never seen by him again.

They followed me out?

A tremble rumbles the forest floor. Startled, the woman puts her hands to the carpet of pine needles, but she doesn't appear alarmed. Iohmar knows the earth shakes here as it does in Látwill, but it must have been much stronger in his mountains to be felt here. Testing his magic against Lor's bond reveals no weakness. The storm is growing.

A nick of rot marks the inside of Iohmar's finger.

It could be mistaken for a splinter, but the papery way it flakes under his touch is unmistakable.

What triggered it? Iohmar has extended no great deal of magic.

He has not so much as *seen* the shadows despite discussing them with this woman. It is not this journey to the human world, for he didn't leave Látwill in the past.

His chest twists until words are a struggle.

"Thank you. I'm grateful you've come to speak to me. You may ask a blessing if you wish." Iohmar hasn't bestowed such a thing upon a human in years but wishes to do so for this gentle woman brave enough to speak to a fae king in his woods.

She blinks. "I do not wish for anything . . ."

Iohmar smiles at the response. "When you do, the crows who hop about your forest will carry it to me. If it is within my power, I will gladly grant it."

"Jonathan," she says, and Iohmar blinks. "My father's name was Jonathan. He wanted you to know."

"I see," Iohmar says, but he doesn't. Not quite. He isn't certain why the human trusted him enough to wish Iohmar to know his name.

"And mine is Martha," she says, fear flickering across her face. What an impression he must've had upon her as a girl, for her to come and bring him her doll. He could ensnare her now with ease, trap her in twilight lands where time does not exist and her human life would rot around her.

"And mine is Iohmar," he says, rising. "You are welcome in these woods if you are ever in need of them."

Once more, he bows, and backs into the sunbeams still splitting the air before the storm.

22

A GROWING STORM

R ain pelts the mountainside when Iohmar retreats to the quiet
warmth of his Halls. He rubs his finger against the tiny
growing wound, hands hidden within the fabric of his sleeves.
His kingsguard pass, but most fae have taken shelter, and they
are following suit. Those still wandering offer him smiles or touch
his robes as he passes.

Strange the shadows followed me from the human world, never to return.
All Iohmar's folk are drawn to his magic in small ways, as Rúnda's
are drawn to hers, but these quiet creatures are oddly attached,
only ever appearing to him and Lor.

Stranger still, the illness has returned.

Iohmar sighs, following the signature of his son's magic to the
opposite side of the mountain, toward the gardens and orchards

beyond. Hours have passed since he left, and Lor will have finished his letter and grown restless. Playing in a downpour isn't an opportunity he'll pass up. This is the first heavy storm of his lifetime. Galen is watching from within the smaller gate leading to the gardens, taking shelter from the sporadic rain under a twist of wisteria vines.

"Your child is becoming drenched," he says as Iohmar joins him.

A rustling of the long grass is all Iohmar sees of Lor until the boy's tuft of pale hair bounces into view, plastered every which way. He waves at them before disappearing.

The mountains tremble, a small thing unlikely to be felt in the human world.

"You did this when you were a child." Galen's expression is soft, eyes gentle, a small smile brightening his face.

Iohmar hates to tell him. He worries so often, and his mood is happy and unburdened at the moment. Days after Iohmar found the ripplings in the heart of the woods, he explained the incident in detail to Galen, including the presence of the shadow child leading him. He wrote Rúnda with the story and was glad for the distance. It was enough to see the grief and fear in Galen's eyes. He was jumpy for many months, even more so than Iohmar. Several times, he caught the old fae gazing toward the deep twilight haze of the woods as if expecting the rippling border to shoot up. It twisted Iohmar's heart.

Finally, Iohmar crept beside him as he gazed out the great window. "They are not spreading. I've returned often. If anything, I believe they've retreated farther."

Galen started, embarrassed to be caught worrying. He smoothed his simple robes. After touching Iohmar's shoulder, he smiled and drifted away. "I know. You have always been diligent and sharp. Since you were a little thing. I am not worried."

He must have been worried, as Iohmar was. He wished to console him, but Iohmar knew no other way to comfort other than to offer the reassurance he had.

The illness will compound his nervous worrying.

Iohmar sighs. Telling Galen is the least of his concerns. Though still small, Lor will notice his father falling ill and will not be dissuaded if put to sleep.

If Iohmar is brave, he will send his crows through the storm to Rúnda.

"Is all well? You seem quieter than usual," Galen says.

"I wasn't aware such a thing was possible."

In his light mood, Galen presses his lips into a withheld smile, stepping closer to pluck leaves off Iohmar's shoulder. He combs his hand through his hair the way Iohmar often does with his son.

"Galen . . ."

"My apologies." Galen straightens his own robes, still unbothered. "How was the human realm?"

"There was a woman waiting. She wanted my attention, sitting on the border of the mountains. I met her father the day I brought Lor home and visited him once after. He saw the shadows in his own woods years ago and told me of it. When he died, he wished his daughter to tell me he never saw the creatures again."

Galen blinks. "That is . . . quite unusual."

"She had innocent intentions. She loved her father; I felt it in her words. I offered her a blessing, but she didn't accept."

"*Very* unusual."

"I took her off guard. I told her she could wish for one later and tell the crows."

"Hmm." Softly, he says, "You *do* seem quieter, Iohmar."

With a sigh, Iohmar offers his hand, keeping his eyes on the rain. Galen's thin, soft hands turn his over. When he finds the mark, Iohmar feels him still. Galen rubs the pad of his finger over the cut with the utmost gentleness. A wash of the healer's magic brushes his own, a warm sensation within his fingers.

"Is there pain?" he asks, concern unhidden.

"No, I wouldn't have noticed had I not seen."

From the corner of his eye, he watches Galen's eyebrows furrow. "You cannot see a connection between this and the previous instances?"

"I've gone over it countless times. I believed it was my strong use of magic, both when I saved Lor and when I broke the earth out of the cavern . . . There is nothing I have expended it upon. The same amount of time may have passed as did between the first two illnesses . . . I've never thought to count the days, so I'm unsure. It is the single correlation I can discern."

It's a frightening implication. *What if the illness continues returning?* Iohmar cannot stomach the concept of being so weakened, if only for a few days—not with the ripplings and shadows and his people to watch over.

What if Rúnda must see me this way?

What if Lor must watch his father fall ill the rest of his life because I broke my magic to save him?

He cannot let this continue. He must *solve this*.

Galen is silent. His disapproval is more distressing than Iohmar appreciates. Perhaps he shouldn't be concerned with the judgment of his childhood caretaker. He was bred a king but knows he has always been far too worrying, too shy, and too frightened. Silence presses on him, helpless exhaustion weighing his limbs. If he were many, many centuries younger, he would lean against Galen for comfort.

If he were many, many centuries younger, his parents would be here for counsel.

They would've counseled him never to risk his magic for a human.

"Shall we call Lor?" Galen asks.

Yes, Iohmar thinks, unable to force the word past his lips. Perhaps the boy needs it explained, the magic and the shadows and the woman in the tunnels. Iohmar planned not to tell him until he was old enough to understand the situation with maturity and consider Iohmar's decisions logically. But perhaps he will never be old enough. Galen did not approve, after all. No number of years would've changed it.

Iohmar took a forbidden human and damaged his magic to save him. No way around the explanation exists. And now the illness is forcing his hand. The thought is bitter. Iohmar doesn't wish to bow to it, feeling unequal to the task.

Slowly, he shakes his head. "Take him to your rooms with you, please. When this has passed, I will think on the correct time and way to explain."

Galen frowns. Iohmar keeps his eyes steady, the expression

of a king.

"Iohmar—"

"He is so little, Galen. Telling him is not the same as telling Rúnda. Even if he isn't frightened by the explanation, he may believe it his fault. One way or another, it will be painful. Do *you* have words to explain in a way which will not wound him?"

Galen swallows, glancing at the shape of the boy bouncing among the dripping trees, too far to hear their words. "No. But it will hurt to keep him from you for days without answering his questions as well. He is part of this, Iohmar. It is because of him you split your magic—"

"You cannot *blame him.*" Iohmar snatches his hand from Galen's. The old fae flinches, and guilt clenches Iohmar's chest. It isn't fair to snap such words. Around him, the vines and roots woven into the walls twitch and curl with the outburst.

"Of course I don't blame him," Galen says, but Iohmar hears uncertainty in his words. "He was just a babe. You know I care for him as I do for you. But it doesn't erase how this began with him. It began when you brought him here, when you decided to break your magic to save him. He should understand . . ."

Galen trails off at Iohmar's sharp expression. *How can I bear Lor believing my suffering is his fault? How can Galen not understand?*

"I don't believe it his fault," Galen repeats, and Iohmar believes him, incapable as they are of lying. "Iohmar, I believe you are making a mistake."

"I know," he says, then amends. "I'll take your words into consideration."

Galen watches the rain. Determination etches into his eyes,

and Iohmar braces himself for the oncoming battle.

"I realize you believe you know best—"

"He is my son. I will protect him."

"And I have been here each day of your life. I would not insist if I didn't believe this would help you both."

Iohmar grinds his jaw. He doesn't wish to be harsh.

Sighing, Galen touches Iohmar's sleeve. "Iohmar, I will explain to the boy if you cannot bring yourself to—"

"You will do no such thing." Iohmar yanks from him, stepping against the opposite wall. Hurt burns his eyes. "I've trusted you with these matters. You do *not* go behind my back because you do not agree with me—"

"I am trying to help. I know you, and—"

"You will not assume to know or speak for me. You are my *servant*."

Galen shrinks. Guilt turns Iohmar's stomach, but he turns his face until the silence threatens to tear a gap in the air. Tears burn his eyes. He hates them. He should not be so easily undone.

Bowing, Galen whispers, "My king."

Iohmar hears rather than watches him leave. Pressing his fingers to his eyes, he attempts to erase the pain from his features. Lor cannot see him in such a way. Shame will not leave him. *Galen was attempting to help, but how else should I respond when he threatens to overrule me?* He was not harsh as he could have been. His parents would've been harsher.

His throat burns.

"Daidí! Look!"

Iohmar smooths his expression in time for Lor to barrel toward him, knocking aside the glistening grasses. He stops short of bumping into Iohmar's legs, instead presenting him with the fawn in his arms.

"What have you found this time?" Iohmar takes the small creature, whispering soothing words when it squirms. It may take all Lor's strength to carry, but it fits neatly within Iohmar's hands. Its rain-soaked brown coat is soft and speckled with white, two large ears flapping. Branches sprout from its back, flowers from the long curve of its neck.

"It broke its leg," Lor says with great seriousness. "You can fix it, right?"

"Of course, but I think you should ask Galen or one of the healers." He places the fawn back into his son's arms. "Now, you know it is yours to care for until it heals."

"I know!" Lor curls his arms around the baby and marches off, several strides to match every one of Iohmar's. "Where's Galen?"

Iohmar forces his expression not to twitch. "I'm not sure. Wandering somewhere. We'll take it to a healer."

"Where did you go?"

"To speak with a human who was entering the edge of our woods."

Lor glances up. He hasn't entered the human world since he was a babe and Iohmar took him to the home of the man and his daughter. It is quite likely he does not remember the situation, but he's heard stories. The boy might understand how different his father feels toward humans than the rest of their kin.

He is still young enough to simply ask, "Why?"

Iohmar anticipated the question but is still unsure how to

answer. "I met one when you were still a babe. His daughter wished to tell me he passed from their world."

"Oh," Lor says, sadness in his voice. "Is it true human lives are very short?"

"Yes." He puts his hand — not the one succumbing to illness — on Lor's head as they walk, fingers combing his hair. "A human can be born, age, and die before you are even grown from infancy. It is their way, as it is ours to live for millennia upon millennia."

"It's sad."

"Indeed it is."

Lor shifts the fawn into one arm so he can take Iohmar's hand with his own. They wander deep into the Halls. Dáithí joins them as they reach the chambers set aside for the healers. He is draped in light clothes and has no need for his weapons, even as ceremony.

"Everyone's settled within the mountain, my lord. And what have we found, little Lor? Another thing to jump about your chambers?"

"Its leg is broken," Lor says, a great deal of importance and magnitude in his tiny voice. Dáithí grins. It isn't the first time Lor's brought home some forest creature, injured or otherwise.

"And I suppose my talents are required?" Leihs approaches from one of the smaller rooms, bowing in a soft swoop. The chambers are round and pale and always precisely clean, bedrooms circling the main area. Leihs has a mate of her own, but a few fae always insist upon venturing into the storms and need a bit of soothing magic in the aftermath. Iohmar nods to her. Her dress is plain and pale, hands free of age though she's half Iohmar's years, a rather significant number. Of all his folk, she is perhaps the least noticeable and most competent at her caring work. Only Galen rivals her healing.

She leads Lor and his new pet to a table, speaking softly. Vines wrapping the arched doorway reach out, clinging to Iohmar's horns and wrists in greeting. Dáithí lingers by his side, chuckling at the leaves obscuring Iohmar's vision.

"Will Queen Rúnda reach the Halls before the storm worsens?" he asks.

"Not likely. The brunt of it is approaching."

She and her folk will take shelter in the trees, away from the raging center of the storm. If Iohmar were to dispatch his crows, she would call the winds to bring her here alone. He can't bring himself to send them.

"Are you well, my sweet lord?" Dáithí asks.

Perhaps he isn't doing a fair job at keeping his expression soft. "Perfectly."

Somehow, it doesn't yet catch in his throat as a lie.

The trees and vines of the mountain are desperate to hold him tight today, and he uses his talons to unravel the little branches with care lest he rip them. One larger branch weaves around his ankle.

Dáithí snorts.

Iohmar levels a glare at him, pulling a vine from his horn before it can fasten his head to the wall. Centuries have passed since his trees ignored his wishes in such a way. Millenia. Dáithí is old enough to remember.

"So grateful I have a kingsguard eager to assist me," Iohmar mutters without annoyance.

Laughing, Dáithí helps extract him while Iohmar sends soothing magic into the trunks and stems.

Something is wrong, he thinks as another tremor shudders against
his bare feet.

Dáithí looks at the ceiling, but after his childhood, Iohmar has
long secured all chambers of the Halls with vines and thick roots.
Even if the shaking were to rival that which buried him, none of
his folk will be in danger so long as they stay within the warmth
of the mountain.

Uncertain, he casts his magic out until he finds Galen's presence. He cannot tell precisely where he is, but nothing seems
amiss.

More vines tug his hair. His head dips. Though the cut of rot
still restricts itself to his finger, exhaustion creeps. It is always his
head affected first; it becomes heavy and impossible to hold up
under the weight of his horns.

"Dáithí," he whispers. "Stay by Lor's side awhile, please. I have
some small things to attend to."

"Of course." Dáithí's expression brightens.

Iohmar touches his shoulder before departing. Earthquakes
rattle the Halls as he makes his way toward his chambers, following the sense of Galen's magic. The few of his folk he passes giggle
and gaze about themselves at the wildness of the earth. Not all
are so plagued by past strangeness as Iohmar. His people, at least,
know he has made these mountains safe for them.

Storm clouds cast the mountain in a shadowed haze, no sunlight
to be found. The Halls are dim, and there's a hazy blue gray to the
air. Warm still, but tinged with energy and the outside gales, the

rich scent of soaked earth finds its way even to the center of the mountain. Iohmar adores this weather even if it brings worry for the safety of his folk.

"Galen?" he asks, entering Galen's chambers beside his own.

It's a simple room thick with plants and flowers. There's a bed and a small ornate wash table in the corner. It's empty.

Iohmar tries his own chambers. The wide window displays the sight of the storm. Outside, trees dance in the wind, throwing themselves against one another, leaves whipping, rain pelting the glass. The mist over the heart of the woods is thicker—near solid—and resistant to the moving air. Crows are huddled against the sill, seeking shelter, so Iohmar eases open the glass long enough to receive a blast of frigid, damp air and for his room to be filled with flocks of inky feathers.

Galen isn't here, but one of the panels in the ceiling window has been moved aside. Iohmar frowns. Galen has never shared Iohmar's fascination with the tunnels and underground hiding places, but his magic is nearby.

"Galen?" He boosts himself above the glass.

The mountain trembles so violently that Iohmar is thrown to the ground.

23

A SPREADING WOUND

Mountain earth trembles, roaring in Iohmar's ears, jarring his bones. He stays frozen on the leaf-strewn floor until the world falls to stillness, only the rain and wind raging. Chills roll over his skin. But he is not a child. He will not be buried.

Casting his magic outward, he finds his people unhurt, Lor and his kingsguard safe if a little shaken. Galen is still nearby, with a faint hint of pain.

"Galen?" he calls, rising with difficulty under the spreading sickness. The cut on his finger is growing. *Does fear quicken its spread?*

Frustrated with the both of them, he slips up the glass window and into the cool of the tunnels. He reinforced the earth here as well, as it's over his chambers and a path he often travels. But not all of it. Not in the places where the deepest dwellers travel. The one time he tried, it frightened the inhabitants.

Maneuvering the path he took toward the tunnels beneath the mountain, Iohmar steps over fallen rocks and crushed crystals, pulling himself free of broken vines clinging to his robes. Worms and insects rip themselves from the earth to follow.

"Galen?" *What is he doing down here? In the middle of a storm?* He knows better.

Here the tunnel has caved. A crack allows him passage. Roots are threading themselves among the stones, slow with lazy panic, tugging at Iohmar.

There. The edge of a sleeve. A sob threatens to lodge itself in his throat.

Sickness grating at his magic, Iohmar calls the vines to lift the stone. *Too slow.* Fistfuls at a time, he tears at the rocks. Sharp tips of roots dig into his skin, recoiling at what they've done, burned by the rage and hurt in Iohmar's magic. He slides his arms under Galen, pulling him to his chest. His breathing is light, eyes closed. Cuts and bruises from fallen stones litter his skin. *What was he* thinking *leaving the mountain?*

"Galen," he whispers, touching his cheek.

Panic wraps itself around Iohmar's heart, an old and familiar sensation. He presses it down, down, down where it belongs. Gathering Galen into his arms, he wraps his magic around the threads of the old creature's soul. Eyes fluttering, Galen whimpers and turns his face into Iohmar's shoulder.

"I found you," Iohmar murmurs. "What were you doing? What were you thinking?"

Shaking ripples the ground. Another quake such as the last is unlikely, but it still spurs Iohmar to his feet, and he stumbles with his body heavy. The tunnel spins, a whirl of dark earth and glowing fragments of crystal. Galen, tall as he is, is not a heavy burden.

"What were you doing down here?"

Galen blinks, eyes closing. One hand clings to Iohmar's robe, so frail and bruised that Iohmar's throat burns fiercer.

"Heard a voice . . ." he whispers, and Iohmar nearly stops in his tracks before slipping down into his chambers.

"A voice? I'm taking you to the healer. What voice did you hear?"

"A voice . . ." he repeats. "She was speaking, but I couldn't understand. I thought . . . she needed help. No one was there . . ."

Iohmar nods. He sensed no other presence in the tunnels until far, far down — not close enough for someone to call out. He considers the shadows but cannot dwell. He will consider it later, when Galen is tended to.

"Leihs?" he calls, returning to the healing rooms. He passes a few of his folk, who gasp and follow in concern for a few steps. Lor and Dáithí are nowhere to be seen — a small relief. Lor shouldn't see Galen broken in his arms.

"My lord — *oh!*"

Leihs rises from opposite the table, where she speaks with another. Iohmar recognizes her lover. Nodding his chin, Iohmar slips into one of the small private chambers and lays Galen upon a bed. Leihs draws the door closed. Quiet covers them, the weight of the storm hidden by the mountain.

"Your hand, my lord . . ."

Turning his arm over, Iohmar finds the cut along his finger has turned to a streak of rot weaving across his palm, disappearing into his sleeve.

"It wasn't—" He cannot lie, cannot tell her the wound is nothing of concern. "It is nothing you can assist with. I'll . . . I'll care for it. Galen is injured."

Her eyes remain crinkled and unconvinced, but she touches a wound upon Galen's shoulder, drawing her fingers across his forehead.

"What happened?"

"He went into one of the tunnels. It collapsed where there was no structure."

She shakes her head, mumbling, "Foolish."

It was. No matter the voice, Galen should've known better. Iohmar supposes he cannot fault him. He has a kind heart, and Iohmar knows he would've done the same.

"He is very weak," Leihs says. "He is far too ancient to be receiving such injuries."

Iohmar knows but cannot force his tight throat to speak. He touches his hand to Galen's, watching his sleeping eyelids and wishing he would wake.

Under his silence, Leihs continues her work. It has been a great time since Iohmar has seen the old fae in a state of little dress. He stares at the long, thin, ink-like markings Galen decorates himself with. His limbs are frail. It is not unusual for a creature of his age and experience to lose the steel in their body. They do not age as humans, and his skin is smooth and free of the signs of time, but his body is thin and brittle, as strong in appearance as soaked paper.

None of the outward injuries are grievous, but Iohmar is unsure how much magic Galen's body expended trying to aid itself. Iohmar feels it slip close to disappearing. He presses his fingers to his eyes. The last time he shared his magic, it was broken to save Lor, tied to his little boy and weakened into illness. It is a sacred thing reserved for him alone. Him and his son.

His eyes are itchy and heavy. Expending his magic now, with the streaks of rot up his arms, would be unwise.

Stepping to the front of the bed, he slips his hands beneath the old fae's hair. Resting his forehead against his, he allows his magic to wash into Galen's limbs.

Leihs starts, her breath sharp. "My king . . . ?"

"Please, keep working," he murmurs.

Floating in the strange place between his own magic and Galen's, Iohmar doesn't think or worry. The outside world is nonexistent. It's a comfortable, familiar sensation. Reminds him of crawling back from the rippling lands with Galen's soothing magic tending his wounds. He doesn't have the presence of mind now to be grieved by the memory. Time slips. He is aware of Galen's body mending under Leihs's touch, his magic stabilizing enough that Iohmar could release it should he wish to. But his illness nags at his limbs and Iohmar doesn't wish to return to conscious thought.

Still, he feels Leihs lay hesitant fingers along his shoulder. Regretfully, he withdraws his magic, being as gentle as possible, easing Galen into his own strength.

Aches grasp his limbs. His horns dip his head. The streaks of rot upon his hand have turned to many up his arms, breaking his pale skin, and he is certain Leihs must see them across his face.

Her eyes are wide when he meets them.

"Do not speak of this to anyone."

Her eyes are so shaken and worried that Iohmar brushes against her magic and its intentions. He finds both concern and the resolve to keep his secret.

"Thank you," he whispers. "Leave us a moment, please."

For a breath, she doesn't move, but then she dips into another slight bow and disappears. Iohmar leans against the bed, staring at Galen's sleeping face, vision blurred. He brushes a finger along the old fae's frail cheek, laying his temple against his forehead, not sharing magic, simply touch. Never has he done such a thing when Galen was awake. It is not proper. Foolish and childlike. But he is relieved, robbed of his pride. Galen will sleep for some time still, healing and returning to his strength, and Iohmar needs to lock himself away within his own chambers before his body betrays him further. Lor is with Dáithí, and it will have to be enough.

He slides a blanket soft as down from the foot of the bed and tucks it up to Galen's chin before slipping unnoticed from the healing rooms.

Iohmar closes the door to his own chambers, and he is alone.

Staring at the peaceful room, he watches silver leaves float from the ceiling to the warm floor, the comfortable bed. Out the window, the storm rages, a mass of warm air, biting rain, and angry clouds. Droplets pelt the glass. Midnight is darkening the world with no moon to light it. Worry secures itself around Iohmar's heart. The last thing he desires is for the illness to take him from Galen and Lor and his people for days to come.

"You are a fool," he mutters, seating himself along the foot of the bed.

A long tear streaks the fine blue fabric of his robe, likely from a sharp rock or the panicking vines. After pushing the heavy fabric from his shoulders, he slips to the floor to unwind the ties on his boots while leaning against the bed frame. The floor is a spongy and pleasant seat.

With Rúnda delayed, Galen healing, and Lor under Dáithí's watchful eye, he will be alone this time. No one will watch him lie helpless, claimed by grieving memories.

Cowering alone in my chambers. Iohmar is sick with himself.

His head spins. He rests his arms upon his knees, dropping his forehead into the crook of his elbow, horns pressing against his muscles.

Footsteps reach him from the hallway—light, gentle steps. His kingsguard, perhaps. He should have secured the door. A soft knock rattles him from his thoughts, but he doesn't rise. If he does not answer, his guard will not enter his chambers without his permission.

"Daidí?" Lor's voice calls, and Iohmar twitches.

He stares at the door, several options fighting in his scattered thoughts. Shadows and strange voices and memories invade his mind whenever the sickness takes hold. His head swims. For the first time, he considers his stomach might twist until it rebels.

But this is Lor, not some memory. Lor's voice. His own little child.

"My lord?" Dáithí calls softly. "Are you here? Lor is looking for you."

Dáithí will sense his presence, and Lor will as well. They know he's here. But if he doesn't speak, Iohmar knows his kingsguard will take the boy away, even if Lor protests.

What will Lor believe when he knows? Will he be hurt I turned him away? Or will terror enter his heart at my appearance? Will he wish he'd never been told the truth?

Iohmar may stay silent and keep this secret to himself.

He closes his eyes. "Let him in, Dáithí. You can join the others."

The door cracks, and a very rain-drenched Lor bounces in, a grin lighting his face, hair still plastered. The fawn is cradled in his arms. He spins in a circle without seeing Iohmar, nudging the door closed with his elbow. "Bye, Dáithí!"

"Good night, Lor." Dáithí's voice is faded behind the door, his presence lessening as he leaves.

"Daidí, did you feel the earthquake?"

Lor freezes halfway between the door and where Iohmar is slumped on the floor. His face goes blank, smile failing.

He takes in the sight of his father and screams.

24

SOME LONG-FORGOTTEN TALES

Iohmar remembers when first he realized his parents could be
frightening.

Remembers his mother contorting magic to offer his father a
lifeline before the rippling lands could swallow him. Remembers
the moon and stars falling empty and lightless, all of Látwill devoid
of time and place for the few moments she took. How her magic
enveloping their world stole each of Iohmar's senses from him,
and how, for a few seconds, he was utterly helpless.

Remembers his father bringing an entire mountain to its knees
when he returned, pushing the creatures back long before the last
battle even began.

Iohmar didn't fear them; he never feared them. But neither
did he see them as when he was a child, innocent and misun-

derstanding of the nature of magic.

Lor's scream is nothing more than a quiet noise, a sudden gasp of surprise. Dáithí, his footsteps having faded, likely doesn't hear. It lasts not even a full breath, but Iohmar flinches nonetheless. Lor stares at him, shock in his eyes, hands frozen around the fawn, and it takes Iohmar too long to find his voice.

"It's all right, Lor," he whispers. It's not enough a lie to stop his words, but his voice tastes bitter in the back of his throat.

Lor blinks, clinging to the tiny deer. Iohmar offers a hand, wanting to comfort him — to comfort them both — but the boy is out of arm's reach. Iohmar's vision spins when he leans forward.

"What's wrong?" Lor's whisper is harsh. His clothes are dripping on the leaves, and Iohmar wants to tell him to change so he'll be warm.

"I . . ." Iohmar doesn't know how to continue, how to tell the truth while keeping the boy unhurt. He invited him in, meaning to tell him, meaning to be braver than he feels, but words have fled his lips. "Sometimes I fall ill. You needn't worry, Wisp."

Lor's eyes wander his body, following the trails of rot. *Does he believe?* Lor knows he cannot lie, but there is a distinct curve of distrust in his frown. Iohmar touches his finger to the flaking paper of his jaw, feeling nothing unusual but knowing the marks are present. Lor isn't meeting his eyes.

"I will be all right, Wisp," he says, his voice far away. He recovered the last two times, so this must be a truth. "I am merely tired."

Lor steps forward, a small movement that doesn't put him within Iohmar's reach. His head cocks, tears turning his eyes to glass. Iohmar hasn't seen the boy cry since the strange night after the cavern so long ago, and neither has he heard him scream. His breath is picking up, and Iohmar feels unequal to the task of soothing. *Is my appearance truly so terrifying to my son?* He expected Lor to be frightened, but not to stay out of his reach.

"Lor," he says, forcing control into his voice, gesturing for him to step closer. "Don't be afraid."

Finally, Lor meets his eyes. "You look like my dreams."

Iohmar blinks. A moment passes before he wraps his head about the words and finds himself more confused than before. Iohmar himself never dreams of falling ill. Even when the sickness began as he crawled with Lor from the caverns, Lor couldn't have seen much of the rotting cuts in the dark, seated on his back, and certainly not in the severity of this. *What put such an image into his mind?*

"What?" he asks, slow and uncomprehending. Something here must be obvious but out of his grasp.

Lor hiccups, holding down sobs. "Are my dreams true?"

Iohmar tries once more to sit forward and reach him, but he catches himself against the edge of the bed before his body can take him down.

"Lor, I don't know what you're speaking of. What dreams? Come here."

Still, he doesn't move from the door. "I dream about you."

"Yes?" Iohmar prompts when he fails to continue. "I dream of you as well. What did you dream?"

"Many things," he whispers.

"Lor, tell me."

He is quiet, little eyebrows pulling together. "Is this why you left me with Dáithí?"

"No, no. I was only looking for Galen."

Lor's frown deepens. Iohmar doesn't understand from where this doubt has sprouted. But those words, at least, are the full truth, not a dance about it.

"What do you dream?" he asks once more.

Lor stares, then glances at the raging storm. He shifts the squirming fawn closer, and his lip trembles. Iohmar wishes so much to gain the strength to rise and snatch the boy into his arms. As it is, he's losing the battle to keep his head upright. He shouldn't have stayed on the floor.

"I . . ." Lor hesitates. "Dream about the caves."

That's not so unusual. Iohmar dreams of them himself. "Yes?"

"And . . . you come looking for me. But you never find me. Sometimes you look at me and walk by and disappear into the dark. And I'm by myself."

Iohmar blinks, and by the time he wraps his thoughts around the words, Lor is continuing.

"Sometimes you turn to dust and float away. It looks like that"—he points skittishly to Iohmar's face—"and I'm buried. And you don't come back. And I wake up."

Buried? Iohmar thinks of the caves burying him when he was a boy. Ascia lost. *Why would Lor dream such things?* Never has Iohmar given him reason to doubt. His heart aches. *Where could my little boy have gained such fears?* He thinks of the nights when Lor climbs under his covers to cuddle within the circle of his arms. *Was he hiding from nightmares?*

"Why didn't you tell me you were having such awful dreams?"

Lor shrugs, turning his face.

Iohmar doesn't believe he's going to receive a better answer. Softly, he asks, "Do you have others?"

"Sometimes," Lor whispers.

"What are they? Are they fair dreams?"

Again, the boy shrugs. His eyes are on the floor and the storm. "They aren't good or bad. Just dreams."

"Lor, tell me. Please."

"Sometimes . . . I dream you're looking at me through a window. It's strange."

"A window?"

"I'm lying somewhere, and all your crows are hopping about. And someone's making noise, but I can't see them. And you're leaning in a window over me and watching. Your eyes are a different color. Your hair too."

Oh.

Oh.

He remembers those first moments? It seems so long ago that Iohmar took him from the human shack. Iohmar's magic must have sealed in the memories when he pulled apart pieces of himself to turn Lor fae. Iohmar doesn't remember his own infancy, but Lor is still so little, and the way he was created was unusual. He even remembers Iohmar's appearance before the broken magic altered him. Perhaps it's possible.

"I have that dream a lot," Lor whispers, eyes fluttering across Iohmar's appearance. "Daidí, what's wrong with you?"

Iohmar sighs. He longs to sleep, body dragging him toward it with every breath, but this is not something to be fixed with silence.

"Sometimes I fall ill, Lor. It has happened before."

"When?"

"Once when you were a little babe. Once after we crawled from the caverns. You were deep asleep."

"Why?"

"I'm not . . . I'm not sure. I believe my magic is quite angry with me." He pauses. Lor still watches, expectant, tears clinging to his eyes. "Some time ago, I split it, which is quite a dangerous thing to do. The threads you feel when you touch magic? Some of my own are tethered to you. Ever since then, it has done this strange thing. I always recover, but I cannot tell you exactly what it is. I do not know myself."

He watches Lor mouth the word *split*. Such things are not known to the boy. Such things weren't known to Iohmar before the woman under the mountain.

"Why did you split it?"

Iohmar's eyes burn. He doesn't allow himself to blink. "When you were a little babe, you were ill and weak. My magic alone could not help, nor could Galen's. You would've died had I done nothing."

"But the trees don't give ill children. All the children the woods give are perfect. Like Rúnda. And Oisín. Everyone says that."

Iohmar closes his eyes, then opens them long enough to say, "I found you in the human world, Wisp."

"Found me?" Lor whispers.

"I . . ." Iohmar starts, then takes a long, deep breath. "Lor, set the fawn on the bed and come here. I will tell you the story."

For a long moment, he doesn't believe Lor will listen. But the boy shuffles to the bedside and places the animal on the blankets before stepping to Iohmar's knees. Catching the rot drifting from his fingers, Iohmar settles his hand on Lor's leg.

He tells him the story.

Beginning to end. From Lor as a helpless little babe to the strange woman beneath the earth who helped Iohmar bind their lives. Confessing to Rúnda was easy as breathing in comparison. Partway through the story, Lor's eyes leave Iohmar's and stay solidly on the floor. Iohmar wishes to abandon the tale, feeling a coward.

Words stick in his throat. *What does Lor think of his human parents? His human life, which would've ended before it'd hardly begun?*

When the tale is finished, Lor's eyes remain on the floor. Iohmar raises his other hand to rest on the boy's side, but the movement spins his head. His vision refuses to focus no matter how he tries. The dim sounds of the storm hurt his ears.

Iohmar can no longer bear to watch the boy turn this over and over in his mind. "Lor," he says, focusing on the word after speaking for so long.

Lor starts. His eyes flicker to Iohmar's. His expression crumples, and he bursts into tears before Iohmar can speak, flowers wilting and drooping from his skin.

Rippling mirrors tearing him was less painful.

Iohmar coughs, gripping Lor's clothes and trying to clear the tightness from his throat. "Lor . . . there is nothing incorrect in being human. You may have been born to different parents, but—"

Lor shakes his head, covering his eyes with the backs of his hands. "I don't care about that!"

Iohmar curses the struggle of raising his arms. A thousand pains could be troubling the boy, and he can't begin to choose one. "Then what is wrong, dearheart?"

Another shake of his head. Iohmar tugs him closer, his light body seeming to hold the weight of a mountain. "Lor—"

" 'Mnotyourson," he mumbles.

"What?"

"You said I was your son . . ." Finally, he stops hiding his face. "You said the forest made me for you. You said I was special because I was yours and the forest made me just for you. But I'm not. I'm not . . ."

Iohmar blinks and blinks. Darkness creeps at the edge of his vision. Dragging Lor another step so he can lock his arms around his back, Iohmar holds him to his chest, uncaring of the sickly cuts that may frighten him.

As gently and clearly as he can, he says, "Lor, you are my son. Because the heart of the woods did not give you to me does not mean you were not a gift."

Lor sniffs, turning his face aside. "But I was special for you . . ."

Tears burn Iohmar's cheeks, but he's afraid to let go of Lor long enough to wipe them. This is not the reaction he expected, not fear of Iohmar's appearance or his human origins. A weight leaves his chest, for the boy hasn't taken the ridiculous idea that the sickness is his fault, but he hates the pain in his voice.

"Do you truly believe I would break my magic for anyone who is not the most precious child in all these lands or the next?"

Lor hiccups, fists pressed against his eyes. Rocking back, he drapes himself against Iohmar's chest, threading his arms about his neck. Iohmar cradles him, eyes closed. His head throbs, and he rests it against Lor's fluffy hair, trying to ease the weight.

"Oh, Lor," he murmurs. "I love you so very much."

Lor doesn't return the words but asks, "Are you going to be all right?"

"Yes . . . I am simply very tired," he says. He's drifting, Lor the single solid weight tethering him to the world. "You are very wet. Too much rain."

It isn't enough. His story isn't enough, especially not when Lor burrows into his shoulder and doesn't speak. *What can I say?* Right now, with his body too heavy to speak or move, it's the only explanation he can offer. He slumps against the foot of the bed, unable to support himself.

I love you, he thinks, then drifts.

25

CENTURIES UPON CENTURIES,
DEEPER AND DEEPER

Time passes, and Iohmar doesn't truly sleep or wake. When Lor maneuvers from his arms, he tries to raise his head and doesn't quite succeed. The boy tugs on his arm.

I can't get up, Wisp, he wishes to say, but he finds his head as iron and his mouth full of feathers.

But he stands. He doesn't intend to and is surprised his legs hold his weight. He wishes to go in the direction Lor needs. Lor needs him, so he must move. He finds himself being tugged by the fingers in one direction until tiny hands press up against his hip.

What is he doing? Slumping atop the bed, he realizes what his son is trying to accomplish. Lor pushes and maneuvers with all his infant strength until Iohmar finds himself tucked under the covers, head on a pillow. Silence. *Did Lor leave?* Iohmar tries to call for him. There's a weight against his leg. The covers lift, and Lor loosens the ties on the front of Iohmar's shirt.

Sweet boy, he thinks as Lor wriggles under his arm as he does in the early-morning twilight.

This is all he is aware of for some time.

As before, Iohmar dreams.

These are much the same, but different. The words are clearer. Sitting in his parents' chambers, he hears their voices. They are not easily discerned, but the quiet ring of them remains in his ears. He is young. His hands are folded within his lap, small child's fingers. Sadness weighs on him. His hair smells of earth and the deep places under the mountain. He went exploring the caves. He does this with Ascia often. His clothes are clean, but he still smells of earth. *Why didn't I wash my hair?*

His mother sits beside him. Pomegranate — the scent she carries on her skin — envelopes him. She's speaking, but not to him, and he doesn't understand. Her fingers brush the top of his head — no, his horn, the aching place where one of them should be. It was broken off.

Yes, it was broken off when the mountain collapsed.

Why am I having such a dream? He hates to think on it. He was so little — too little to have done anything. His friend was buried while he was found. He hates this dream, even as he watches the soft shape of his father moving about the small warm chambers. They will be Iohmar's chambers eventually. No, he sealed these rooms away to their ghosts, taking his own bedroom as the chambers of a king. One day, when even he is old enough to pass from these twilight lands, his will be Lor's.

"Daidí?" he hears himself say. How strange. By such an age— barely younger than Lor, he must've been—Iohmar no longer called his father by the informal title. Athair, it always was. *Why am I switching back?*

His father's hand touches his cheek. It's warm and smells of candle wax. Either his hand is damp or Iohmar's cheeks are. Daidí is saying something now too. Exhaustion lines his fair features. Still, the words are a haze, an echoing, weightless dream.

Iohmar remembers it as an apology.

Another dream. It must be, for Lor is not with him, and the orchard is silent. He searches for the boy, testing the strings binding their magic and finding none. He sits in the roots of his mother's tree. It is a large thing, recently filled with her magic. The trees grow all their lives before taking on their inhabitants. Iohmar's is somewhere within these rows of bluish limbs, growing wide, reaching for the sky. He searched for it as a child, as many children do. Never to be found. It is not meant to be, not until his final days.

His body aches. It's not the strange illness, but a familiar physical pain: wounds. He puts his hand within his shirt and finds the raw, unhealing things war gifted him. Bandaged. He should tell someone. Galen, certainly. The old fae will fuss and tend to him as if he's a child. He wishes to feel as such.

Centuries upon centuries of life. But his parents are dead, alongside many of his folk. He is the oldest in their Halls now. No, there is Galen. Galen is still with him, the presence of his magic a bright spark beneath the mountain, dimmed by grief.

A little boy. Iohmar's legs don't carry him far. He weaves among the crystals and mushrooms dwelling beneath his parents' mountain.

Ascia follows.

A crossroads in the tunnel presents itself. Ascia creeps beside him, twirling the hem of the green-brown dress matching her skin and hair, and heads to the left.

Deeper. Deeper.

Iohmar "plays" prince so Ascia can play princess. Brother and sister. Grand adventurers protecting the great mountain and its Fair Halls. She's the only child he's ever met, the only one so young as he, and he loves this game.

Deeper.

She is a child of the heart of the woods, not the daughter of anyone. Iohmar learned recently how this works and is even happier to play brother and sister. After all, she came from the woods his parents serve. No one knows who begged the trees to gift her, but it matters little. They are Iohmar's trees as they are his parents'. He feels their life force at all times. Feels the wind. The animals. Insects. His folk and their kin.

Which makes her his best friend to protect. A little sister of some sort, even when they aren't playing adventurers.

Deeper.

He can feel the mountain.

Deeper.

He can feel the mountain tremble.

Ascia speaks. It's an echoing, weightless noise. Down a crack in the earth, he sees a great cavern. White pillars like great bones rise to greet them, and he forgets the unrest in the earth.

"Look what I can do!" Ascia slips down first. Shadows move about her, nudging the space wider at her call. Iohmar follows. Darkness is a safe, warm beast.

This is a new talent; Ascia is learning her magic. It's wonderful. He believes it's very apt a fae born of his woods has a magic so similar to his yet so unique. Playing brother and sister is a very good thing indeed.

Ascia slides down a pillar. Iohmar balances atop one and wonders if he can make the jump to the next. Only the faintest flicker of the mountains and woods above reaches him. They must be very deep in the earth.

The mountain trembles.

Ascia looks up at him, a pinprick of light below where her skin casts off the darkness around her as Iohmar's gathers the light, and cocks her head. She does this often, her ear resting on her shoulder when she's curious.

Iohmar feels older for a moment — centuries upon centuries

older — and can't understand why.

He looks up, and the mountain trembles around him.

He lies on the floor. His bed is behind him, ground carpeted with leaves brittle and dead. It is not his room, not truly. His parents' chambers should be his own. No. He doesn't want them. He shouldn't be in their chambers. It is their room and shouldn't yet be his.

Perhaps he should rise and lie on the blankets. Certainly, he should tend to his people. Make an appearance if not speak to them. Be their king beneath the earth. After all, his body now bears the wounds of protecting them and their home.

But he's been crying for hours. What a terror he'll look. Galen is seated on the ground beside him. Somehow, at some point, Iohmar's head came to rest on the caretaker's lap. The old fae is petting his hair, touching fingers along his back and torso, sending soothing warmth along the healing skin. Iohmar cannot move away.

He's reacting as a child.

But Galen wept when Iohmar did. He supposes, then, it can't be too shameful a thing. He allowed the old creature to tend to his wounds after a time.

I must rise. He knows he should. He is king beneath the earth.

His body will not leave the floor, neither does Galen move him, and they remain as such through the darkest hours of midnight.

Iohmar observes the human child through the window. The mother he found far in the woods and deep beneath the earth. Crows surround him, swarm before his eyes and land atop his head and shoulders and feet. Their beaks peck his hands. Their cries are soft and curious. Beady eyes turn upon the human babe.

The king's own eyes flicker to the man in the corner unknowing of his sunlight presence. A human matter was hardly worth him leaving the mountain. He should've wandered home the moment he met the men on the path. They spoke to him of their troubles. Their human lives are so short, so insignificant and small. *Is this truly worth my magic and concern?*

A coo reaches his ears. The human thing grins at him. He sees Iohmar. Even in the sunlight. Children must react differently to his magic.

Quietly, the babe gurgles, reaching for him with infinitely small grasping fingers.

Iohmar leans his horns in the cracked window frame.

His daidí kisses his forehead and speaks. Iohmar cannot hear the words. His head is full of down. Words drift over him like heavy water, like floating in Rúnda's sea.

How can I have such memories? He is a little thing, a child with a mountain collapsed upon him.

"I'm sorry. I'm so sorry," his daidí tells him, because it has been days and days since the earth collapsed, and no one ever found her.

Iohmar likes to step through sunbeams. *Ascia called shadows to her, didn't she? Or was it the earth itself? What were the last words she spoke to me?*

She must have slipped away from him forever. One day, will he slip into a sunbeam and never return to his body? Will he never be anything other than dust motes and warm light, nowhere and everywhere at once? Covering his mountains and his woods and his people, his daidí and mhamaí. He will circle the sun and the moon and her stars.

He will be something other than this strange thing he is.

The king beneath the earth leaves a bundle of twigs in place of the babe. Handling such a delicate thing is odd. Fae children are not so breakable, so soft. The babe is small, fitting within his palm and fingers.

He tests his magic against the child's, for all humans have at least a scrap of it, a shred of light and warmth to fuel their life. What he finds is as small and weak as the child itself. It's concerning, but it further assuages his uncertainty at taking the boy. The child will be safe in Látwill until he finds a suitable home.

Round human eyes gaze at him, a fawn lost in the evening light, a wisp of weight in his palm. The boy smiles, and Iohmar's lips twitch.

He tucks the creature into the crook of his left elbow with care. There are no more tears, nothing in the silence but the existence of the woods, the flapping of his crows, and the harsh movements from the vile thing within the shack that has the gall to call itself human.

He thinks of the bundle of twigs and the child it will mirror while the real babe lies safe in his arms. A terrifying death. A fitting end to a creature which committed so horrible a murder. Iohmar need not monitor the magic or think on it for it to take effect.

With a rustle and sweep of his robes, he leaves the cursed bundle in the makeshift crib fit for no loved thing. He melts into the woods, followed by a shaft of sunlight and a flock of gossiping crows.

26

RIPPLINGS AND SHADOWS

Iohmar wakes, and the storm greets him against the window. Curled in the space between his arms and chest is Lor, his head under Iohmar's chin. His finger runs the softest circle around his horn—the broken one.

Such strange dreams. They return to him in the slow trickle of a stream. Grasping them all at once is difficult. *How did I come to be in bed? Did Lor move me?*

Stretching his hands, he finds the marks still present, grains of rot drifting from his skin. They fade before settling upon anything. His joints are stiff but move when requested, his head lighter, his talons regrown.

A weight sits against his legs, and he raises his head to see the rescued fawn curled into a makeshift nest. The knobby creature flaps its ears at him, velvet nose wrinkling. A twig from its back pokes his ankle through the blanket. Iohmar sighs, content. Hesitantly, he brushes his fingers through Lor's hair, not wishing to disturb him.

Lor rubs his face into Iohmar's shoulder before peering up, sleepy. Breath whispers upon his cheeks.

"I see you've put on dry clothes." Iohmar's voice is cracked and thick, but words obey him.

Lor nods.

"I am sorry I fell asleep."

"It's all right. I like sleeping here."

Warmth blooms in Iohmar's heart, but he remembers an earlier consideration. "Because you have bad dreams?"

"Sometimes. But I still just like it here." His fingers move down to Iohmar's cheek. "Are you all right now? You still look sick."

"Not entirely, but I am very much improved." Telling the full truth is a relief. Hours or days have passed in a blur, but already his body feels less wounded than the previous experiences — quicker to recover, even if worse at the outset. He remembers wishing to hold Lor close when they lay on the forest floor, but his arms hadn't the strength, and the boy was deep in sleep.

Are you helping me? Iohmar wonders, watching Lor's eyes trail his face and hair.

"Sometimes I have dreams you are fighting someone. Not with those stick swords you and Rúnda play with, just with your magic. You always look sad."

The warmth in Iohmar's heart constricts. He curls Lor tighter to him while the boy's hand travels to a section of skin along

Iohmar's chest.

"Are those dreams where you got these?"

Lor's fingers brush one of the many pale scars. Iohmar doubts Lor has seen such disfigurements on others — not enough to register its gravity. Injuries are tended to with haste in Iohmar's Halls, and don't often leave traces.

"Yes, I received those fighting."

"So that dream is true?"

"Perhaps. Not the exact memory, I would assume. You were not there to remember, after all."

"There were mirrors everywhere."

Mirrors. Ripplings.

Iohmar shudders. "Yes, a real memory."

"And the dream of you looking at me through the window, that's true." It isn't a question.

"Yes," he says, quieter. The pain of the conversation is fresh. He wishes to take it from Lor, keep it all as his own burden. Such is a nonexistent magic.

"Does that mean the other things are true?"

"What things?"

"When . . . I'm in the caves and you can't find me? Or you disappear?"

"No, no, no. I will always find you. I cannot tell you where those dreams came from, but I assure you, they are not true."

For a moment, he fears Lor will not believe. There is no smile to his eyes, but Lor nods. Believes him.

"I am sorry you had such frightening dreams, Wisp. You could have told me of them."

"I like some of them. I have many where you carry me around. I think I'm a baby and you carry me everywhere. It's very nice."

Tears prickle Iohmar's eyes. Weeping is ridiculous, but he nuzzles his nose into Lor's hair. For a while, they lie in silence, Iohmar drifting. His eyes remain heavy with sleep. He thinks of dozing. Visiting Galen tugs at him, but he isn't sure standing is wise. His strength is returning, but curled under piles of blankets with his head on a pillow is simple. He may crumble the moment he attempts sitting.

"Daidí?"

"Hmm?"

"I have another dream sometimes. When I'm dreaming about the caves. I don't understand."

His voice is hesitant, and Iohmar's relieved he's confiding in him. "Yes? Tell me."

"I hear people speaking to me," Lor says, and Iohmar blinks awake. "A lot of times it's a woman, and she's the one I can understand. She's realer. She's a shadow, and she doesn't have a face I can see, but she looks at me and calls me your name, and I can still tell she's looking at me."

Iohmar remembers the night in the caves when the shadows dragged them down, how a voice spoke his name to Lor. He never claimed it was a woman's voice. And the woman in the tunnels he first approached to save Lor was faceless and shrouded in shadow. She treated Iohmar as if he were his father.

"Is this the same voice you heard in the caves?"

"I think so. I don't remember very well. It's strange."

"And she calls you by my name?"

Lor nods. "Sometimes she sounds older, like you. Sometimes like me. I think it's the same person. All she says is your name . . ."

A little girl. Iohmar stares out the window, unseeing of the raging storm. The shadows took the form of a child when they led him to the ripplings in the heart of the woods, but the voice wasn't familiar.

And the woman in the tunnels whose involvement he dismissed because of her pure intentions was nameless and faceless, pure magic dwelling in the dark. But many dwell in shadows; Iohmar himself takes to them as he does sunlight. He felt the grip of her hand certain enough, but her heartbeat was a thin, threading thing, strange and small for a large fae.

The voice called Lor by Iohmar's name. The woman treated Iohmar as if he were his father.

Galen heard a girl's voice below the mountain, calling for help.

He considers Ascia, her voice and face brought to the surface by dreams.

She made creatures of shadow.

He remembers them now. It could've been a false dream, his ill mind playing cruel tricks, putting her together with the shadows and the woman simply because he is worrying. But all the other memories brought to the surface by the sickness have been real.

He searched for her for so long. *So long.* So long after he'd followed her beneath the earth, exploring below the surface, in the deepest places of Látwill, where most fae won't venture.

Great dragon bones.

"Oh . . ." he whispers.

He raises his head from the pillows, propping himself onto

his elbow. His head spins, but his body doesn't heave the way he expected. Lor starts, gazing up at him.

"Daidí?"

Such magic isn't possible. *It isn't possible.* But these woods and mountains are forever changing, unknown magic surfacing even his parents and grandparents did not understand. Those shadows following him, their tiny life force hearts and lack of speech. The woman in the tunnels without a face disappearing once she helped him, once she expended a great deal of her magic. He put from his mind the idea of her causing the shadows. Perhaps he was correct. Perhaps she is the shadows.

He worms around Lor, tossing aside the covers. Dizziness takes momentary hold, but he's steadier on his feet than when last he was awake.

"Daidí, what are you doing?" Lor stumbles when he drops to the floor and veers around the foot of the bed after Iohmar.

Iohmar takes from the closet a robe not torn or specked with Galen's blood and unlatches the window where the tunnel collapsed a short time ago.

"Daidí?"

"Lor, go to the healing rooms and sit with Galen, yes? I will return shortly."

"But where are you goin—what's wrong with Galen?"

Oh. Iohmar forgot the boy already left the healing chambers. "He was injured a bit by one of the earthquakes. He will be perfectly fine, Wisp."

And Lor is giving him those same eyes again, the ones when he cannot understand all languages, or when Iohmar told him of the illness. They look much older and slightly as if he realizes Iohmar isn't telling him the full story. His doubt twists into Iohmar like a blade. *How do I make the boy understand?*

"Is this about the woman's voice?" he asks.

"Yes," Iohmar says. He means not to continue but finds himself saying, "I believe I know why she's calling you by my name."

"Why?" His voice is a whisper.

Iohmar doesn't know how to explain the strange instinct fallen upon him. "I believe someone needs help."

"I want to go with you."

"You want to go far underground? Into all those tunnels?" After his terrible dreams, Iohmar is certain this will dissuade him.

Lor opens and closes his mouth several times, then finally says, "If I'm with you, I'm not afraid of tunnels."

Iohmar's resolve weakens. He does not believe a great deal of danger exists in the places below the earth. If nothing else, the trembling mountain is of no danger while Iohmar is beside him, but he is uncertain. But the woman spoke to Lor, a great deal more than Iohmar heard from the shadows. Whatever magic clings to him, it is drawn to Lor equally. If he brings him, if they search for the shadows together, perhaps Iohmar will gain greater luck.

Still, he hesitates. "Lor . . ."

"Is the girl real? If you're going to help her, I want to help too."

Sweet boy, Iohmar thinks. One hand still holding the pane of glass, he gestures for Lor to come closer. His son threads his hand between Iohmar's fingers and gazes up at him with troubled little eyes. Perhaps he needs this as dearly as Iohmar.

"You must never leave my side. Some magic is very strange

even to me. Do you understand?"

Lor nods, and Iohmar believes he grasps the gravity. Pushing up the glass, he lifts Lor through the opening, then slips up after him and lowers the window into place.

He has taken Lor to the mountains by these paths several times, but never into the tunnels since he was a babe. When he turns to the tunnels sloping downward, Lor's hand finds his, but he doesn't make a sound, skin glowing faintly as Iohmar's once did. They pass the crumbled earth and weave down tunnels until the worms wriggling out to greet their king have gone and the shimmering crystals have faded to a handful every few hundred steps.

Iohmar is breaking a promise by returning. But, if he is correct, he doesn't believe such a slight will be held against him.

Last time he ventured so far, Lor in his arms, Iohmar followed the strongest taste of magic. It is gone now. Iohmar attempts to navigate by memory. The creatures he passes are familiar, and they greet him with the same hesitant respect. There is no sign of the strange monster that threatened them when last they traveled here.

"Where are we going?" Lor asks, his voice the softest whisper.

"To find the woman who helped save you. At least, to try. She seemed to disappear after, so I'm hoping to find a hint."

"She was all the way down here? What does she have to do with the little girl talking to me?"

Iohmar is uncertain how to explain. "When I was a boy— younger than you, even—there was another child who lived in the Fair Halls."

Lor's eyes are upon him. Other children are not a foreign

concept to the prince, but he's had few with whom to play.

"She was a child of the heart of the woods, and we played often. She was much a younger sister to me. She was strong with her magic as I was, but she was still learning, and we were both young enough it didn't mean much. We hadn't much control over it, as you don't. But we liked to play in these tunnels. She could see places in the dark even I could not, so we spent a great deal of time down here. We thought tunnels were much more adventurous than places in the sunlight."

"What happened to her?"

"When we were still younger than you, we were exploring deep in the tunnels. We found a cavern. Sometimes the earth shifts, as it did earlier, and we were both buried very, very deep. My daidí and mhamaí and many others searched for us. They found me."

Lor stares. Quietly, he asks, "No one found your friend?"

"No. Even her magic disappeared, and when I woke, my parents told me she was lost, though they continued searching for a time. I wandered here many decades hoping to find her, thinking her magic did something to save her, let her live under the earth. I thought if I came searching, she'd find me. I never found the caverns again. Never found a trace of her . . ." Iohmar pauses. To himself, he says, "It was so long ago."

"Do you think the little girl . . . ?" Lor doesn't finish, but Iohmar understands.

"Perhaps her magic left traces. I was her best friend . . ."

Perhaps she's calling out to him. *Somehow.* He must find the meaning behind the shadows. He has a clue now, something which may lead him to the shadows, a method of speaking to them, perhaps. Nothing fits it all together in perfect pieces, but he learned long ago of magic's uncanny nature. Evidence walks beside Iohmar, holding his fingers. Evidence is upon Iohmar's skin, drifting flecks of rot, his magic turning itself inside out as it heals.

Rounding a corner, Iohmar comes to the place he is certain the woman dwelled, a cozy round home of roots burrowed into the earth. Lor bumps into the backs of his legs when he stops.

Iohmar puts his hand to the thick vines encrusting the round portion of the wall.

Extending his magic, he finds it solid and twined tight as knots. He could unwind it should he wish but would find an empty hole. Whatever strong magic once dwelled here, Iohmar finds sad traces lingering in the roots.

"Daidí?" Lor copies the touch, but Iohmar doubts his magic is developed enough to understand.

"The woman dwelled here," Iohmar murmurs. "She has been gone some time."

Lor drops his hand and gazes about. Only the soft glow of his skin lends light. Even the luminous crystals have disappeared. The scent of earth and cold hangs thick. A small flying creature wriggles through the air as a worm squirming in water, bumping into Lor's cheek before passing. It continues down the tunnels, deeper than Iohmar has gone since he was a child. He watches it long after it's disappeared.

When he was a child. *If I continue far enough, will I reach the cavern?*

"What are we doing now?" Lor asks, still blinking at the ceiling.

Iohmar follows his gaze but finds nothing of interest. He

wanders a few steps in the direction the creature flew. Lor hurries after, the weight of his hand on Iohmar's robes. They continue a dozen paces. A dozen more.

Deeper. Deeper.

Iohmar stops. His heart aches. He stares into the darkness.

"Are you there?" he whispers, the weight of Lor's eyes upon him. Silence embraces them. Iohmar wishes it could be so easy as to ask.

Rocks tumble gently. Turning, he finds pebbles disturbed along the floor. He stands over them, reaching out to brace himself against the stone.

He stumbles, and his shoulder bumps against the edge of a different tunnel. Moments ago, he passed by this section of the wall and found it solid. Stretching his hand before him, he finds nothing opposing.

"Lor, come closer," he says, and the boy's light reveals a long stretch of tunnel leading upward. Iohmar frowns. He pictures their location beneath the mountain and what direction the tunnel leads — not toward the human land or Rúnda's. If he is correct, it leads not quite toward the heart of the woods, but nearer to the permanent border of the rippling lands.

His skin crawls.

"This wasn't here a moment ago," Lor whispers.

"No."

Iohmar casts a glance back at the chill tunnel. He gazes into this one, which leads to the surface. The shadows can manipulate earth — enough so to pull him and Lor into the caverns — as Ascia's magic was beginning to do. *Why would they lead me away?*

A flicker of movement deep in the tunnel draws his eye. He knows the shape of the shadows and the terror of the ripplings enough to know them apart. These are the creatures he's ventured to find.

"Come," he says, scooping Lor to his chest. Lor locks his arms and legs about him in a heartbeat. Louder, he calls, "I'm following you."

His body is stronger now, whether from Lor's magic or these underground places, he isn't certain, but the movement doesn't cause him to tremble. Ducking into the tunnel, he climbs.

It is hours before starlight reaches him. Iohmar raises his head and finds the end to the tunnel, fresh air and flowers upon the breeze. Lor shifts, blinking at the pale light after so long in dark.

Iohmar climbs into a meadow, and the storm is silent.

Over his shoulder, the outline of his mountain cuts the sky, and he need not search the tree line to know the ripplings are here, so close his scars weigh against his skin. Lor clings to his shoulder, unaware of a deep mark there, but Iohmar doesn't readjust.

"Why are we here?" Iohmar breathes, turning his back to the mountain to face the line of trees concealing the barrier. Moonlight catches in reflective shimmers.

"Daidí, there she is."

He points, and Iohmar finds, among the trees and grasses, the shadow child who led him to the heart of the woods.

"Iohmar," it says in a voice he recognizes, then slips into the trees. Her voice echoes in his ears.

Ascia, he wants to say, to scream, but the word catches in his chest.

He can't bear to be here — not so close to their barrier, not with his son in his arms. He hates for Lor to know these nightmare creatures told of in stories, hates for Lor to see him crumble under memories and fears.

"We have to follow her," Lor whispers, little eyes troubled. Iohmar squeezes him tighter, tight enough no monster can touch him, and steps toward the rippling border.

27

A LONG-UNFORGOTTEN WAR

Past the trees, ripplings greet him.

Several dozen are poised behind their barrier, small and inconsequential beside his power, but enough to turn his legs to petals and his fingers to ice. He recognizes the one at the heart of the woods, larger, gazing at him with a faceless body, something unforgettable in the way it contorts about itself. As before, the shadow girl is nowhere to be seen, but he believes she watches.

She led him to the ripplings before; there must be a reason now.

"Why are you here?" he asks.

Never has he expected an answer, and he doesn't this time. Perhaps the shadow will answer. Some of the closest trees are withered at their smallest branches, and he shoves down immediate and unhelpful rage.

When Lor sees them, his breath hitches, arms tightening around Iohmar's neck. "Those are the creatures in my dreams. The ones that hurt you."

Again, Iohmar's eyes burn. He refuses to blink. "Yes. They will not harm you, Wisp."

The creature cocks its head at him, a strangely familiar gesture. Iohmar knows they are not one in the same, the shadows and the ripplings, but he wonders where this thing could've learned such a gesture if not from the woman in the caves, looking at him and cocking her head like a bird.

"You wish for me to be here," Iohmar says. Though he isn't certain it's true, he must speak. "What do you wish of me?"

What can I expect? His father's first interactions were in friendship, and they were met with pain. Their only thought is to consume.

He thinks of his father and mother, their lives slow and soft in their trees, and steps so close to the border that he feels the chill of it upon his cheeks. "What do you want —"

"Help . . ."

Iohmar twitches, jerking back so sharply that his ill body nearly gives. Lor yelps and clings to his horn. Catching himself against a tree, Iohmar stares. His eyes ache. Heartbeats throb behind his ears. It spoke to him.

It *spoke*.

In a sharp, soft voice so much like tinkling glass that Iohmar could almost believe it gentle.

"Daidí?" Lor asks, voice trembling, and Iohmar maneuvers him from his side to between his shoulder blades, arms curled under him. His body is between the ripplings and his little boy.

"Help," he repeats. His voice is incorrect, echoing, but he will not back away further. With force, he steps toward the border. Some of the small creatures disappeared, frightened by his sudden reaction. The largest one, the one that spoke, shifts but does not flee.

"When did you learn our tongue?" Iohmar asks.

It almost appears nervous, the way it twists and shifts, and the part of it that could be a face turns every which way.

"Your tongue is . . . uneasy . . . difficult . . ."

Numb, Iohmar finds himself nodding. They are *speaking* to each other. His eyes won't stop burning.

"When? How?"

"After you were frightened of me . . ."

Frightened. In the heart of the woods, Iohmar encountered this one. He *was* frightened. Terrified. And the creature realized.

"The little shadow taught us . . ."

Little shadow. Iohmar searches for the shadow girl, finding nothing but the darkness opposite the moonlight.

"Is she one of you?"

"No . . ."

Iohmar didn't believe so. Not when her name is caught in his throat.

"How did she teach you?"

"She . . . sat at our border and spoke long things until we understood her words . . . one by one . . ."

"Did she tell you her name?"

A long silence stretches. "Name . . . I do not understand . . ."

They have no names for one another?

"It matters not."

Iohmar finds himself approaching the border, the chill of it upon his skin, face close to the creature separated from him by his and his parents' magic, sealing it away. He is so near he could breach the border and place his fingers upon it, watch them shrivel as his father's did.

"How do you need help?" he asks. His voice trembles worse than his fingers. Lor's warmth against his back, head on his shoulder, grounds him. Subtly, he presses his cheek to the boy's temple and takes reassurance in the small, even breaths.

"We . . . are starving . . ."

Starving. Iohmar glances about, takes in the sight of the trees nearest the border with branches shriveled and vines turned to nothing where the creatures pressed past their barrier. If Iohmar were to let them, all his mountains and forests would be as the rippling lands, empty and voided, husks of trees bereft of life.

"You consume living things to survive," he says, then realizes he should have understood sooner, that it was not harm but thoughtless hunger, even if such a discernment would've made no difference. "When we fought . . . do you realize you killed . . . ?"

Killed his parents. His folk. Reduced those dwelling in Rúnda's land to a few hundred and those in the Fair Halls to even smaller a number.

"Why did you attack us?"

"We did not . . ."

The creature shifts, and Iohmar senses its words are unfinished. He waits. Waits.

"We did not . . . realize . . . The ones before us . . . consumed so fast . . . We aren't certain . . ."

It doesn't finish, but Iohmar understands. These are individual creatures. The ones that first wounded his father, that pressed into Látwill and brought grief upon them, were killed by Iohmar's own hand.

These are new. Younger creatures. Not the same.

"I know you . . ." it says. "You are the one who shattered us . . ."

"Yes."

"Because we shattered the ones who created you . . ."

Athair. Máthair. "Yes."

Lor's breath hitches. He knows the story in a vague sense, knows the life of his grandparents cherished within the orchard. The horrid details have been kept to Iohmar's heart, and he wonders what Lor could think of such things.

"We are not created by our own . . . We simply . . . happen . . ."

Iohmar nods and does not trust his voice. They have no family but understand loss enough to know Iohmar took from them as they took from him and his kin.

"Is that one . . . created by you . . . ?"

With a start, he tightens his arms around Lor, then touches a hand back to Lor's ear. "Yes, this one is my own."

Lor's arms turn unbreakable around his neck. He kisses Iohmar's cheek.

A soft noise echoes along the remaining creatures. Nonthreatening. Past them, Iohmar gazes at the shrouded emptiness of their lands, devoid of life and warmth, a chill unbearable to his own kin. They feed on life, and Iohmar pushed them back to ensure they did not consume all the lands of Látwill.

Closing his eyes, he forces himself to breathe deep, filling his lungs tight.

He can assist. He is king beneath the earth. Shadow and sunlight and all living beings answer his call.

These are not the same creatures who took his world and left him in threads.

Not the same.

"I can help," he whispers, then says firmly, "if you can learn not to wound us. I can encourage your lands to grow. But you cannot eat away at them immediately, or nothing will last."

A shiver of light passes along the border, moonlight breaking the trees. The creature shifts toward him, near touching the border, and Iohmar locks his muscles so he won't flee.

"You will help . . . ?" It sounds like a question, hopeful, and the burning in Iohmar's eyes turns to tears. He can't bring himself to hate this thing. He isn't sure which is a worse pain.

"Yes. It will take some time, but yes."

His trees are close. Animals have gathered to his presence, keeping their safe distance from the ripplings. Murmuring, Iohmar calls from the nearest blossoming tree a small fruit, round and soft and sweet, near crushing it between his fingers.

The barrier is chill to the back of his hand, like pressing his fingers into the crunch of the snow capping far-off mountains. Shivers run up his arm and along his skin. With his hand through, the border grasps his wrist, his fingers so near the rippling monster that he sees the reflection of his dark talons along the mirrors of its body. He balances the fruit in his palm and does not allow himself to recoil.

Carefully, a filament of the creature's form stretches. Should it touch his skin, Iohmar's fate will be much the same as his father's. He is ready to cast Lor aside from him should the creature take hold. But it does not. Gripping the fruit, it coils itself around the small offering, leaving Iohmar untouched. He withdraws his hand to the warm, storm-heavy air of the woods.

"I'll return," he says, then wonders if the creature understands the break in his voice. Hundreds of shimmering bodies return to the heart of their lands.

Iohmar retreats until the chill of the barrier no longer brushes his skin. His fingers tremble. Gently, he slips Lor to the mossy ground, fearful of collapsing under him. He stares at the soil, at the fallen leaves, and doesn't remember how to move.

After a time, Lor asks, "Daidí?"

Iohmar sobs. On his knees, he presses the back of his arm to his lips, trying to stifle the sound, to not do these things before his child. It doesn't help. Lor's fingers brush his hair. Tugging on Iohmar's arm, he pushes himself onto his lap and curls there, petting both Iohmar's cheeks with his tiny hands.

"I'm sorry you don't have your daidí and mhamaí anymore," he whispers. His eyes are red, and Iohmar is unsure when the boy began crying. He puts his forehead against Lor's shoulder, trying not to choke on his breath. Speaking seems impossible.

"But you have me, so it's okay, right?" Lor's voice is small.

Iohmar crushes him to his chest, pressing his face into the boy's neck. Animals nuzzle him, circling the two in concern. Iohmar rocks Lor in the pile of moss, kissing him along his ear and cheek and silken hair.

"Yes," he says when he can breathe enough to speak. "Yes, I have you, so everything is beautiful."

"Love you, Daidí."

Iohmar believes him. "Mmm, I love you, Wisp."

"I know."

Iohmar nearly laughs, but his throat is closed, and his body aches from magic and strain and weeping. He holds Lor so tight he wonders if the boy can breathe and watches the rippling border, empty until he can return and coax life from the ground.

"Daidí?" Lor's voice is a whisper, conspiratorial, eager.

"Hmm?"

"The shadow girl is here."

Hope presses against his rib cage. Raising his head, Iohmar finds the trees to his left full of moving shadows. The featureless shape of a child is among them, hidden behind the trunk of a tall, fat tree.

"Thank you," he says, partially to Lor, and partially to the shadow for showing him the other creatures of these lands needing help. "I believe I know who you are," he murmurs, brushing at the midnight moths swarming their king and prince. He reaches out, fingers still stained with their magic from so many years ago. "But I need you to show me. Somehow. Do you understand?"

For a moment, they continue their sinuous dance among the trees and ferns. When she slips to his side, Iohmar feels the bird-quick pulse of a heartbeat before she's near enough to touch. She stands outside his grasp. Lor wriggles higher in Iohmar's lap to get a better look.

"Iohmar?" she asks in a voice soft as spring earth, cocking her head to her shoulder.

"Yes," he says and isn't sure he knows how to believe.

A hand of shadow rests in his, not large enough even to cover his palm.

He closes his fingers and asks, "Ascia?"

She shatters into a thousand shadows, and Iohmar's world disappears under the weight of a mountain.

28

DOWN AMONG DRAGON BONES

Iohmar remembers in bits and pieces those days he's become so practiced at forgetting. How it felt to be buried within the mountain, the force of the earth upon him, not crushing his small body yet trapping him nonetheless.

Cold and warmth in the air. A strange passing of time. The sensation of his father's magic nearby before he was found. His mother next. And Galen. And many of his other folk who came to the aid of their prince.

How strange it was to bask in sunlight once more. The sight of the collapsed boulders at the base of the fair mountain which would one day be overgrown in ruin.

How it felt to wake again as if for the first time.

Wake again. Wake again.

Wakes again.

Iohmar is falling. Lor's sharp cry is nearby, and he is gone from Iohmar's arms. No balance exists to the falling. No up or down. The earth itself is about him.

Shadows swirl, hands and fingers grasping and tugging, pulling him every which way. Fabric tears. They grip his fingers and horns and hair. He can't push them away.

Separated from Lor, there is no light, no direction. Soil fills his eyes and mouth. He needs to breathe, needs a moment of calm long enough to call to his own magic, but it is scrambled as his thoughts.

He coughs, spits, and says, "Stop," in a voice too garbled and full of grit to sound his own.

Lor is calling to him, falling alongside him somewhere close and far.

Catching as much breath as he can, he calls, "Ascia, stop!"

The world falls still.

Coughing, he shoves at the soil suffocating his face, ears ringing as the roar of the falling earth is silenced. Blinking and wiping dirt from his eyes, he finds this place—still surrounded by stone and ground—dark as ever.

"Lor?" he calls, then louder, "Lor!"

"Daidí?" comes the meek response, the boy's voice thick with tears. Relief is too strong for Iohmar to be worried. He presses his hand through the soil in the direction of the voice. It is soft here, not as the tunnels full of hard-packed stone, almost warm as loam baking in the midday sun.

The shadows cling but do not hinder his digging.

With a few moments of fumbling and another sobbing call from Lor, Iohmar's hand finds a face, then a shoulder, then a familiar hand. A rough tug brings the boy into his pocket of air. Lor coughs and cries as Iohmar curls him into an embrace. His tiny arms grasp tight, and he nuzzles his face into Iohmar's neck.

"It's all right. I have you, dearheart," Iohmar whispers. Lor grips his horn as he did when the ripplings frightened him, his skin shedding pale leaves and petals.

Their space in the soil is hardly large enough for Iohmar to curl within, legs still buried, Lor pressed against one wall while Iohmar's back is cramped against the other. His horns are snarled within the loose earth above his head. The shadows swirl through his hair and between his fingers, attempting to worm within the nonexistent space between his chest and Lor's. They no longer take shape, and his skin crawls, trapped within the confined space.

"Ascia?" he asks, unable to raise his voice above a whisper.

His head spins. *How could it have happened?* He searched for her for so long. So many years he spent wandering tunnels and spreading his magic far as it would reach into the darkest depths.

In the end, it took her own magic to find him, even if she didn't recognize how greatly he'd changed.

The shadows tighten, and Iohmar's stomach plunges as the soil beneath him gives way. With a sharp drop and a cry of surprise from Lor, Iohmar crashes to a solid floor. The air is knocked from his lungs, and his head rings. Pebbles dig into his back. His shoulder blades ache.

He groans and thinks vaguely of cursing.

King beneath the earth, indeed.

Lor's breaths are quick, but a brush against his magic confirms he isn't hurt so much as frightened, held safely atop Iohmar's chest. Iohmar sits and gazes about now that Lor's soft glow has returned.

His own skin shimmers as it did in childhood, though the dark of his talons and stained fingertips remains.

"Daidí . . . ?" Lor hiccups. "You're glowing too."

"Yes . . ."

The boy's hands comb Iohmar's hair with great gentleness. "Your hair is a different color."

Pulling a handful over his shoulder, Iohmar gazes at it in the pale light. It is indeed the color it once was, autumn hued. For a moment, panic reaches him, and he tests the bonds of magic with his son. But they remain strong and stable as ever. Stronger, perhaps, with the streaks of rot fading and his strength returning. He is alive, powerful, Lor a tiny mirror to him.

Lor sits back enough to look into Iohmar's face. His hands touch his temples. "Your horns are different."

Other fae alter their appearance, but Lor is unused to it in his father. His eyebrows pull together as he inspects the change.

"Are they paler?"

Lor nods. "Like your hair. And those trees atop the mountain."

Birch trees. Before his magic changed, his horns were autumn hued and streaked with the color of birch bark, as Lor's soft skin. Unwilling to release the boy, he gets his feet under him. Hesitantly, he stretches his magic into the surrounding cavern. It responds happily to his call, the sharp and intense presence of his forest and mountains and rising sunlight and all his fair folk above them. Warmth spreads at the rising sun, and he lets his mind return to the dark of the cave.

"What is it you wish to show me?" he asks the gathering shadows, and they press into him. Iohmar turns and allows them to guide his steps. Lor doesn't flinch at their touch, but his arms are tight about Iohmar's neck.

Darkness reveals great pillars of pale bones. Iohmar knows this place, recognizes it now. This place he forgot.

He stares up at the great pillar of a rib he once stood upon.

"It's a dragon," Lor whispers, head turned enough to see, cheek pressed to Iohmar's.

"Yes."

The shadows push and push, and Iohmar allows himself to be led among the bones and past the great skull. Toward the end of the cavern, he finds the second half of the rib cage buried in the wall. Boulders are piled, and it takes Iohmar a moment to realize the skeleton was not always buried.

Once, two children played down among dragon bones and were buried deep.

Spreading his palm to the fallen rocks, he stretches his magic. The shadows press him near flat against the wall, and this place has a soft, strange magic he did not find when last they fell. It's the faint familiarity he sensed but was unable to identify.

"Was there another cave-in after the one that buried you and your friend?" Lor asks as Iohmar kneels and sets him on the ground.

"I believe it's the same one," Iohmar murmurs. The shadows

hum, and his fingers tremble once more. *What do they wish me to see?*

Lor touches the rocky wall as Iohmar does, but his eyebrows furrow. "I don't feel anything."

"You're young."

Iohmar moves the largest of the rocks he can budge without collapsing the pile surrounding the bones. A waiting quiet falls across the cavern, only the crackle of rocks coming loose. The shadows dip in and about the crevices before Iohmar's hands, shifting the earth in small liquid movements, the same way they pulled him into the cavern. Lor watches him with wide, serious eyes before digging at the smaller stones alongside him.

The magic grows stronger. Pausing, Iohmar listens to the spark of warmth. It is much the same as testing his bonds with Lor. He finds a flame of life, smothered in its place buried so deep.

Tears blur his vision.

Stepping back, he brings his magic from the warm light of the surface, digging deeper and deeper through layers of mountains and tunnels and earth. The ground rumbles. Stones crack. Lor weaves one arm around his knee.

Roots crack the ceiling and sprout from the walls, entire trees undoing themselves to answer his call. Little burrowing creatures he has no name for wriggle about his feet and into the collapse of cavern before him. No light makes its way so deep, not yet. Vines and roots weave through the walls, stabilizing uncertain earth the shadows could not shift alone, removing boulders and stones until there is nothing left but a pocket of soft earth where the magic is sharpest.

He lets it rest.

Lor squeezes his knee. Not even when they were first trapped did his son see such a display. Iohmar realizes how inhibited his magic had been. The illness was creeping upon him without his realization, but now it is fading.

The shadows swarm the pocket created from the collapsed mountain, still partially concealed. Iohmar sheds his cumbersome robes and slides beneath the dark crack, the light from his skin unable to break the dense swarm of shadows. His hand finds first the giant bone embedded in the stone, then fingers little enough to be Lor's, warm and soft. He holds his breath; there's not enough room among the clay to cry. Wrapping an arm about the tiny form, he slides the two of them out into the vast cavern, his and Lor's light cutting the dark enough to see.

"It's a girl?" Lor asks, voice rising in surprise. "A *real* girl?"

Iohmar sits, cradling the child's head, peering at her small face.

It isn't possible, he thinks, extending his magic so far that he touches the orchard above, the presence of his parents slow and unaware. *They searched for her. I searched for her. This isn't possible. Isn't possible . . .*

A sob cracks his chest, and he swallows it down.

"Ascia?" he asks, taking her face between his hands. She fits in his grasp as Lor does. She is so young. They were both so young.

"Is she your friend?" Lor asks. "But she's little like me . . ."

Iohmar can't respond. He brushes his magic across hers, worried to wake her but frightened to allow her to sleep. Her eyelids flutter. She blinks at him. For the life of him, Iohmar tries to remember the color of her eyes but can't picture it. They're green when she stares up at him, and he wishes he weren't dirty and disheveled and weeping over her, frightening.

As soon as she wakes, her shadows return to her, some dissolving into her skin, some swirling close. Her face scrunches. She glances around, turns her eyes to him, and asks, "Årelang?"

Iohmar blinks tears. He doesn't remember when last someone spoke his father's name.

"No," he whispers as gently as he can manage. "It's me, Ascia. I'm Iohmar."

Almost smiling, she says, "You're not Io—"

Her eyes find his horns among his hair, a feature neither his father nor his mother had. He raises a hand to them, then shows her his long talons.

"It's me," he repeats. "I'm Iohmar. It's me."

She sits, still grasping one horn. Eyes far away, she puts a hand in the pocket of her moss-green dress and pulls out a small stone.

Not a stone, he realizes as she holds it to eye level. It's the tip of horn that was broken off him so long ago when he brought Lor to the strange woman of shadow.

The form Ascia's magic took on as it wandered the tunnels, lost.

Didn't the woman shatter into a thousand shadows before I lost consciousness? Iohmar's own magic has a life of its own, tethered to him. Ascia's does as well, and hers was trapped here, a child even when taking the form of someone as ancient as he.

Following him about his woods, trying to lead him back.

Ascia seems confused by the presence of the broken horn, a deep pinch to her eyebrows as she stares between it and Iohmar.

"You aren't Iohmar," she says, but she's looking at Lor.

The boy shakes his head, and Iohmar says, "He's my son. Lor.

He's my little boy."

That is why she called Lor by my name. He is near the same age Iohmar was when they were buried. And though he doesn't share Iohmar's features, there is a significant slope to his face matching Iohmar's, and their magic, now bonded, carries the same presence and feel.

"You're grown up," Ascia whispers, her eyes finding Iohmar's.

"Yes," he says, then gathers her into his arms so she doesn't see him weep.

She weaves her arms about his neck much as Lor does, and there is a crack of tears in her voice. "Why are you grown?"

"I don't know," Iohmar says, though his age is not the strange magic that has been working all these centuries. He puts his hand to the crown of her head and gives her the emotions of how greatly he missed her.

Lor stares at them, lip trembling. Iohmar offers his arm and holds each of them tight.

"I'm sorry," he tells Ascia. "I thought I lost you. I searched for so long. I'm sorry. I'm so sorry."

29

A BURST OF LIGHT

When Iohmar rises, he calls to his magic.

Ascia's shadows swarm, tucking into her skin. Some remain, weaving between Iohmar's legs and arms, swirling about his neck. Lor grips Iohmar's hand with both of his, and Iohmar cradles Ascia in his other arm.

His magic floods each and every place he can reach, a circle of warmth and growth spreading out and up to the world above. His forests are calm and exhausted from the storm, basking in twilight. A crack spreads in the earth, so vast and deep Iohmar's skin warms in the soft glow.

The cavern cracks. Branches and vines and all manner of living greenery wrap around them, and they leave the sunlight to touch the dragon bones for the first time in millennia.

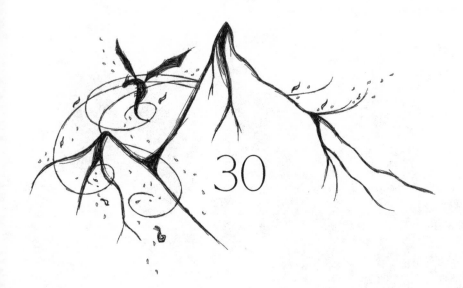

ATOP MOUNTAINS,
AMONG ORCHARDS

Iohmar rests in the willow chair alongside his bed—the one Galen frequents—and watches the children sleep. Nothing exists to guard them from, not here in the sanctuary of his chambers, but he cannot tear his eyes away.

Ascia is tucked into one side, Lor the other, both swimming in blankets and sleeping deep as the trees. Two ears pop up between them where the fawn nests.

Once they reached the mountain, Lor pieced together the story. "I dreamt of you," he told Ascia when Iohmar first sat them on the edge of his bed.

She gazed at him strangely, head on her shoulder—an expression Iohmar now remembers in earnest—and said, "I dreamt of you too."

Iohmar didn't know what to expect—for he's certain now Ascia's magic caused his son his terrible dreams, even if she didn't realize it herself—but watched as Lor flung his arms about her and said, "You're going to stay with us now."

Hot tears sit along his cheeks. Iohmar scrubbed his face clean of dirt and the remnants of weeping once the children fell into sleep. These are fresh. He didn't heal the cut he created in the mountainside, letting the sun reach the giant bones forever, but cast his magic upon it, dissuading others from venturing too close.

Iohmar rests his head against the back of the chair. He tests the strings of his magic against theirs. They are free of dreams, frightening or otherwise. Snippets of color dance behind his eyes. Extending it further, he finds Galen stronger. His people are well, some nurturing cuts and bruises from venturing into the gales. Many wander the now-calm trees. He dozes, continuing his pass of magic along the lands.

Far within the mountains and deep woods, the rippling borders are peaceful, awaiting him.

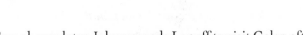

Some hours later, Iohmar sends Lor off to visit Galen after a dozen requests. Once alone, he follows the bright trace of Ascia's magic.

He woke when she slipped from the chamber door but kept his eyes closed and his breathing soft. He fears allowing her out of his sight, overly sensitive, but knows in his heart nothing in the Fair Halls will harm her. Now that she is here alongside him, her magic is familiar and strong, easy to monitor.

It is bright noon, and the sunlight soaks Iohmar's skin, welcoming him with vigor. As he leaves the shelter of the Halls, his crows flock, and he shoos at them to leave a path to walk along. Small creatures float about, drifting away when he sends a wash of magic over them.

She's sitting at the peak of the mountain, atop a stone bathed in sunlight jutting high enough for her to see over the trees.

They came here often as children.

A handful of years ago, Iohmar sat atop the great stone at night, whispering his thanks to the shadows.

Her magic greets his, shadows dancing around her and rising to see him. He welcomes them with sunlight, sparkles and slivers of midnight sliding across the mountaintop. She smiles. In the daylight, with her face cleaned, freckles show on her cheeks. Her ears are narrow, carrying the same uncanny nature as Iohmar and Rúnda and Lor and all their kin who have been both under the earth and over the sky.

"You are so grown," she says again, and hearing her speak turns him into a little child for the briefest moment.

"I know. Horrifying, isn't it?"

She smiles, plucking a dandelion fae from the air. "How did my magic do so many strange things when I didn't know?"

Time has never been a linear beast, and he accepts the change, though it is not with ease. He did not know such an aberration in magic could exist, but insisting it should not be possible would do nothing for either of them. Sadness is present in Ascia's magic, but warmth and love are as well.

"I do not entirely know," he admits, standing below the rock so they are face-to-face. "It protected you. Perhaps it was doing all it could because it was buried and frightened for you and could not save you on its own."

"I didn't know it worked in such a way."

"Neither did I. The older I become, the more I grasp, but I will never understand the extent of these lands."

"Has your magic ever done something so strange?"

"It causes me dreams, yes. It has never taken physical forms and intentions outside my own, but I was never buried as long as you."

"But you were buried too?" she asks, gazing up at him. "I remember you being there and the mountain shaking. I don't think any of the things I remember after were real."

"I was buried. My athair found me. They searched for you, both my parents. As did I. For so long."

She grasps his finger in her tiny fist.

"What are the other things you remember?"

A little divot forms between her eyebrows. "I remember nothing for a great deal of time. It didn't even feel long. A handful of days here and there.

"Sometimes I couldn't speak. Then I could, but only small words. And sometimes I saw you and tried to call out . . . but I thought . . . thought Lor was you. You were too big to be you. Sometimes I could talk, but only if I didn't stray too far from the cavern. I dreamt I spoke to you . . . well, to Lor. Then the mountain was trembling, and I tried to call for help."

Iohmar nods, encouraging. Hers were the words Galen heard in the tunnels.

"I had so many dreams of you. About those big monsters made of glass and reflections hurting you. And the monsters were in your woods, so I wanted to tell you. I talked to them because I didn't want them to hurt you again, and they talked back."

Iohmar's breath catches. He bites the inside of his lip to hide the trembling. "Those were real things. Your shadows led me to the monsters, and you teaching them to speak allowed them to ask for help."

"But they hurt you? Was that real?"

"Yes, some of them did. Some did not, and those ones needed help."

Her eyes lower. She presses her hand to the place above his heart. "You have a wound here."

Iohmar moves the fabric of his robe aside until marred skin is visible. She touches a scar as Lor did, as if she's trying to pet a moth's wing, and he does not remove her hand.

"I saw you fighting," she tells him, and his heart aches. *Did Lor share all Ascia's dreams?*

"I'm sorry. I wish you hadn't seen."

She continues watching the scar but drops her hand. "I wish you hadn't been there. I had dreams about Lor too."

Iohmar tries to smile. "He dreamt of you as well."

"Why?"

"I'm not sure. It was your magic wandering the tunnels that helped me save him when he was a babe. Some of you is likely tied to him, as I am."

"How did my magic know such things?"

Iohmar shakes his head. "I'm unsure. You may never know.

Perhaps it could move threads of mine because it was so disconnected from you. Your magic I spoke with is still a part of you, after all, even if it seemed a grown woman. I remember it scattering after helping me. I believe it was weakened as I was. It's regrowing now, enough you were able to find me, and perhaps it'll strengthen once more."

Putting a hand in her pocket, she pulls out the tip of his horn, then holds it out to him. "May I keep this?"

Iohmar turns it over in his fingers, amused by its presence, and places it back in her palm. "Of course."

She takes a shuddering breath. When her fingers brush his, the shadows staining his fingers drain back into hers. "I'm frightened."

"I know."

"None of the people I passed were familiar to me."

Such is a pain Iohmar understands. "I know, dearheart. But you do not need to be frightened. Come with me. There is a place I wish to show you."

He offers his arms, and she scoots to the edge of the rock, grasping her hands about his neck. After pulling her close, Iohmar steps into the nearest beam of sunlight.

In the orchard, Iohmar sits within the tangled roots of his parents' trees. Ascia puts her hand on the nearest trunk. Red poppy petals run between her fingers.

"Your parents were very sweet to me," she tells him.

Her chin trembles, and Iohmar offers his arms for her to nuzzle into. He doesn't trust his voice. They stay long enough that the bright hour of midday fades to twilight afternoon. The bright spark of Lor's magic leaves the mountain and grows stronger. When he appears among the trees, he hops the creek and finds a place against Iohmar's side to curl up.

"Hi," he says to Ascia, and she maneuvers around to smile at him.

"How is Galen?" Iohmar asks.

"Sleepy. He told me if you got in trouble while he was asleep that he will be very, very cross. Then he closed his eyes again, so I sat on the bed with him for a little bit."

Iohmar smiles. Relief lodges like a stone in his throat.

"Galen?" Ascia asks, grinning with such joy that Iohmar's smile is easy. This is a name she knows, for she loves the old caretaker as Iohmar does.

"Yes, Galen. He is still here with us. And I should visit him."

"I want you to stay here," Lor says, his voice muffled under Iohmar's arm.

"Me too," Ascia says.

And Iohmar can't rise under such a weight. "A little while then," he says, putting an arm around each. Ascia sends shadows dancing among the grasses, and Lor plucks flowers sprouting from between his fingers. Iohmar watches him close his eyes and concentrate to call upon the magic more and more resembling his father's.

When he sends out his own, he finds Rúnda and her folk close enough for him to watch over, maneuvering the sleepy woods. Her presence unknots something in his chest.

"What happens now?" Ascia asks.

After everything, it seems a silly question, a child's worry.

"Do you not wish to stay with me?"

"I wish it very much."

"Then that is what you shall do, little princess."

Both children smile up at him.

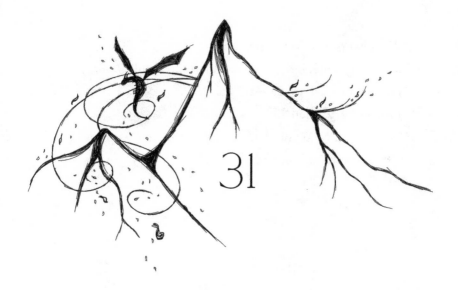

31

A FEW STOLEN KISSES

Leihs greets him at the entrance of the healing chambers, offering another bow. Her eyes flick across his healed skin, and
she nods to herself.

"He's awake. And cranky."

"Returning to himself then," Iohmar says, ducking into the
private room as her soft laugh follows. He slides the door shut.

A window in the corner has been cast open, and gentle sunlight
washes in. Iohmar visited once, the evening before, after sitting
with Lor and Ascia, only to find the old caretaker asleep. Now, the
room is bright and happy. Galen sits on the edge of the bed, fuss-
ing with the ties on his shirt. He is still frail, more so than usual,
but color has returned to his skin, warmth to his magic. Sensing
Iohmar, he gazes up with a start as if he's Lor and has been caught

stealing sweets from the kitchens.

"Iohmar," he says, enough uncertainty to his voice that Iohmar's heart constricts. He caused such pain and wishes deeply to heal it over.

He smiles and hopes it is as gentle as he intends.

"Your hair is different," Galen states, too surprised to sound properly emotionless. "Your horns . . . Lor visited, and he said something happened but wouldn't explain."

"He said you fell asleep on him."

"Yes, well . . ." Galen huffs, eyebrows furrowed at the window. Iohmar manages not to appear too amused.

"It is all very strange and complicated. I will show you first; it will be easier. Then I will explain. We are all well now."

Suspicion touches Galen's eyes, and Iohmar deserves it.

"I see," Galen says, abruptly nervous, returning to fiddling with the ties on his shirt, not meeting Iohmar's eyes. "Iohmar . . . I realize I stepped across a boundary. I know I am not your father or mother and I have no right to speak to you how I did, and I should never have threatened to overrule you. I simply . . . I have always . . . I have been watching over you since you were a little babe yourself, and I . . . I've always . . . I—"

Iohmar crouches between Galen's knees, taking the shirt strings from his fingers. After unknotting them, he weaves them into the proper pattern. He hasn't trimmed the needle sharpness of his talons since the illness and is careful to avoid Galen's butterfly-fragile skin.

Galen's eyes remain downcast, fingers folding and unfolding, and Iohmar searches for words until he's finished the ties.

"What I said was quite cruel," he murmurs. "You were doing as you should have done. I am not my parents. Often, I believe I should more resemble them. Sometimes I am glad for the difference. You are not to me what you were to them. You have been very much a father to me. Were you to become nervous in my presence, it would break my heart. Please, do not be, not because I say foolish things when I am frightened."

Galen blinks. His lips press into a line. Iohmar sees his reflection in his silver eyes. Once has Iohmar seen him weep, when he held him in his arms on the floor of his chambers, when the war was over and his parents were no longer with them.

Gently, he curls his finger to dry the underside of the old fae's eyes. "I hope you might forgive me."

"Oh, Iohmar . . ."

Iohmar finds himself drawn into an embrace. Resting his head against Galen's shoulder, he circles his arms around his middle, rocking them, eyes closed. He has never felt competent at soothing anyone save for Lor, but Galen is content to cling to him. With hesitation, he pets his hair, combing it about his horns, and Iohmar allows him much longer than he would usually tolerate.

Leaning back, he rests their foreheads together and tests the strings of his magic, comforted by Galen's responding with strength.

"Come to the gardens with me. The sunlight will make you stronger."

Galen sniffs. Iohmar rubs under his own burning eyes and takes Galen by the arms to steady him on his feet.

"Are you going to explain?" Galen's voice still shakes as he glances at the ground, but the pain has eased from his eyes.

"Yes, yes. I'm unsure how you believe I would get away with keeping secrets from you. You glare them out of me."

Grumbling, Galen straightens his clothes and takes the robe Iohmar drapes across his shoulders. They stroll from the healing rooms through the quiet Halls with arms looped. All Iohmar's kin are wandering the gardens and nearby woods, basking in the sun and the quiet of the mountains. Lor and Ascia he left for his kings-guard to keep watchful eyes upon, though any threats he feared are no longer worthy of concern. Ascia's magic was calling for his help and has returned to her now that she is no longer in danger. The rippling borders are quiet, awaiting Iohmar's visit.

They walk the Halls toward the bright gardens, and Iohmar tells Galen the tale.

Vines reach lazy tendrils around his toes and legs, and Iohmar pulls his hands away lest he become trapped. Nearby trees sway, shedding leaves that catch in his hair and the threads of his robes. Deer wander close, sprouting flowers. Badgers and foxes and things with no names, graceful of limb, pass by. Túirt appeared once, keeping his distance, before returning to his plums. Iohmar shoos away the smaller fae thoughtless enough to approach the rippling barrier and digs his magic deeper into the earth.

He presses his fingers into the soil, which is still warm from the noon sun. The air is humid and rid of the storm.

The rippling creature he spoke with rests opposite the border, shifting in a squat roundish circle, a tiny reflective puddle in the empty land. Delicately, Iohmar unweaves the threads of his magic binding the barrier until enough is left for his forest to grow past, though not enough to let the creatures' dead lands into the lush fields. They can press their consuming bodies past, as always, with great determination, but this creature — Iohmar has yet to fit a name to it — has sworn they will keep their peace, as Iohmar has sworn to help.

The trees take some convincing but bow under the will of their king. He will let no harm befall them even in these other lands, offering leaves and flowers and fruits but nothing more. Sprouts push past the gray topsoil. Usually, Iohmar lets his woods grow at their own pace, allows flowers to bloom when they wish and animals to do as they please. Creatures of Látwill cannot pass into the rippling lands, but he encourages the shoots to grow. Saplings rise to the height of human men. Flowers bud. Grasses spread seeds.

A finger of water bubbles as diamonds from the roots of a new tree, trickling into the dead lands until Iohmar can no longer see where it travels. He spreads the growth along the rippling side of the border and lets the forest alone to grow with its own sweet time. He will return often to ensure it takes to the lands. Should the need arise, he will provide warmth with his own magic.

"You must be slow with it," he tells the creature tugging away at individual petals of a yellow tulip. "If you consume it all at once, it will not continue to grow."

"We will . . . take care . . ."

Iohmar nods.

A brush against fallen leaves draws him. In the shade of the trees, Rúnda folds her fingers together, eyes soft, watching. Her hair is wild from the winds, dress ruffled from travel. She's once more taken to wearing gems in her ears, glittering things of pure silver.

Ages seem to have passed since he last drank in the sight of her. He considers how she would react to him springing upon her but feels sheepish.

"How long have you been there?"

"A short time. You were engrossed."

Indeed he was. Bringing such magic to the surface of the dead lands was no easy task. His head spins, and his limbs burn pleasantly from the power.

"Quite the rainstorm you brought down. Sulking about something?"

Iohmar presses his lips together. The storm was Látwill's creation, but Iohmar could cause one of his own if he chose. He has in the past. Once or twice.

"I had a splinter."

She's trying not to laugh, and Iohmar gestures to the mossy ground. Grasses swish about her legs. Her eyes flicker to the rippling lands, expression sharp as fine iron for a moment. Heat slides up his skin when she sits pressed to his side.

"Did you speak to Galen when you arrived?"

"Yes. He explained you were here and what you were doing. He seemed a tad overwhelmed."

"I dumped quite a long tale upon him this morning," Iohmar

says, remembering Ascia throwing herself into the old fae's arms and Galen bursting into tears a moment later.

"Hmm."

Rúnda watches the rippling creature pluck individual grasses slowly, without greed. It doesn't appear interested in them. Soon, Iohmar will bring Ascia here, and she can meet the creatures her magic taught to speak.

Rúnda's fingers find the backs of his. Her words are a whisper. "You are doing a brave thing."

Tears burn his eyes. He has been an inexcusable amount of ridiculous these past days.

Their kiss is so soft that he could be caressing the wings of a butterfly—a few stolen kisses hidden among the spring grasses. She closes her eyes and leans the bridge of her nose against his, their faces tucked together. Warm wind curls her hair and tickles it across his cheeks.

"I do not believe my illness is something that will fade," he tells her, speaking soft enough that it doesn't feel as if he's breaking the surrounding magic. "I do not believe it will ever be accustomed to the way it is threaded to Lor's life. I am strong as ever when I recover, but it was not the shadows that caused it. My appearance was different because of them—they clung to my skin—but this illness . . . it was my own actions, a change in my own magic, and I believe it will return."

Rúnda raises her face to his.

"I fear it a little. I . . . cannot help the feeling," he tells her. "But it is not something to dread, not even something to be upset over. It is simply how my magic heals itself. I realize I have not told you as much about it as I could have, but I will answer any question you ask. And . . . if you wish it, I will send my crows when I am ailing. It would . . . comfort me, for you to be by my side."

Her eyes shimmer, lips quirking. "You are very loved, Iohmar."

He presses his lips to the soft skin in the corner of her eye, allowing himself to be held. "As are you."

"I think this is a ploy to see me more often."

"Once more, you've seen through my ruse."

"Hmm."

"Come with me. I wish for you to meet Ascia."

Her eyebrows knit together. "I know that name. You've spoken it before. Long ago."

"Yes," he says, rising and pulling her in the direction of a sunbeam breaking the twilight sky.

"Oh no," she says, digging her bare feet into the soil. "This turn is mine, king beneath the earth."

Iohmar smiles.

Tugging him into the clearing, she wraps her arms about his chest. He tugs her to him. Gales rise, twining their clothes, tangling Iohmar's hair about his horns. Winds sweeps them up with chill hands, whipping them back toward the great mountain and over the sky.

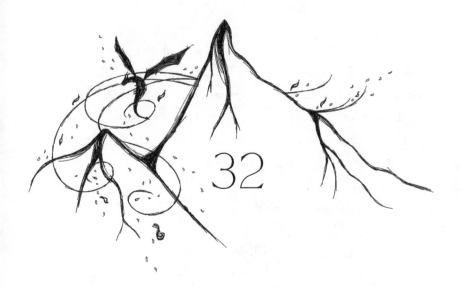

32

THE END

Seven crows fly to their king beneath the earth.

They speak to him of humans and strange magic, of jewels they collect from mortal lands.

Iohmar sits at his desk and listens to their gossip. When he is ill and Lor is nestled in the covers beside him, he lets them sit on his wrists and cackle on and on as Ascia perches on Galen's knee and draws, her shadows slipping into dark spaces of his room, watching over him. Sometimes, he holds Galen's hand. Rúnda shoos the birds when they become pests.

They speak of the rippling lands and their growing trees and spreading waters, of Rúnda's ships sailing the great, wild waves, of vast deserts and the moments when the trees in the heart of the woods wake from their slumber and sing. And once or twice they bring him news of great flying beasts impossibly like dragons in places far and far from the king beneath the earth.

They do not speak of sunlight or bring news of shadows, for those dwell within his mountain.

THANK YOU FOR READING!

Thank you so much for reading *Under the Earth, Over the Sky*! Leaving a review on Amazon, Goodreads, or any other platform you prefer helps support this book and reach new readers!

To follow along with more of Emily McCosh's works, you can sign up for her author newsletter at *oceansinthesky.com* to be the first to learn about new releases, artwork, unreleased content, and any other nerdy book news.

ABOUT THE AUTHOR

Emily McCosh is a graphic designer and writer of strange things. She currently lives in California with her two parents, two dogs, one tree swing, and innumerable characters who need to learn some manners. Her short fiction has appeared in *Beneath Ceaseless Skies*, *Shimmer Magazine*, *Galaxy's Edge*, *Flash Fiction Online*, *Nature: Futures*, and elsewhere.

Her fantasy and science fiction collection, *All the Woods She Watches Over: Stories & Poetry*, and was a finalist for the Next Generation Indie Book Awards, and she publishes an ongoing web novel titled *In Dying Starlight*.

Find her online on her writing YouTube channel and TikTok full of wild writing skits and bookish content.

Website: oceansinthesky.com

YouTube: Emily McCosh

TikTok: emilymccosh

Instagram: emily_mccosh

Facebook & Twitter: @wordweaveremily

ACKNOWLEDGMENTS

As always, the biggest of thanks to my parents, for being the most supportive two people on the planet. To my Mom, for reading all my drafts, and listening to my ramblings about the publishing industry and my too-many story ideas. To my Dad, for being hilarious, clever, and for first encouraging me to write.

A big thank you to my wonderful editor, Natalia, for whipping this manuscript into shape. And to my beta readers: Deborah, Zaq, Kino, Freya, Saf, and Aven. Your feedback was incredibly helpful and your commentary gave me life.

I would be remiss if I didn't mention this book was written greatly to the music of Ludovico Einaudi, M83, Gang of Youths, Mumford & Sons, Of Monsters and Men, and The Irrepressibles.

And finally, turn the page for a big thank you to all the amazing folks who believed in this book and supported it on Kickstarter!

ACKNOWLEDGMENTS

Thank you to everyone on Kickstarter who has supported this project and given it so much love. I could not have had such an amazing book launch without every single one of you.

Seedling

Spoon Douglas
Fallon Somer-Guynn
Clare Hardager

CJ Milacci
Rachel Morley
Jack Holder

J. Elias Epp
Dustin Laughlin
E. S. Dickenson

Flower Sprout

Michelle Cooper
Stewart C Baker
Melissa Craven
Anthea Sharp
Jill Vance
Victoria Besner
Stephanie Owen
Joshua C. Chadd
Jamie Dockendorff
Deanna Stanley
pjk
Jak Lore
Katalin Ceskel
Bethany Tomerlin
Prince

Melissa Showers
Jan Birch
Niklas Nord
Karyne Norton
Lidija Smertinaite
Elizabeth Davis of
Dead Fish Books
Thomas Bull
Noarvara
Christian Bell
ScribeTheMad
Mattia Gualco
Brittany Gugel
Justin Fike
Helen Patrice

Julia OGara
rinibeeny
Charlotte E. English
Marcia Zina Mager
Ellysa Hermanson
Alexandru Nedel
Michelle Meyering
Zachary Kelley
Jon Paul Anthony Hart
Chris Brimmage
J.D.L. Rosell
Frank G Greene
dana
Hristina Popova
Debra

Susan S.
Ivo
Rachel Bryant
Michelle Valentine
Lesly

Jason Link
Katrina James
Regina Garowen
Lisa Ciccarello
Eli

Stephany
Rebecka Thim
André Laude
Jonathan Mendonca

Sapling

Tea
Alexandra Fluskey
Rahy Ayrin
Dara
Jordan Grace
Racheile R
Teya Martin
Brandon Chapman
Lori Lea
Blebbo
HardWorkLucky
Noah Blackburn
Missy Beal
Qkelly820
Elizabeth Long
Emily Lynn
Mitzi M
Mikhaila
Crag-Chaderton
Andromeda
Taylor-Wallace
Bunni Daniel

Jackie Argyropoulos
Brooks Moses
D. Ekle
Viima Taimi
Xilenoy75
Sherricka K.
Nicole Payne
Juliana F
Braden Dougherty
Lauren M.
Taylor Ewing
Chris
Lucretia Swanson
Stacy Shuda
Ali Costa
Amber Fae
Therena Carlin
Erik T Johnson
Richard Valdez
Gabriel Casillas
Merissa Mayhew
Jamie Buckley

Aileen Sapp
Fia
Selena L. Rice
Abigail E. Williams
Miriam Kitson
Heather B. Proffer
Sarah Steinweg
Vulpecula
Joseph A Williams
Kylie W.
Casey T.
H Melendez
Katie Rahlfs
Quail
Rav
Tim Stroup
Jenna Lynn
Ellis Winter
L Panzarella
Tracie Lucas

Forest Glade

Cassandra Stubbs
Buller
Nicole Hopkins
Samantha Mitchell

M. Dick
Melissa Ford
Jacqueline Armour
Maysha R.

Rachel Kennedy
Samantha Kitchel
Sunny
Tracey

Kris Hamilton
Erin Pou
Jeff Chandler
Mel Green-Allen
Teagan Plain
Stephanie M.
Madalyn Cooke
Emily Renee Eikost

Haley A
Rachel Wieczorkowski
Abigail Spears
Maggie Musclow
Asierleigh Richards
Reece
Jessie R Seager
Katherine Scheper

Rachel Arrighi
Katie Gale
Cleo Yaz
Kaylee
Jocelyn Faydenko
Janine Lü
Caitlyn B.

Ancient Tree

Deborah L. Davitt
Adam Cole
Tess Kinniburgh
Covington
Eliza Tilton
Becca Taylor
Christian H.
Luis K Penn
Gwendolyn
Woodschild
Monica Kim
Hailey Christine
Chappell
Shiro
Eliza Williams

Syn
Andrew Liddell
Cassie Black
Ashley Cruz
Zachary Moore
Nicolette Andrews
Gunthermation
Pamela Lowery
Kit Brannen
Addi Lea
Liz Carlberg
AmBaby - Alexandra
Eden Van Wyhe
Christina Berry
Miranda Harding

Katie Carmichael
Red Valkyrie
Daniel Blatt
Lauren Frost
Kim-Marie H.
Stephanie Diaz
Lezli Robyn
Kay
Sam Vermillion
Arielle Ross
Luke
Leeloo Velazquez
Bjørg Sandbeck

Ancient Forest

Jaymee Crowell
Alexa Lee
Zaq Cass
Cassidy Logan
Glenn Hiramatsu
Matthea W. Ross
Austin Hoffey

Elizabeth Neyman
Katie Holland
Aerie
Diego Riley
Megyn "Crimson"
MacDougall
Alissa Müller

Samantha Kuxhaus
Kathryn Vandrey
CP Jones
Carissa F.
Cody L. Allen
Lauren Engle
Piper Arington

J. Sessions
Jeramie Vens
Sissel K. H. Rasmussen
Scott R.
I. Clara Luca
Kaizad P.
Quinn Kohut
Michelle White-Huff
Charity Diaz Peres
David Edmonds
Chelsea Allen
Paloma Egido
Tori Carlini
Julian Someguy

McKayla Boyd
Kali Atwell
Xio Reyes
Kimberly Lingley
Brian Weicker
Morgan Freeman
Stuart Day
Edward A Maher III
Carson Prestegard
Caitlin Millsaps
Foss Waters
Caleb Slama
Gabrielle
Aidan M

Carrie Magerl
Mary Divin
Joshua Struss
Morgan Stoneman
Elizabeth Ryner
Molly Kawamoto
Nellie Cole
Terry E Roberts
Jonathan Cole
Gladys Derelly
Lemesurier
Haji Muhammad
Fuad Ghazali Hj
Aminorashid

Great Mountain

Sunny Side Up
Slifer274
Rebekah Post
Hana Engel
Karissa Tedrow
Julie Alviar
Kyra York
Samantha Landström
Michael E. Noll
Wildon
Karima
Doug Erling
Will Rodd
Katy Keller
Jamieson McKenzie
Olia
Pace Willisson
Jeffrey M. Johnson

Cirdan
Joshua Yates
Robert Pritchard
Cape Girl
Annie Williams
Rebecca Cruz
Rod Cressey
Jon Marshburn
Patrick Hoover
Jerome p. Anello
Kaitlin Heinz
Jaycee Smith
Rae Yocum
In Memory of
Shantara Belisle
Donna Kualii
Nicole Matamala
Jacob Tashoff

Misha Coleman
Elisabeth Schwaiger
Robert Brown
Hannah Lantz
Ro Raviv
Michael Yeh
Corrin Odell
Kristie Lynn C.
Heather Burns
Jalle Van
Goidsenhoven
Sarah A. G.
Jordan Williams
Victoria Brown
Olivia Burnette
Justin Greer
Nicole Fraser
Kathryn Craig

Mighty Dragon

Sofia Bennani T.
Audrey Priest
Savaril
A. Marquez
Jenn Falls
Karen M
Millennia Bayless
Breanna Martinez
Tiffany Gaustad
Devin Wood
Emilee K

Bella Bliss
Kristin Hendrick
Marisa Naples
Adrienne Hiatt
Lillie Deas
Bryan Dossen
Taryn L.
Sabrina D
Cassidy Browning
Holly Wunsch
Kehle and Cole

Alicia T. Stoesser/
Kiwri/Nattwinged
Matúš Matula
Crystal Oldham
Chase n Darla Guymon
Hannah Coffee
Mia Power
Leomaris
Yasmin Bhatti